Things got blurred for a while. When they clarified, I realized that I had come out from under the influence.

When I had entered the room, I must mention, I had been clad in a quiet grey suit with powder blue socks matching the neat tie and melting, as it were, into the tasteful suede shoes. And now, by Jove, I'm blowed if I wasn't wearing knickerbockers and stockings! And then suddenly I caught sight of my face in the mirror . . .

LAUGHING GAS
P. G. Wodehouse

"Wodehouse is absolutely the best . . . A genius."
—Wilfrid Sheed

LAUGHING GAS

P. G. Wodehouse

BALLANTINE BOOKS • NEW YORK

ISBN 0-345-25156-3-195

Manufactured in the United States of America

First Ballantine Books Edition: May 1972
Second Printing: April 1977

Chapter 1

I HAD just begun to write this story, when a literary pal of mine who had had a sticky night out with the P.E.N. Club blew in to borrow bicarbonate of soda, and I thought it would be as well to have him vet what I'd done, in case I might have foozled my tee-shot. Because, except for an occasional anecdote in the Drones smoking-room about Scotsmen, Irishmen, and Jews, and even then I generally leave out the point, I've never told a story in my life. And the one thing all the cognoscenti stress is that you must get started right.

So I said: 'I say, can I read you something?' and he said: 'If you must,' and I said: 'Right ho.'

'I am trying to get down on paper,' I said, 'a rather rummy experience that happened to me about a year ago. I haven't got very far yet. I start with where I met the kid.'

'What kid?'

'The kid I met,' I said, and kicked off as follows:

The kid was sitting in one arm-chair. I was sitting in another. His left cheek was bulging. My left cheek was bulging. He was turning the pages of the *National Geographic Magazine*. So was I. In short, there we both were.

He seemed a bit restless, I thought, as if the *National Geographic* wasn't holding him absolutely spellbound. He would put it down for a minute and take it up for a minute and then put it down for a minute again, and it was during one of these putting-it-down-for-a-minute phases that he looked over at me.

'Where,' he asked, 'are the rest of the boys?'

At this point, my literary pal opened his eyes, which he had closed in a suffering sort of way. His manner was that of one who has had a dead fish thrust under his nose.

'Is this bilge,' he asked, 'to be printed?'

'Privately. It will be placed in the family archives for the benefit of my grandchildren.'

'Well, if you ask me,' he said, 'the little perishers won't be able to make head or tail of it. Where's it all supposed to be happening?'

'In Hollywood.'

'Well, you'll have to explain that. And these arm-chairs. What about them? What arm-chairs? Where?'

'Those were in a dentist's waiting-room. That's where the kid and I met.'

'Who is this kid?'

'He turns out to be little Joey Cooley, the child film star, the Idol of American Motherhood.'

'And who are you?'

'Me?' I said, a bit surprised, for we had been at school together. 'Why, you know me, old man. Reggie Havershot.'

'What I mean is, you've got to introduce yourself to the reader. He doesn't know by intuition who you are.'

'You wouldn't let it gradually dawn upon him in the course of the narrative?'

'Certainly not. The first rule in telling a story is to make it thoroughly clear at the outset who's who, when, where, and why. You'd better start again from the beginning.'

He then took his bicarbonate and withdrew.

Well, then, harking back and buckling down to it once more, my name, as foreshadowed in the foregoing, is Reggie Havershot. Reginald John Peter Swithin, third Earl of Havershot, if you want to be formal, but Reggie to my pals. I'm about twenty-eight and a bit, and at the time of which I am writing was about twenty-seven and a bit. Height six feet one, eyes brown, hair a sort of carroty colour.

Mark you, when I say I'm the third Earl of Havershot, I don't mean that I was always that. No, indeed. I started at the bottom and worked my way up. For years and years

I plugged along as plain R. J. P. Swithin, fully expecting that that would be the name carved on my tombstone when the question of tombstones should arise. As far as my chances of ever copping the title went, I don't suppose I was originally more than about a hundred-to-eight shot, if that. The field was full of seasoned performers who could give me a couple of stone.

But you know how it is. Uncles call it a day. Cousins hand in their spades and buckets. And little by little and bit by bit, before you know where you are – why, there you are, don't you know.

Well, that's who I am, and apart from that I don't know that there is much of interest to tell you *re* self. I got my boxing Blue at Cambridge, but that's about all. I mean to say, I'm just one of those chaps. So we'll shift on at once to how I happened to be in Hollywood.

One morning, as I was tucking away the eggs and bacon at my London residence, the telephone rang, and it was old Horace Plimsoll asking if I could look in at his office on a matter of some importance. Certainly, I said, certainly, and off I went. Only too pleased.

I liked old Plimsoll. He was the family lawyer, and recently, what with all the business of taking over and all that, we had been seeing a good deal of one another. I pushed round to his office and found him, as usual, up to the thorax in bills of replevin and what not. He brushed these aside and came to the surface and looked at me over his spectacles.

'Good morning, Reginald,' he said.

'Good morning,' I said.

He took off his spectacles, polished them and put them on again.

'Reginald,' he said, giving me the eye once more, 'you are now the head of the family.'

'I know,' I said. 'Isn't it a scream? Have I got to sign something?'

'Not at the moment. What I wished to see you about to-day has to do with a more personal matter. I wished to point out to you that, as head of the family, certain responsibilities devolve upon you, which I feel sure you will not neglect. You have obligations now, Reginald, and those obligations must be fulfilled, no matter what the cost. *Noblesse oblige.*'

'Oh, ah?' I said, not liking the sound of this much. It began to look to me like a touch. 'What's the bad news? Does one of the collateral branches want to dip into the till?'

'Let me begin at the beginning,' said old Plimsoll. He picked a notice of distraint or something off his coat sleeve. 'I have just been in communication with your Aunt Clara. She is worried.'

'Oh, yes?'

'Extremely worried, about your Cousin Egremont.'

Well, of course, I tut-tutted sympathetically, but I can't say I was surprised. Ever since he grew to man's estate, this unfortunate aunt has been chronically worried about the lad under advisement, who is pretty generally recognized as London W.1's most prominent souse. For years everybody has been telling Eggy that it's hopeless for him to attempt to drink up all the alcoholic liquor in England, but he keeps on trying. The good old bull-dog spirit, of course, but it worries Aunt Clara.

'You know Egremont's record?'

I had to think a bit.

'Well, one Boat Race night I saw him put away sixteen double whiskies and soda, but whether he has beaten that since or not —'

'For years he has been causing Lady Clara the gravest concern. And now —'

I raised a hand.

'Don't tell me. Let me guess. He's been bonneting policemen?'

'No. He —'

'Throwing soft-boiled eggs at the electric fan in the better class of restaurant?'

'No. He —'

'Not murder, surely?'

'No. He has escaped to Hollywood.'

'Escaped to Hollywood?'

'Es-caped to Hollywood,' said old Plimsoll.

I didn't get his drift, and said so. He continued snowing.

'Some little while ago, Lady Clara became alarmed at the state of Egremont's health. His hands were shaky, and he complained of spiders on the back of his neck. So, acting on the advice of a Harley Street specialist, she decided to send him on one of these cruises round the world, in the hope that the fresh air and change of scene —'

I spotted the obvious flaw.

'But these boats have bars.'

'The bar-attendants had strict orders not to serve Egremont.'

'He wouldn't like that.'

'He did not like it. His letters home – his almost daily wireless messages also – were full of complaints. Their tone was uniformly querulous. And when, on the homeward journey, the boat touched at Los Angeles, he abandoned it and went to Hollywood, where he now is.'

'Golly! Drinking like the stag at eve, I suppose?'

'Direct evidence on the point is lacking, but I think that one may assume such to be the case. But that is not the worst. That is not what has occasioned Lady Clara this excessive perturbation.'

'No?'

'No. We have reason to believe – from certain passages in his latest communication – that he is contemplating matrimony.'

'Yes?'

'Yes. His words leave no room for doubt. He is either betrothed or on the verge of becoming betrothed to some young woman out there. And you know the sort of young women that abound in Hollywood.'

'Pippins, I have always been given to understand.'

'Physically, no doubt, they are as you describ-. But they are by no means suitable mates for your cousin Egremont.'

I couldn't see this. I should have thought, personally, that a bird like Eggy was dashed lucky to get any girl to take him on. However, I didn't say so. Old Plimsoll has a sort of gruesome reverence for the family, and the remark would have hurt him. Instead, I asked what the idea was. Where did I come in? What, I asked, did he imagine that I could do about it.

He looked like a high priest sicking the young chief of the tribe on to noble deeds.

'Why, go to Hollywood, Reginald, and reason with this misguided young man. Put a stop to all this nonsense. Exert your authority as head of the family.'

'What, me?'

'Yes.'

'H'm.'

'Don't say "h'm".'

'Ha!'

'And don't say "ha". Your duty is plain. You cannot shirk it.'

'But Hollywood's such miles away.'

'Nevertheless, I insist that it is incumbent upon you, as head of the family, to go there, and without an instant's delay.'

I chewed the lower lip a bit. I must say I couldn't see why I should go butting in, trying to put a stopper on Eggy's – as far as I could make out – quite praiseworthy amours. Live and let live is my motto. If Eggy wanted to get spliced, let him, was the way I looked at it. Marriage might improve him. It was difficult to think of anything that wouldn't.

'H'm,' I said again.

Old Plimsoll was fiddling with pencil and paper – working out routes and so on, apparently.

'The journey is, as you say, a long one, but perfectly simple. On arriving in New York, you would, I understand, take the train known as the Twentieth Century Limited to Chicago. A very brief wait there —'

I sat up.

'Chicago? You don't go through Chicago, do you?'

'Yes. You change trains at Chicago. And from there to Los Angeles is a mere —'

'But wait a second,' I said. 'This is beginning to look more like a practical proposition. Your mention of Chicago opens up a new line of thought. The fight for the heavyweight championship of the world is coming off in Chicago in a week or so.'

I examined the matter in the light of these new facts. All my life I had wanted to see one of these world's championships, and I had never been able to afford the trip. It now dawned upon me that, having come into the title and trimmings, I could do it on my head. The amazing thing was that I hadn't thought of it before. It always takes you some little time to get used to the idea that you are on Easy Street.

'How far is it from Chicago to Hollywood?'

'Little more than a two days' journey, I believe.'

'Then say no more,' I said. 'It's a go. I don't suppose for a moment that I'll be able to do a thing about old Eggy, but I'll go and see him.'

'Excellent.'

There was a pause. I could see that something else was coming.

'And – er – Reginald.'

'Hullo?'

'You will be careful?'

'Careful?'

He coughed, and fiddled with an application for soccage in fief.

'Where you yourself are concerned, I mean. These Hollywood women are, as you were saying a moment ago, of considerable personal attractions . . .'

I laughed heartily.

'Good Lord!' I said. 'No girl's going to look at me.'

This seemed to jar his reverence for the family. He frowned in a rebuking sort of way.

'You are the Earl of Havershot.'

'I know. But even so —'

'And, if I am not mistaken, girls have looked at you in the past.'

I knew what he meant. A couple of years before, while at Cannes, I had got engaged to a girl named Ann Bannister, an American newspaper girl who was spending her holiday there, and as I was the heir apparent at the time this had caused some stir in the elder branches of the family. There was a considerable sense of relief, I believe, when the thing had been broken off.

'All the Havershots have been highly susceptible and impulsive. Your hearts rule your heads. So —'

'Oh, right ho. I'll be careful.'

'Then I will say no more. *Verbum* – ah – *sapienti satis.* And you will start for Hollywood as soon as possible?'

'Immediately,' I said.

There was a boat leaving on the Wednesday. Hastily throwing together a collar and a toothbrush, I caught it. A brief stay in New York, a couple of days in Chicago, and I was on the train to Los Angeles, bowling along through what I believe is called Illinois.

And it was as I sat outside the observation car on the second morning of the journey, smoking a pipe and thinking of this and that, that April June came into my life.

The general effect was rather as if I had swallowed six-pennorth of dynamite and somebody had touched it off inside me.

Chapter 2

THESE observation cars, in case you don't know, are where the guard's van is on an English train. You go through a door at the end on to a platform with a couple of chairs on it, and there you sit and observe the country-side. Of which, of course, there is no stint, for, as you are probably aware, there's a lot of America, especially out in the Western districts, and once you get aboard a train for Los Angeles you just go on and on.

Well, as I say, on the second morning of the journey I was sitting on the observation platform, observing, when I was stunned by the door opening.

That's not quite right, of course, and when I fix and re-vise I must remember to polish up that sentence. Because I don't mean the thing got me on the head or anything like that. What stunned me was not the door opening, but what came through it. Viz., the loveliest girl I had ever seen in my life.

The thing about her that hit the spectator like a bullet first crack out of the box was her sort of sweet, tender, wistful gentleness. Some species of negroid train-attendant had accompanied her through the door, carrying a cushion which he put down in the opposite chair, and she thanked him in a kind of cooing, crooning way that made my toes curl up inside my shoes. And when I tell you that with this wistful gentleness went a pair of large blue eyes, a perfectly modelled chassis, and a soft smile which brought out a dimple on the right cheek, you will readily under-stand why it was that two seconds after she had slid into the picture I was clutching my pipe till my knuckles stood out white under the strain and breathing through my nose in short, quick pants. With my disengaged hand I straightened my tie, and if my moustache had been long enough to twirl there is little question that I would have twirled it.

The coloured brother popped off, no doubt to resume the duties for which he drew his weekly envelope, and she sat down, rather like a tired flower drooping. I dare say you've seen tired flowers droop. And there for a few moments the matter rested. She sniffed the air. I sniffed the air. She watched the countryside winding away. So did I. But for all practical purposes we might have been on different continents.

And the sadness of this was just beginning to come over me like a fog, when I suddenly heard her utter a sharp yowl and saw that she was rubbing her eye. It was plain to the meanest intelligence that she had gone and got a cinder into it, of which there were several floating about.

It solved the whole difficult problem of how I was ever going to break down the barriers, if you know what I mean, and get acquainted. It so happens that if there is one thing I am good at, it is taking things out of eyes – cinders, flies, gnats on picnics, or whatever it may be. To whip out my handkerchief was with me the work of a moment, and I don't suppose it was more than a couple of ticks later before she was thanking me brokenly and I was not-at-all-ing and shoving the handkerchief up my sleeve again. Yes, less than a minute after I had been practically despairing of ever starting anything in the nature of a beautiful friendship, there I was, fixed up solid.

The odd thing was, I couldn't see any cinder, but it must have been there, because she said she was all right now and, as I say, started to thank me brokenly. She was all over me. If I had saved her from Manchurian bandits, she couldn't have been more grateful.

'Thank you ever, *ever* so much,' she said.

'Not at all,' said I.

'It's so awful when you get a cinder in your eye.'

'Yes. Or a fly.'

'Yes. Or a gnat.'

'Yes. Or a piece of dust.'

14

'Yes. And I couldn't help rubbing it.'

'I noticed you were rubbing it.'

'And they say you ought not to rub it.'

'No, I believe you ought not to rub it.'

'And I always feel I've got to rub it.'

'Well, that's how it goes.'

'Is my eye red?'

'No. Blue.'

'It feels red.'

'It looks blue,' I assured her, and might have gone on to add that it was the sort of blue you see in summer skies or languorous lagoons, had she not cut in.

'You're Lord Havershot, aren't you?' she said.

I was surprised. The old map is distinctive and individual, but not, I should have said, famous. And any supposition that we had met before and I had forgotten her was absurd.

'Yes,' I said. 'But how —?'

'I saw a photograph of you in one of the New York papers.'

'Oh, ah, yes, of course.' I recalled that there had been blokes fooling about with cameras when the boat arrived at New York. 'You know,' I said, giving her a searching glance, 'your face seems extraordinarily familiar, too.'

'You've probably seen it in pix.'

'No, I've never been there.'

'In the pictures.'

'In the ... Good Lord!' I said. 'You're not April June, are you?'

'Yes.'

'I've seen dozens of your pictures.'

'Did you like them?'

'I loved them. I say, did you say you'd been in New York?'

'Yes. I was making a personal appearance.'

'I wish I'd known.'

'Well, it wasn't a secret. Why do you wish you had known?'

'Because ... Well, I mean to say ... Well, what I mean is, I rather hurried through New York, and if I'd known that you were there I – er – I wouldn't have hurried.'

'I see.' She paused to tuck away a tendril of hair which had got separated from the main body and was blowing about. 'It's rather draughty out here, isn't it?'

'It is a bit.'

'Suppose we go back to my drawing-room and I'll mix you a cocktail. It's nearly lunch-time.'

'Fine.'

'Come along, then.'

I mused to some extent as we toddled along the train. I was thinking of old Plimsoll. It was all very well, I felt, for old Plimsoll to tell me to be careful, but he couldn't possibly have anticipated anything like this.

We reached the drawing-room and she rang the bell. A negroid bloke appeared – not the same negroid bloke who had carried the cushion – another – and she asked for ice in a gentle voice. He buzzed off, and she turned to me again.

'I don't understand English titles,' she said.

'No?' I said.

'No,' she said. 'There's nothing I enjoy more than curling up with a good English book, but the titles always puzzle me. That New York paper called you the Earl of Havershot. Is an Earl the same as a Duke?'

'Not quite. Dukes are a bit higher up.'

'Is it the same as a Viscount?'

'No. Viscounts are a bit lower down. We Earls rather sneer at Viscounts. One is pretty haughty with them, poor devils.'

'What is your wife? A Countess?'

'I haven't got a wife. If I had, she would be a Countess.'

A sort of faraway look came into her eyes.

'The Countess of Havershot,' she murmured.

'That's right. The Countess of Havershot.'

'What is Havershot? The place where you live?'

'No. I don't quite know where the Havershot comes in. The family doss-house is at Biddleford, in Norfolk.'

'Is it a very lovely place?'

'Quite a goodish sort of shack.'

'Battlements?'

'Lots of battlements.'

'And deer?'

'Several deer.'

'I love deer.'

'Me too. I've met some very decent deer.'

At this point, the ice-bearer entered bearing ice. She dropped the live-stock theme, and started to busy herself with the fixings. Presently she was in a position to provide me with a snort.

'I hope it's all right. I'm not very good at making cocktails, I'm afraid.'

'It's fine,' I said. 'Full of personality. Aren't you having one?'

She shook her head, and smiled that soft smile of hers.

'I'm rather old-fashioned. I don't drink or smoke.'

'Good Lord! Don't you?'

'No. I'm afraid I'm very quiet and domestic and dull.'

'No, I say, dash it. Not dull.'

'Oh, but I am. It may seem odd to you, considering that I'm in pix, but I'm really at heart just a simple little home body. I am never happier than among my books and flowers. And I love cooking.'

'No, really?'

'Yes, really. It's quite a joke among my friends. They come to take me out to some party, and they find me in my kitchen in a gingham wrapper, fixing a Welsh rarebit. I am never happier than in my kitchen.'

I sipped my snootful reverently. Every word that she uttered made me more convinced that I was in the presence of an angel in human shape.

'So you live all alone at – what was the name of the place you said?'

'Biddleford? Well, not exactly. I mean, I haven't really

17

checked in yet. I only took over a short while ago. But I suppose I shall in due season settle down there. Old Plimsoll would have a fit if I didn't. He's our family lawyer, you know, and has views on these things. The head of the family has always hung out at the castle.'

'Castle? Is it a castle?'

'Oh, rather.'

'A real castle?'

'Oh, quite.'

'Is it very old?'

'Definitely moth-eaten. One of the ruins that Cromwell knocked about a bit, don't you know.'

That faraway look came into her eyes again. She sighed.

'How wonderful it must be, having a lovely old home like that. Hollywood is so new and . . . garish. One gets so tired of its garishness. It's all so —'

'Garish?'

'Yes, garish.'

'And you don't like it? I mean, you find it too garish?'

'No, I don't like it. It jars upon me terribly. But what can I do? My work lies there. One has to sacrifice everything to one's work.'

She sighed again, and I felt that I had had a glimpse of some great human tragedy.

Then she smiled bravely.

'But let's not talk about me,' she said. 'Tell me about yourself. Is this your first visit to America?'

'Yes.'

'And why are you going to Hollywood? You are going to Hollywood, I suppose? Not getting off somewhere before Los Angeles?'

'Oh, no, I'm bound for Hollywood all right. On business, as you might say, more or less. You see, a splash of family trouble has arisen. There's a cousin of mine making rather an ass of himself in those parts. You haven't run into him, by any chance, have you? Tall, butter-coloured-haired chap named Egremont Mannering?'

'No.'

'Well, he's in Hollywood and, from all accounts, planning to get married. And what we feel, knowing Eggy, is that the bride-to-be is probably some frightful red-hot mamma. In which event, it is imperative that a spanner be bunged into the works. And I was told off to come along and do it.'

She nodded.

'I see. Yes, I don't wonder you are anxious. Most of the girls in Hollywood are terrible. That is one of the things that make the place so uncongenial to me. That is why I have so few real friends. I know people think me prudish, but what is one to do?'

'I see what you mean. Bit of a problem.'

'Rather than mix with uncongenial people who think about nothing but wild parties, I prefer to be lonely. Though, after all, can one ever be lonely if one has one's books?'

'True.'

'And flowers.'

'Quite.'

'And one's kitchen, of course.'

'Absolutely.'

'But here we are, talking about me again! Go on telling me about yourself. Was it just to find your cousin that you came to America?'

'Not exactly. I rather saw my way to killing two birds with one stone, as it were. There was this heavyweight championship fight on in Chicago, and I particularly wanted to see it.'

'You really enjoy watching fights?'

'I know what you mean,' I said. 'Nine times out of ten they're absolute washouts, of course. But this one was a corker. It was worth coming four thousand miles just to see that fifth round.' The recollection of it stirred me deeply, and I had to rise in order to illustrate. 'It had been pretty good even before that, but in the fifth everything just boiled over. The champion managed to work his man into a neutral corner and copped him squarely on the nose. The challenger came back with a beauty to the eye. They clinched. The referee broke them. Champion to chin, challenger to lower ribs. Another clinch. Break. In-fighting all over the ring. Challenger landed lightly, champ to nose again, then right on the smush. Blood flowing in quarts, and the air thick with teeth and ears and things. And then, just before the bell went, the champ brought one up from the floor . . .'

I broke off here, because she had fainted. I had thought at first, when she closed her eyes, that she had done so merely in order to listen better, but this was apparently not the case. She slid sideways along the seat and quietly passed out.

I was gravely concerned. In the enthusiasm of the moment I had forgotten the effect my narrative might have on this sensitive plant, and I was not quite certain what was the next move. The best way, of course, of bringing round a swooned subject is to bite the ear, but I couldn't very well bite this divine girl's ear. Apart from anything else, I felt I didn't know her well enough.

Fortunately, before I was called upon to take any steps, her eyelids fluttered and she gave a little sigh. Her eyes opened.

'Where am I?' she murmured.

I looked out of the window.

'Well, I'm a stranger in these parts myself,' I said, 'but I think somewhere in New Mexico.'

She sat up.

'Oh, I feel so mortified!'

'Eh?'

'You must think me so silly, fainting like that.'

'My fault entirely. I oughtn't to have dished the dreadful details.'

'It wasn't your fault. Most girls would have enjoyed it. Though I think there is something terribly unfeminine . . . Go on, Lord Havershot, what happened after that?'

'No, no. I wouldn't dream of telling you.'

'Do. Please'

'Oh, well, putting the thing in a nutshell, he soaked him on the button, don't you know, and his day's work was done.'

'Could you get me a glass of water?'

I leaped to the bottle. She sipped in a fluttering sort of way.

'Thank you,' she said. 'I feel better now. I'm sorry I was so silly.'

'You weren't silly.'

'Oh, but I was. Terribly silly.'

'You weren't silly at all. The whole episode reflects great credit on your womanly nature.'

And I was about to add that I had never in my puff beheld anything that had stirred me more deeply than the way she had turned her toes up, when the negroid bloke poked his nose in at the door and announced that lunch was served.

'You go along,' she said. 'I'm sure you must be starving.'

'Aren't you coming?'

'I think I'll just lie here and rest. I still feel ... No, you go along.'

'I should like to kick myself.'

'Why?'

'For being such a chump. Sullying your ears like that.'

'Please! Do go and get your lunch.'

'But will you be all right?'

'Oh, yes.'

'You're sure?'

'Oh, yes, really. I shall just lie here and think of flowers. I often do that — just lie around and think of flowers. Roses, chiefly. It seems to make everything beautiful and fragrant again.'

So I pushed off. And as I sat eating my steak and fried, I put in some pretty intensive thinking between the mouthfuls.

Of course I saw what had happened. These volcanic symptoms were unmistakable. A chap's heart does not go pit-a-pat, as mine was doing, for nothing. This was the real thing, and what I had taken for a strong man's passion when I had got engaged to Ann Bannister two years ago had been merely Class B stuff. Yes, there was no getting away from it. At long last Love had wound its silken fetters about Reginald Havershot.

I had suspected this from the first. The very moment I had set eyes on this girl, I had received the distinct impression that she was my soul-mate, and everything that had passed between us had made me more certain on the point. It was that sweet, tender, gentle wistfulness of hers that had got in amongst me to such a marked extent. I suppose this is always the way with beefy birds like me. Something draws us instinctively to the fragile flowerets.

It was in a sober, thoughtful spirit that I polished off the steak and put in a bid for deep-dish apple pie with a bit of cheese on the side.

Chapter 3

AND I'll tell you why I was sober and thoughtful. It was because I recognized that this, as they say in the stories, was not an end but a beginning. I mean to say, it was all very well to have fallen in love at first sight, but that didn't take me very far. Where, I was asking myself, did I go from there? What of the future? In other words, what steps was I to take in order to bring about the happy finish? The fact had to be faced that if banns were ever to be put up and clergymen were ever to say 'Wilt thou, Reginald?' some pretty heavy work lay ahead of me. In no sense could the thing be looked upon as a walkover.

You see, I have kept it from you till now, but there are certain defects in my personal appearance which prevent me being everybody's money where the opposite sex is concerned. I am no flier in the way of looks. Externally, I take after the pater, and if you had ever seen the pater you would realize what that means. He was a gallant soldier and played a hot game of polo, but he had a face like a gorilla – much more so, indeed, than most gorillas have – and was, so I am informed, affectionately known to his little circle of cronies as Consul, the Almost Human. And I am his living image.

These things weigh with girls. They shrink from linking their lot with a fellow whose appearance gives the impression that at any moment he may shin up trees and start throwing coconuts.

However, it was too late to do anything about that now. I could only hope that April June would prove to be one of those rare spirits who can pierce the outer husk, as it were, and penetrate to the soul beneath. Because I haven't got such a bad soul, as souls go. I don't say it's the sort of soul you would write to the papers about, but it's well up to the average.

And I'm bound to say that, as the days went along, I found myself perking up a bit. I seemed to be making progress. No one could have been matier than April during my first week in Hollywood. We motored together, bathed together, and had long talks together in the scented dusk. She told me all about her ideals, and I told her all about the old homestead at Biddleford and how Countesses were presented at Court and had the run of the Royal Enclosure at Ascot and a lot of other things she seemed interested in. And there was absolutely nothing in her manner to suggest that she was in any way repelled by the fact that I looked as if I belonged in Whipsnade.

In fact, to cut a long story short, her chummy attitude so encouraged me that by the end of the first week I had decided to chance my arm and have at it.

The occasion I selected for pressing the button and setting the machinery in motion was a party she was giving at her house on Linden Drive. She explained that she didn't like parties, as they seemed to her hollow, but that a girl in her position was expected to give one every now and then, particularly if she had been away for a while.

It was to be one of those jolly Beverly Hills outdoor dinner parties, where you help yourself at the buffet, squash in anywhere, and top of the meal by diving into the swimming-pool. The proceedings were to begin somewhere after nine and before ten, so I rolled up at about nine forty-five.

This, as it turned out, was on the early side. A few scattered couples had arrived and were strolling about under the coloured lanterns, but April was still dressing and the orchestra hadn't started to play and altogether it was apparent that there was going to be a bit of a lull before the revelry got into high.

In these circs, it seemed to me that the best way of passing the time would be to trickle over to the table where the drinks were and brace myself with one or two. In view of what lay before me, I wanted to feel at the top of my form – which I wasn't at the moment, owing to having been kept awake a good deal during the night with a touch of toothache.

As I approached the table, I noticed that my idea of going and doing a bit of stoking up, though good, was not original. It had occurred also to a tall, slender bloke with butter-coloured hair. He was standing there in a rooted sort of way, as if he meant to take a lot of shifting, and he seemed to be putting a good deal of custom in the way of the bar-tenders. And there was something about him, something in his technique as he raised and lowered his glass, which somehow struck me as oddly familiar. Also, I felt I had seen that hair before. And the next moment I had identified him.

'Eggy!' I cried.

He had just emptied his glass as I spoke, which was fortunate, for at the sound of my view-halloo he leaped about six inches in the air. Returning to earth, he leaned towards the chap behind the bar, his bosom heaving a bit.

'I say,' he asked in a low, trembling tone, 'you didn't hear a voice then, by any chance, did you?'

The chap said that he thought he had heard someone say something about eggs.

'Oh, you did hear it?'

'Eggy, you old ass,' I said.

This time he turned, and stood staring at me. His face was drawn and anxious.

'Reggie?' he said, in a doubting sort of way.

He blinked a couple of times, then put a hand out and prodded my chest cautiously. As his finger touched solid shirt-front, a look of relief spread over his features.

'Phew!' he said.

He asked the chap behind the bar for another Scotch, and it was not until he had received and taken a liberal swig of this that he spoke again. When he did, his voice was grave and reproachful.

'If you know me a million years, Reggie, old man,' he said, wiping a bead of persp. from his brow, 'never do a thing like that again. I thought you were thousands of miles away, and when I heard your voice, all ghastly and hollow ... calling my name ... like a ruddy banshee ... It's the one thing I'm scared of, hearing voices,' he said. 'I'm told that till you do that you're all right, but once the voices start coming it's the beginning of the end.'

He shuddered and finished the rest of his drink at a gulp. This appeared to complete the cure, for he became easier in his manner.

'Well, well, well,' he said, 'so you're here, are you, Reggie? Ages since I saw you last. Six months come Sheffield Wednesday, or thereabouts. What on earth are you doing in Hollywood?'

'I came to see you.'

'You did?'

'Yes.'

'Pretty cousinly. Have a spot. I can recommend the Scotch. Bar-bloke, would you be so good as to mix a Scotch and soda for my relative here and the same for me.'

I attempted to dissuade.

'I wouldn't have any more.'

'You haven't had any yet.'

'If I were you, I mean. You're sozzled already.'

'Half sozzled,' he corrected, for he is rather exact in these matters.

'Well, half sozzled, then. And it's only ten o'clock.'

'If a man isn't half sozzled by ten o'clock, he isn't trying. Don't you worry about me, Reggie, old man. You don't understand the wonders of the Californian climate yet. So superbly bracing is it that day by day in every way you can put away all you want to, and not a squawk from the old liver. That's what they mean when they speak of California as an earthly Paradise, and that's why trainloads of people are pouring in all the time from the Middle West with their tongues hanging out. I expect that's why you came here, isn't it?'

'I came to see you.'

'Oh, yes. You told me that, didn't you?'

'Yes.'

'And did I say it was cousinly?'

'Yes.'

'And so it is. Most cousinly. Where are you staying?'

'I've got a bungalow at a place called the Garden of the Hesperides.'

'I know it well. Have you a cellar?'

'I've got a bottle of whisky, if that's what you mean.'

'It's precisely what I mean. I shall make a point of looking you up. A fellow can't have too many oases. Meanwhile, drink hearty and have another.'

Something about all this had been puzzling me, and now I discovered what it was. On the train, I remembered, I had spoken of Eggy to April, and she had specifically stated that she didn't know him. Yet here he was, at her house, throwing his weight about like a reveller in a comic opera.

'What are you doing here?' I asked, resolved on probing this mystery.

'Having a dashed good time,' he responded heartily, 'and all the better for the sight of your honest face. Delightful, seeing you again, Reggie. Later on, you must tell me what brought you to California.'

'You don't know April June?'

'April who?'

'June.'

'What about her?'

'I was saying, you don't know her.'

'No, but I'd love to. Any friend of yours. If she is a friend of yours.'

'This is her party.'

'It does her credit.'

'You weren't invited.'

His face cleared.

'Now I understand. Now I see what you're driving at. Good heavens, laddie, you don't have to be invited to go to people's parties in Hollywood. You just saunter along till you see coloured lanterns, and walk in. Many of my happiest evenings have been spent as the guest of people who didn't know me from Adam and hadn't a notion I was there. But, by an odd chance, I'm not gate-crashing to-night. I was brought here. What did you say that name was? April —?'

'June.'

'That's right. It all comes back to me. My fiancée is April June's press agent, and she brought me here.'

I felt that this was a good opportunity of tackling this fiancée business. I had been wondering how to bring it up.

'I wanted to talk to you about that.'

'About what?'

'About this engagement of yours.'

I spoke pretty crisply, with a goodish amount of head-of-the-family-ness, for the old conscience was prodding me a bit. I felt I had been letting Horace Plimsoll and my Aunt Clara down rather badly. I mean to say, they had sent me out here to find this bird and reason with him, and I had been out here a week without giving him a single thought. Since I had got off the train at Los Angeles he had absolutely passed from my mind. It just shows what love can do to you.

He weighed the remark carefully.

'Engagement?'

'Yes.'

'My engagement?'

'Yes.'

'What about it?'

'Well, what about it?'

'Happiest man in the world.'

'Aunt Clara isn't.'

'This Aunt Clara being who?'

'Your mother.'

'Oh, the mater? Yes, I know her. Should we drink to the mater?'

'No.'

'Just as you say. Though it seems a bit uncivil. Well, what's wrong with the mater? Why isn't she the happiest man in the world?'

'Because she's worrying herself pallid about you.'

'Good Lord, why? I'm all right.'

'What the devil do you mean, you're all right? You ought to be ashamed of yourself. You go sneaking off to Hollywood, and I find you here, mopping up the stuff like a vacuum cleaner . . .'

'Aren't you being a bit pompous, old man?'

The point was well taken. I was, of course. But it seemed to me that pomposity was of the essence. I mean to say, you can't tick a bloke off properly unless you come over a bit mid-Victorian.

'I don't care if I am. You make me sick.'

A look of pain came into his face.

'Is this Reginald Havershot speaking?' he said reproachfully. 'My cousin Reginald, who on New Year's Eve two years ago, in the company of myself and old Stinker Pomeroy, broke twenty-three glasses at the Café de l'Europe and was thrown out kicking and screaming —'

I checked him with a cold gesture. My great love had purified me so intensely that it was loathsome to me to listen to these reminiscences of what had happened to my baser self two years ago.

'Never mind that,' I said. 'I want to know about this business of yours. How long have you been engaged?'

'Oh, a certain time.'

'And are you going to get married?'

'My dear chap, that's the whole idea.'

It was a little difficult to know what to say. Old Plimsoll had told me to exercise my authority, but I didn't see how it was to be done. Eggy had plenty of money of his own. If I had threatened to cut him off without a shilling, he would simply have asked to be shown the shilling, pocketed it, thanked me, and carried on according to plan.

'Well, if you're going to get married,' I said, 'you'd better stop drinking.'

He shook his head.

'You don't understand, old man. I can't stop drinking.

I have a shrewd idea that this girl got engaged to me in order to reform me, and pretty silly she would feel if I went and reformed on my own. You can see how it would discourage her. Probably she would lose interest and chuck me. You've got to think of these things, you know. The way I look at it, the safe, sane, and sound policy is to keep reasonably pie-eyed till after the ceremony and then sober up by degrees during the honeymoon.'

It was a theory, of course, but I hadn't time to go into it then.

'Who is this girl you're engaged to?'

'Her name is . . .' He paused, and his brow wrinkled. 'Her name . . . Now, if you had asked me that an hour ago – nay, even half an hour ago . . . Ah!' he said, perking up. 'Here she comes in person. She'll be able to tell us.'

He waved cordially at someone behind me. I turned. A slimmish sort of girl was coming towards us across the lawn. I couldn't see if she was pretty or not, because her face was in the shadow. She waved back at him.

'Hello, Eggy. There you are. I thought you would be.'

Something in her voice caused me to start and gaze narrowly at her as she came into the light. And at the same moment something in the cut of my jib caused her to start and gaze narrowly at me. And in half a tick we were gazing narrowly at each other – she at me, I at her. And in half a tick after that our last doubts were dispelled.

Reading from left to right, we were myself and Ann Bannister.

Chapter 4

'ANN —!' I cried.

'— Bannister!' cried Eggy, slapping his forehead. 'I knew it would come back. It was on the tip of my tongue all along. Hullo, Ann. This is my cousin, Reggie.'

'We have met.'

'You mean before this moment?'

'A long time before this moment. We're old friends.'

'Old friends?'

'Very old friends.'

'Then, obviously, a small drink is indicated. Bar-bloke —'

'No,' said Ann. 'You get right away from that bar.'

'But aren't we going to celebrate?'

'No.'

'Oh?'

'You go and take a walk round the block, Egremont Mannering, and don't come back till your brain is like a razor.'

'My brain is like a razor.'

'Two razors, then. Off you go.'

There had always been something compelling about Ann. I had noticed it myself in the old days. She was one of those small, brisk, energetic girls, abundantly supplied with buck and ginger, who have a way of making the populace step around a bit. Eggy trotted off like a lamb in a his-not-to-reason-why manner, and we were alone together.

We stood in silence for a moment. I was brooding on the past, and I suppose she was, too.

Just to keep the record straight, I'd better tell you about this past that we were brooding on. This Ann Bannister, as I said, was a newspaper girl, and I had met her when she was taking a holiday at Cannes. We became chummy. I asked her to marry me. She right-hoed. So far so good.

And then, quite unexpectedly, the engagement went and busted itself up. One moment, it was buzzing along like a two-year-old, and was all gas and gaiters. The next, it had come a stinker.

What happened was this. One night, we were sitting side by side on the terrace of the Palm Beach Casino, watching the silver moon flood the rippling Mediterranean, and she squeezed my hand, and I leaned towards her tenderly, and she leaned towards me, waiting for the loving observation which she had every reason to suppose would emerge, and I said:

'Gosh! My feet hurt!'

Well, they did, I mean to say. Even as I leaned towards her, they had given me a sudden twinge of acute agony. I was trying out a new pair of dress shoes that night, and you know what patent leather can do to the extremities. But, undoubtedly, I should have chosen another moment for introducing the topic. She took it rather hard. She seemed upset. In fact, she turned away, and petulantly, at that. So, thinking to heal the breach, I bent forward to plant a gentle kiss on the back of her neck.

Well, that was all right, of course – I mean to say, as an idea. The trouble was that I forgot that I had a lighted cigar in my mouth, and when the fact was drawn to my attention, it was too late. Leaping like a scalded kitten, she began calling me a soulless plugugly and breaking off the engagement. And next day, when I called at her hotel with flowers to take the matter up again, I found that she had left. Yes, she had gone out of my life.

And here she was, two years later, back again.

I'm bound to say I was a bit embarrassed at finding myself *vis-à-vis* with this chunk of the days that were no more. It's always embarrassing to run unexpectedly into a girl you used to be engaged to. I mean, you don't quite know how to comport yourself. If you look chirpy, that's not much of a compliment to her. Whereas, if you look mouldy, you feel that she's patting herself on the back and saying: 'Aha! I thought losing me would make the poor clam think a bit!' and that offends a fellow's pride. I suppose the wheeze really is to have one of those cold, inscrutable faces you read about in books.

She, on her side, women having the gift more than men, had already pulled herself together.

'Well!' she said.

A pleased smile had come into her face, and she was looking at me as if I had been just some fairly mere acquaintance who meant nothing much in the scheme of things, but whom she was quite glad to see.

'Well, fancy meeting you here, Reggie!'

I saw that this was the right attitude. After all, the dead past is the dead past. I mean to say, the heavy stuff was over between us. At the time when she had severed relations, the thing had, of course, stuck the gaff into me to quite a goodish extent. I won't say that I had not been able to sleep or touch food, because I've always slept like a log and taken my three square a day, and not even this tragedy could break the habit of a lifetime, but I certainly had felt a bit caught in the machinery. Sombre, if you know what I mean, and unsettled, and rather inclined to read Portuguese Love Sonnets and smoke too much. But I had got over all that ages ago, and we could now meet on a calm, friendly footing.

So I spoke, as she had done, with an easy cordiality.

'Me, too,' I said. 'Fancy meeting you here.'

'How are you?'

'Oh, I'm fine.'

'The feet quite all right?'

'Oh, quite.'

'Good.'

'You're looking well.'

She was, too. Ann is one of those girls who always look as if they had just stepped out of a cold bath after doing their daily dozen.

'Thanks. Yes, I'm all right. What has brought you to Hollywood, Reggie?'

'Oh, this and that.'

There was a slightish pause. I felt a bit embarrassed again.

'So,' I said, 'you're affianced to old Eggy?'

'Yes. I do seem to run in the family, don't I?'

'You do a bit.'

'Do you approve?'

I considered this.

'Well, if you ask me,' I said, 'I think it is a far, far better thing that Eggy is doing than he has ever done. But where do you get off? Doesn't this open up a pretty bleak future for you?'

'Why? Don't you like Eggy?'

'I love him like a brother. One of my oldest pals. But I should have thought that for domestic purposes someone who was occasionally sober would have suited you better.'

'Eggy's all right.'

'Oh, he's all *right*. He enjoys it.'

'There's lots of good stuff in Eggy.'

'Quite. And more going in every minute.'

'His trouble is that he has always had too much money and too much spare time. What he needs is a job. I've got him one.'

'And he's accepted office?'

'You bet he's accepted office.'

I was rather overcome.

'Ann,' I said, 'you're a marvel!'

'How so, Mister Bones?'

'Why, making Eggy work. It's never been done before.'

'Well, it's going to be done now. He starts to work to-morrow.'

'That's splendid. One feels a certain pang of pity for whoever it is he's starting to work for, but that's splendid. The family were worried about him.'

'I don't wonder. I can't imagine anybody more capable

34

of worrying a family than Eggy. Just suppose if Job had had him as well as boils!'

The garden was beginning to fill up now, and several thirsty souls had come prowling up to the table like lions to the drinking-hole. We moved away.

'Tell me about yourself, Ann,' I said. 'You're working hard all the time, of course?'

'Oh, yes. Always on the job – such as it is.'

'How do you mean, such as it is? Don't you like it?'

'Not very much.'

'But I should have thought it would just have suited you, being a press agent.'

'A what?'

'Eggy told me you were April June's press agent.'

'He was a little premature. That's what I'm hoping to be, if all goes well, but nothing's settled yet. It all depends on whether something comes off or not.'

'What's that?'

'Oh, just an idea I've got. If it works out as I'm hoping she says she will sign on the dotted line. I shan't know for a couple of days. In the meantime, I'm a sort of governess-companion-nursemaid.'

'A what?'

'Well, I don't know how else you would describe the job. Have you ever heard of Joey Cooley?'

'One of these child stars, isn't he? I have an idea April June told me something about him being in her last picture.'

'That's right. Well, I look after him. Tend him and guard him and all that.'

'But what about your newspaper work? I thought you worked on newspapers and things.'

'I did till a short while ago. I was on a Los Angeles paper. But the depression has upset everything. They let me go. I tried other papers. No room. I tried free-lancing, but there's nothing in free-lancing nowadays. So, having to eat, I took what I could. That's how I come to be governess-companion-nursemaid to Joey.'

35

I must say I felt a pang. I knew how keen she had been on her work.

'I say, I'm frightfully sorry.'

'Thanks, Reggie. You always had a kind heart.'

'Oh, I don't know.'

'Yes, you did. Pure gold and in the right place. It was your poor feet that let you down.'

'Oh, dash it, I wish you wouldn't harp on that.'

'Was I harping?'

'Certainly you were harping. That's the second time you've dug my feet up. If you knew what gyp those shoes were giving me that night ... I thought they were going to burst every moment like shrapnel. ... However, that is neither here nor there. I'm awfully sorry you're having such a rotten time.'

'Oh, it's not really so bad. I don't want to pose as a martyr. I'm quite happy. I love young Joseph. He's a scream.'

'All the same, it must be pretty foul for you. I mean, I know how you must want to be out and about, nosing after stories and getting scoops or whatever you call them.'

'It's sweet of you to be sympathetic, Reggie, but I think I'm going to be all right. I'm practically sure this thing I was speaking of will come off – I don't see how there can be a hitch – and when it does I shall rise on stepping-stones of my dead self to higher things.'

'Good.'

'Though, mind you, there's a darker side. It won't be all jam being April June's press agent.'

'What! Why not?'

'She's a cat.'

I shuddered from stem to stern, as stout barks do when buffeted by the waves.

'A *what*?'

'A cat. There's another word that would describe her even better, but "cat" meets the case.

I mastered my emotion with an effort

'April June,' I said, 'is the sweetest, noblest divinest

girl in existence. The loveliest creature you could shake a stick at in a month of Sundays, and as good as she is beautiful. She's wonderful. She's marvellous. She's super. She's the top.'

She looked at me sharply.

'Hullo! What's all this?'

I saw no reason to conceal my passion.

'I love her,' I said.

'What!'

'Definitely.'

'It can't be true.'

'It is true. I worship the ground she treads on.'

'Well, for crying in the soup!'

'I don't know what that expression means, but I still stick to my story. I worship the ground she treads on.'

She went into the silence for a moment. Then she spoke in a relieved sort of voice.

'Well, thank goodness, there isn't a chance that she'll look at you.'

'Why not?'

'It's all over Hollywood that she's got her hooks on some fool of an Englishman. A man called Lord Havershot. That's the fellow she's going to marry.'

A powerful convulsion shook me from base to apex.

'What!'

'Yes.'

'Is that official?'

'Quite, I believe.'

I drew a deep breath. The coloured lanterns seemed to be dancing buck and wing steps around me.

'Good egg!' I said. 'Because I'm him.'

'What!'

'Yes. Since we – er – last met, there has been a good deal of mortality in the family and I've copped the title.'

She was staring at me, wide-eyed.

'Oh, hell!' she said.

'Why, "oh, hell"?'

'This is awful.'

'It is nothing of the kind. I like it.'

She clutched my coat.

'Reggie, you mustn't do this. Don't make a fool of yourself.'

'A fool of myself, eh?'

'Yes. She'll make you miserable. I may be going to depend on her for my bread and butter, but that shan't stop me doing my best to open your eyes. You're such a sweet, simple old ass that you can't see what everybody else sees. The woman's poison. She's frightful. Everybody knows it. Vain, affected, utterly selfish, and as hard as nails.'

I had to laugh at that.

'As hard as nails, eh?'

'Harder.'

I laughed again. Whole thing so dashed absurd.

'You think so, do you?' I said. 'Funny you should say that. Extremely funny. Because the one thing she is is gentle and sensitive and highly strung and so forth. Let me tell you of a little episode that occurred on the train. I was describing round five of the recent heavyweight championship contest to her, and when I came to the bit about the blood her eyeballs rolled upwards and she swooned away.'

'She did, did she?'

'Passed right out. I never saw anything so womanly in my life.'

'And it didn't occur to you, I suppose, that she was just putting on an act?'

'An act?'

'Yes. And it worked, apparently. Because now I hear that you follow her everywhere she goes, bleating.'

'I do not bleat.'

'The story going the round of the clubs is that you do bleat. People say they can hear you for miles on a clear day. My poor Reggie, she was just fooling you. The woman goes to all the fights in Los Angeles and revels in them.'

'I don't believe it.'

'She does, I tell you. Can't you see that she was simply making a play for you because you're Lord Havershot? That's all she's after – the title. For heaven's sake, Reggie, lay off while there's still time.'

I eyed her coldly and detached my coat from her grasp.

'Let us talk of something else,' I said.

'There's nothing else I want to talk about.'

Then don't let's talk at all. I don't know if you realize it, but what we're doing is perilously near to speaking lightly of a woman's name – the sort of thing chaps get kicked out of clubs for.'

'Reggie, will you listen to me?'

'No. I jolly well won't.'

'Reggie!'

'No. Let's drop the subj.'

She gave a little sigh.

'Oh, very well,' she said. 'I might have known it would be no use trying to drive sense into a fat head like yours ... April June!'

'Why do you say "April June" like that?'

'Because it's the only way to say it.'

'Well, let me tell you I resent your saying "April June" as if you were mentioning the name of some particularly unpleasant disease.'

'That is the way I shall go on saying "April June".'

I bowed stiffly.

'Oh, right ho,' I said. 'Please yourself. After all, your methods of voice production are your own affair. And now, as I observe my hostess approaching, I will beetle along and pay my respects. This will leave you at liberty to go off into a corner by yourself and say "April June", if you so desire, till the party is over and they lock up the house and put the cat out.'

'They don't put her out. She lives here.'

I made no reply to this vulgar crack. I felt that it was beneath me. Besides, I couldn't think of anything. I moved away in silence. I could feel Ann's eyes on the back of my neck, like Eggy's spiders, but I did not look round.

I pushed off to where April was greeting a covey of guests and barged in, hoping ere long to be able to detach her from the throng and have a private word with her on a tender and sentimental subject.

Well, of course, it wasn't easy, because a hostess has much to occupy her, but eventually she seemed satisfied that she had got things moving and could leave people to entertain themselves, so I collared a table for two in a corner of the lawn and dumped her down there. And we had steak and kidney pie and the usual fixings, and presently we started wading into vanilla ice-cream.

And all the while my determination to slap my heart down before her was growing. Ann's derogatory remarks hadn't weakened me in the slightest. All rot, they seemed to me. As I watched this lovely girl shovelling down the stuff, I refused to believe that she wasn't everything that was perfect. I braced myself for the kick-off. At any moment now, I felt, it might occur. It was simply a question of watching out for the psychological moment and leaping on it like a ton of bricks the second it shoved its nose up.

The conversation had turned to her work. She had said something about her chances of doing a quiet sneak to bed at a fairly early hour, because she was supposed to be on the set, made up, at six on the following a.m. for some retakes; and the mere idea of being out of the hay at a time like that made me quiver with tender compassion.

'Six o'clock!' I said. 'Gosh!'

'Yes, it's not an easy life. I often wonder if one's public ever realize how hard it is.'

'It must be frightful.'

'One does get a little tired sometimes.'

'Still,' I said, doing a spot of silver-lining-pointing, 'there's money in it, what?'

'Money!'

'And fame.'

She smiled a faint, saintly sort of smile and champed a spoonful of ice-cream.

'Money and fame mean nothing to me, Lord Haver-shot.'

'No?'

'Oh, no. My reward is the feeling that I am spreading happiness, that I am doing my little best to cheer up this tired world, that I am giving the toiling masses a glimpse of something bigger and better and more beautiful.'

'What ho,' I said reverently.

'You don't think it silly of me to feel like that?'

'I think it's terrific.'

'I'm so glad. You see, it's a sort of religion with me. I feel like a kind of priestess. I think of all those millions of drab lives, and I say to myself what does all the hard work and the distasteful publicity matter if I can bring a little sunshine into their drab round. You're laughing at me?'

'No, no. Absolutely not.'

'Take Pittsburgh, for instance. They eat me in Pittsburgh. My last picture but one grossed twenty-two thousand there on the week. And that makes me very happy, because I think of all those drab lives in Pittsburgh being brightened up like that. And Cincinnati. I was a riot in Cincinnati. People's lives are very drab in Cincinnati, too.'

'It's wonderful!'

She sighed.

'I suppose it is. Yes, of course it is. All those drab lives, I mean. And yet is it enough? That is what one asks oneself sometimes. One is lonely now and then. One feels one wishes one could get away from it all and be just an ordinary happy wife and mother. Sometimes one dreams of the patter of little feet . . .'

I waited no longer. If this wasn't the psychological moment, I didn't know a psychological moment when I saw one. I leaned forward. 'Darling,' I was just about to say, 'stop me if you've heard this before, but will you be my wife?' when something suddenly went off like a bomb inside my head, causing me to drop the subject absolutely.

It happened in a flash. One moment, I was all fire and

41

romance, without a thought for anything except that the girl who was sitting beside me was the girl I loved, and that I was jolly well going to put her in touch with the facts: the next, I was hopping round in circles with my hand pressed to my cheek, suffering the tortures of the damned.

Whether by pure spontaneous combustion, or because I had inadvertently taken aboard too large a segment of ice-cream, the old Havershot wisdom tooth had begun to assert its personality.

I had had my eye on this tooth for some time, and I suppose I ought to have taken a firm line with it before. But you know how it is when you're travelling. You shrink from entrusting the snappers to a strange dentist. You say to yourself 'Stick it out, old cock, till you get back to London and can toddle round to the maestro who's been looking after you since you were so high.' And then, of course, you cop it unexpectedly, as I had done.

Well, there it was. A fellow can't pour out his soul under those conditions. In fact, I don't mind admitting that at that juncture all thoughts of love and marriage and little feet and what not had passed for the nonce completely out of my mind. With a hasty word of farewell, I left her sitting and proceeded to the chemist's shop by the Beverley-Wilshire Hotel in quest of temporary relief. And next day I was in the dentist's waiting-room, about to keep my tryst with I. J. Zizzbaum, the man behind the forceps.

So here we are again at the point where, if you remember, I originally wanted to start the story, only my literary pal headed me off. There I was, as I told you, sitting in an arm-chair, and across the room in another arm-chair, turning the pages of the *National Geographic Magazine*, was a kid of the Little Lord Fauntleroy type. His left cheek, like mine, was bulging, and I deduced that we were both awaiting the awful summons.

He was, I observed, a kid of singular personal beauty. Not even the bulge in his cheek could conceal that. He had large, expressive eyes and golden ringlets. Long lashes hid these eyes as he gazed down at his *National Geographic Magazine*.

I never know what's the correct course to pursue on occasions like this. Should one try to help things along with a friendly word or two, if only about the weather? Or is silence best? I was just debating this question in my mind, when he opened the conversation himself.

He lowered his *National Geographic Magazine* and looked across at me.

'Where,' he asked, 'are the rest of the boys?'

Chapter 5

His meaning eluded me. I didn't get him. A cryptic kid. One of those kids, who, as the expression is, speak in riddles. He was staring at me enquiringly, and I stared back at him, also enquiringly.

Then I said, going straight to the point and evading all side issues:

'What boys?'

'The newspaper boys.'

'The newspaper boys?'

An idea seemed to strike him.

'Aren't you a reporter?'

'No, not a reporter.'

'Then what are you doing here?'

'I've come to have a tooth out.'

This appeared to surprise and displease him. He said, with marked acerbity:

'You can't have come to have a tooth out.'

'Yes, I have.'

'But I've come to have a tooth out.'

I spotted a possible solution.

'Perhaps,' I said, throwing out the suggestion for what it was worth, 'we've both come to have a tooth out, what? I mean to say, you one and me another. Tooth A and Tooth B, as it were.'

He still seemed ruffled. He eyed me searchingly.

'When's your appointment?'

'Three-thirty.'

'It can't be. Mine is.'

'So is mine. I. J. Zizzbaum was most definite about that. We arranged it over the phone, and his words left no loophole for misunderstanding. "Three-thirty," said I. J. Zizzbaum, as plain as I see you now.'

The kid became calmer. His alabaster brow lost its

44

frown, and he ceased to regard me as if I were some hijacker or bandit. It was as if a great light had shone upon him.

'Oh, I. J. Zizzbaum?' he said. 'B. K. Burwash is doing mine.'

And, looking about me, I now perceived that on either side of the apartment in which we sat was a door.

On one of these doors was imprinted the legend:

I. J. ZIZZBAUM

And on the other:

B. K. BURWASH

The mystery was solved. Possibly because they were old dental college chums, or possibly from motives of economy, these two fang-wrenchers shared a common waiting-room.

Convinced now that no attempt was being made to jump his claim, the kid had become affability itself. Seeing in me no rival for first whack at the operating-chair, but merely a fellow human being up against the facts of life just as he was, he changed his tone to one of kindly interest.

'Does your tooth hurt?'

'Like the dickens.'

'So does mine. Coo!'

'Coo here, too.'

'Where does it seem to catch you most?'

'Pretty well all the way down to the toenails.'

'Me, too. This tooth of mine is certainly fierce. Yessir!'

'So is mine.'

'I'll bet mine's worse than yours.'

'It couldn't be.'

He made what he evidently considered a telling point.

'I'm having gas.'

I came right back at him.

'So am I.'

'I'll bet I need more gas than you.'

'I'll bet you don't.'

'I'll bet you a trillion dollars I do.'

It seemed to me that rancour was beginning to creep into the conversation once more, and that pretty soon we would be descending to a common wrangle. So, rather than allow the harmony of the proceedings to be marred by a jarring note, I dropped the theme and switched off to an aspect of the matter which had been puzzling me from the first. You will remember that I had thought this kid to have spoken in riddles, and I still wanted an explanation of those rather mystic opening words of his.

'You're probably right,' I said pacifically. 'But, be that as it may, what made you think I was a reporter?'

'I'm expecting a flock of them here.'

'You are?'

'Sure. There'll be camera men, too, and human interest writers.'

'What, to see you have a tooth out?'

'Sure. When I have a tooth out, that's news.'

'What!'

'Sure. This is going to make the front page of every paper in the country.'

'What, your tooth?'

'Yay, my tooth. Listen, when I had my tonsils extracted last year, it rocked civilization. I'm some shucks, I want to tell you.'

'Somebody special, you mean?'

'I'll say that's what I mean. I'm Joey Cooley.'

Owing to the fact that one of my unswerving rules in life is never to go to a picture if I am informed by my spies that there is a child in it, I had never actually set eyes on this stripling. But of course I knew the name. Ann, if you remember, had spoken of him. So had April June.

'Oh, ah,' I said. 'Joey Cooley, eh?'

'Joey Cooley is correct.'

'Yes, I've heard of you.'

'So I should think.'

'I know your nurse.'

46

'My what?'

'Well, your female attendant or whatever she is. Ann Bannister.'

'Oh, Ann? She's an all-right guy, Ann is.'

'Quite.'

'A corker, and don't let anyone tell you different.'

'I won't.'

'Ann's a peach. Yessir, that's what Ann is.'

'And April June was talking about you the other day.'

'Oh, yeah? And what did she have to say?'

'She told me you were in her last picture.'

'She did, did she?' He snorted with not a little violence, and his brow darkened. It was plain that he was piqued. Meaning nothing but to pass along a casual item of information, I appeared to have touched some exposed nerve. 'The crust of that dame! In *her* last picture, eh? Let me tell you that *she* was in *my* last picture!'

He snorted a bit more. He had taken up the *National Geographic Magazine* again, and I noted that it quivered in his hands, as if he were wrestling with some powerful emotion. Presently the spasm passed, and he was himself again.

'So you've met that pill, have you?' he said.

It was my turn to quiver, and I did so like a jelly.

'That what?'

'That pill.'

'Did you say "pill"?'

' "Pill" was what I said. Slice her where you like, she's still boloney.'

I drew myself up.

'You are speaking,' I said, 'of the woman I love.'

He started to say something, but I raised my hand coldly and said 'Please,' and silence supervened. He read his *National Geographic Magazine*. I read mine. And for some minutes matters proceeded along these lines. Then I thought to myself: 'Oh, well, dash it,' and decided to extend the olive branch. Too damn silly, I mean, a couple of fellows on the brink of having teeth out simply sitting

47

reading the *National Geographic Magazine* at one another instead of trying to forget by means of pleasant chit-chat the ordeal which lay before them.

'So you're Joey Cooley?' I said.

He accepted the overture in the spirit in which it was intended.

'You never spoke a truer word,' he replied agreeably. 'That's about who I am, if you come right down to it. Joey Cooley, the Idol of American Motherhood. Who are you?'

'Havershot's my name.'

'English, aren't you?'

'That's right.'

'Been in Hollywood long?'

'About a week.'

'Where are you staying?'

'I've a bungalow at the Garden of the Hesperides.'

'Do you like Hollywood?'

'Oh, rather. Topping spot.'

'You ought to see Chillicothe, Ohio.'

'Why?'

'That's where I come from. And that's where I'd like to be now. Yessir, right back there in little old Chillicothe.'

'You're homesick, what?'

'You betcher.'

'Still, I suppose you have a pretty good time here?'

His face clouded. Once more, it appeared, I had said the wrong thing.

'Who, me? I do not.'

'Why not?'

'I'll tell you why not. Because I'm practically a member of a chain gang. I couldn't have it much tougher if this was Devil's Island or the Foreign Legion or sump'n. Do you know what?'

'What?'

'Do you know what old Brinkmeyer did when the contract was being drawn up?'

'No, what?'

'Slipped in a clause that I had to live at his house, so that I could be under his personal eye.'

'Who is this Brinkmeyer?'

'The boss of the corporation I work for.'

'And you don't like his personal eye?'

'I don't mind him. He's a pretty good sort of old stiff. It's his sister Beulah. She was the one who put him up to it. She's the heavy in the sequence. As tough as they come. Ever hear of Simon Legree?'

'Yes.'

'Beulah Brinkmeyer. Know what a serf is?'

'What you swim in, you mean.'

'No, I don't mean what you swim in. I mean what's downtrodden and oppressed and gets the dirty end of the stick all the time. That's me. Gosh, what a life! Shall I tell you something?'

'Do.'

'I'm not allowed to play games, because I might get hurt. I'm not allowed to keep a dog, because it might bite me. I'm not allowed in the swimming-pool, because I might get drowned. And, listen, get this one. No candy, because I might put on weight.'

'You don't mean that?'

'I do mean that. It's in my contract. "The party of the second part, hereinafter to be called the artist, shall abstain from all ice-creams, chocolate-creams, nut sundaes, fudge, and all-day suckers, hereinafter to be called candy, this to be understood to comprise doughnuts, marshmallows, pies in their season, all starchy foods, and twice of chicken." Can you imagine my lawyer letting them slip that over!'

I must say I was a bit appalled. We Havershots have always been good trenchermen, and it never fails to give me a grey feeling when I hear of somebody being on a diet. I know how I should have felt at his age if some strong hand had kept me from the sock-shop.

'I wonder you don't chuck it.'

'I can't.'

'You love your Art too much?'

'No, I don't.'

'You like bringing sunshine into drab lives in Pittsburgh and Cincinnati?'

'I don't care if Pittsburgh chokes. And that goes for Cincinnati, too.'

'Then perhaps you feel that all the money and fame make up for these what you might call hideous privations?'

He snorted. He seemed to have as low an opinion of money and fame as April June.

'What's the good of money and fame? I can't eat them, can I? There's nothing I'd like better than to tie a can to the whole outfit and go back to where hearts are pure and men are men in Chillicothe, Ohio. I'd like to be home with mother right now. You should taste her fried chicken, southern style. And she'd be tickled pink to have me, too. But I can't get away. I've a five years contract, and you can bet they're going to hold me to it.'

'I see.'

'Oh, yes, I'm Uncle Tom, all right. But listen, shall I tell you something? I'm biding my time. I'm waiting. Some day I'll grow up. And when I do, oh, baby!'

'Oh what?'

'I said "Oh, baby!" I'm going to poke Beulah Brinkmeyer right in the snoot.'

'What! Would you strike a woman?'

'You betcher I'd strike a woman. Yessir, she'll get hers. And there's about six directors I'm going to poke in the snoot, and a whole raft of supervisors and production experts. And that press agent of mine. I'm going to poke him in the snoot, all right. Yessir! Matter of fact,' he said, summing up, 'you'd have a tough time finding somebody I'm not going to poke in the snoot, once I'm big enough. I've got all their names in a little notebook.'

He relapsed into a moody silence, and I didn't quite know what to say. No words of mine, I felt, could cheer this stricken child. The iron had plainly entered a dashed sight too deep into his soul for a mere 'Buck up, old bird!' to do any good.

However, as it turned out, I would have had no time to deliver anything in the nature of a pep talk, for at this moment the door opened and in poured a susurration of blighters, some male, some female, some with cameras, some without, and the air became so thick with interviewing and picture-taking that it would have been impossible to get a word in. I just sat reading my *National Geographic Magazine*. And presently a white-robed attendant appeared and announced that B. K. Burwash was straining at the forceps, and the gang passed through into his room, interviewing to the last.

And not long after that another white-robed attendant came and said that I. J. Zizzbaum would be glad if I would look in, so I commended my soul to God, and followed her into the operating theatre.

Chapter 6

I. J. ZIZZBAUM proved to be rather a gloomy cove. He looked like a dentist with a secret sorrow. In reply to my 'Good afternoon,' he merely motioned me to the chair with a sombre wave of the hand. One of those strong, silent dentists.

I, on the other hand, was at my chattiest. I am always that way when closeted with a molar-mangler. I dare say it's the same with you. I suppose one's idea is that if one can only keep the conversation going, the blighter may get so interested that he will shelve the dirty work altogether in favour of a cosy talk. I started in right away.

'Hullo, hullo, hullo. Here I am. Good afternoon, good afternoon. What a lovely day, what? Shall I sit here? Right ho. Shall I lean my head back? Right ho. Shall I open my mouth? Right ho.'

'Wider, please,' said I. J. Zizzbaum sadly.

'Right ho. Everything set for the administration of the old laughing gas? Good. You know,' I said, sitting up, 'it's years since I had gas. I can't have been more than twelve. I know I was quite a kid, because it happened when I was at a private school, and of course one leaves one's private school at a very tender age. And, talking of kids, who do you think I met in the waiting-room? None other than little Joey Cooley. And it's an odd coincidence, but he's having gas, too. Shows what a small world it is, what?'

I broke off, abashed. It did not need the quick wince of pain on I. J. Zizzbaum's mobile face to tell me that I had made a bloomer and said the tactless thing. I could have kicked myself.

Because it had suddenly flashed upon me what the trouble was and why he was not this afternoon the sunny I. J. Zizzbaum whose merry laugh and gay quips made him, no doubt, the life and soul of the annual dentists' convention. He was brooding on the fact that the big prize in the dentistry world, the extraction of little Joey Cooley's bicuspid, had gone to his trade rival, B. K. Burwash.

No doubt he had been listening in on all that interviewing and camera-clicking, and the shrill cries of the human interest writers as they went about their business must have made very bitter hearing – rubbing it in, I mean to say, that old Pop Burwash was going to get his name on the front page of all the public news-sheets and become more or less the World's Sweetheart, while all he, Zizzbaum, could expect was my modest fee.

It was enough to depress the most effervescent dentist, and my heart bled for the poor bloke. I hunted in my mind for some soothing speech that would bring the roses back to his cheeks, but all I could think of was a statement to the effect that recent discoveries in the Congo basin had thrown a new light on something or other. I had this on the authority of the *National Geographic Magazine.*

It didn't seem to cheer him up to any marked extent. Not interested in the Congo basin, probably. Many people aren't. He simply sighed rather heavily, levered my jaws a bit farther apart, peered into the abyss, sighed again as if he didn't think highly of the contents, and motioned to his A.D.C. to cluster round with the gas-bag.

And presently, after a brief interlude during which I felt as if I was being slowly smothered where I sat, I was off.

I don't know if you are familiar with this taking-gas business. If you are, you will recall that it has certain drawbacks apart from the sensation of being cut off in your prime by stoppage of the windpipes. It is apt to give you unpleasant dreams and visions. The last time I had had it, on the occasion which I had mentioned in my introductory remarks, I remember that I had thought somebody was shoving me down into the sea, and I had a distinct illusion of being pried asunder by sharks.

This time, the proceedings were still rummy, but not quite so bad as that. The sharks were not on the bill. The stellar role was played by little Joey Cooley.

It seemed to me that he and I were in a room rather like the waiting-room, only larger, and as in the real waiting-room, there were two doors, one on each side.

The first was labelled:

I. J. ZIZZBAUM

The other:

B. K. BURWASH

And the Cooley kid and I were jostling one another, trying to get through the Zizzbaum door.

Well, any chump would have seen that that wasn't right. I tried to reason with the misguided little blighter. I kept saying: 'Stop shoving, old sport; you're trying to get into the wrong room,' but it wasn't any use – he simply shoved the more. And presently he shoved me into an arm-chair and told me to sit there and read the *National Geographic Magazine*, and then he opened the door and went through.

After that, things got blurred for a while. When they clarified somewhat, I was still sitting in a chair, but it was a dentist's chair, and I realized that I had come out from under the influence.

The first thing I saw was I. J. Zizzbaum in his white coat. He was regarding me with a kindly smile.

'Well, my little man,' he said, in a fatherly sort of way. 'Feeling all right?'

And I was just about to ask him what the dickens he meant by calling me his little man – for the Havershots, though matey, have their sense of dignity, when I suddenly perceived that we were not alone. The room was absolutely crammed.

Ann Bannister was there, standing on the other side of

54

me, but I didn't object to that. If she had somehow got wind of this operation of mine and something of the old love and affection still lingered in her bosom, causing her to want to be with me in my hour of trial, well, that was all right. Dashed decent of her, I felt. But I strongly resented the presence of all these other birds. I mean to say, perfect strangers have no right to come flocking round a chap when he's having a tooth out. Then, if ever, he is surely entitled to a spot of privacy.

There was a whole mob of them, and I had a sort of vague feeling I'd seen them before somewhere. Some were male, some female. Some had cameras, some hadn't. I sat up, feeling a bit huffy. I was surprised at I. J. Zizzbaum allowing them on the premises, and I was just going to tell him so – and I didn't intend to mince my words – when I made a rather odd discovery – to wit, that the chap in the white coat wasn't I. J. Zizzbaum. Somebody different altogether.

And I was about to enquire into this, when I discovered something else. Something that made me draw in my breath quickly with a startled 'What ho!'

When I had entered the waiting-room, I must mention, I had been clad in a quiet grey suit with powder-blue socks matching the neat tie and melting, as it were, into the tasteful suède shoes. And now, by Jove, I'm blowed if I wasn't wearing knickerbockers and stockings. And then suddenly I caught sight of my face in the mirror and saw that it was of singular beauty, topped off with golden ringlets. And the eyes staring into mine were large and expressive and had long lashes.

'Hell!' I cried.

Well, I mean to say, who wouldn't have? I saw right away what had happened. Someone, as the poet says, had blundered. Joey Cooley and I must have gone under gas at exactly the same moment and, owing presumably to some bad staffwork during the period when we were simultaneously sauntering about in the fourth dimension, or

55

whatever they call it, there had been an unforeseen switch. The impetuous young cuckoo had gone and barged into my body, and I, having nowhere else to go, had toddled off and got into his.

His fault, of course, the silly ass. I had told him to stop shoving.

Chapter 7

I SAT staring at myself in the mirror, and was still in full goggle when the bird in the white coat who had called me his little man – B. K. Burwash, I took him to be – stepped forward.

'You'll want this, eh?' he said, still speaking in that fatherly manner, and I saw that he was holding out a little cardboard box.

I continued to goggle. I hadn't any time for cardboard boxes. I was still trying to adjust myself to this new twist in the scenario.

A bit breath-taking, the whole affair, you will agree. Of course, I had read stories where much the same sort of thing had happened, but I had never supposed that a chap had got to budget for such an eventuality as a possible feature of the programme in real life. I know they say you ought to be prepared for anything, but, I mean, dash it!

Besides, it all seemed so sudden. In the stories there had always been a sinister scientist who had messed about with test-tubes, or an Egyptian sorcerer who had cast spells, and the thing had taken weeks, if not months. If quick service was desired, you had to have a magic ring or something. In either case, you didn't get results casually like this – out of a blue sky, as it were.

'The tooth,' explained B. K. Burwash. 'You'll want to keep it.'

I trousered the box absently, a proceeding which brought a howl of protest from the mob. The simple action seemed to get them all worked up.

There was a babble of voices.

'Hey!'

'Don't put that away.'

'We want to get a shot of you looking at it.'

'Sort of musing over it.'

'Hold it up and kind of smile at it.'

'Like as if you were saying to yourself: "Well, well!"'

'Have you a statement for the Press?'

'What do you think of the political situation?'

'Has the President your confidence?'

'What is the future of the screen?'

'Give us a message for the people of America. Something snappy with a heart-throb in it.'

'Yay. And how about your favourite breakfast food?'

I had always known Ann Bannister as a girl of character and decision, and I must say my heart warmed to her at this juncture. She took the situation in hand right away and startled hustling them out as if she had been a bouncer in a waterfront pub who had just taken office and was resolved to make good.

'Give the poor child a chance, can't you?' she cried. 'What's the idea of worrying him at a time like this? How would you like it?'

The fellow who had asked for a message to the people of America said that it was as much as his job was worth to go back to the office without one.

Ann remained firm.

'I'll give you all the messages you want,' she said. 'I'll give you anything you like, only get out of here.'

And she went on hustling them out, and presently, by sheer personal magnetism, had cleared the room, and B. K. Burwash and I were alone.

'Quite a lot of excitement,' said B. K. Burwash. 'Ah, well, the penalties of Fame!'

He smiled as he spoke – the jolly, beaming smile of a dentist who, in addition to pouching a nice fee, knows that he has just had about a thousand dollars' worth of free advertisement.

I was not able to share his merry mood. The dazed feeling passed off, leaving me all of a twitter. I could see now that I had gone and got myself into a very nasty jam.

I mean to say, life's difficult enough as it is. You don't

want to aggravate the general complexity of things by getting changed into a kid with knickerbockers and golden curls. A nice thing it was going to be if this state of affairs proved to be permanent. Bim, obviously, would go any chance I might have had of leading April June to the altar. A girl in her position wasn't going to walk up the aisle with a kid in knickerbockers.

What, too, would the fellows at the Drones say if I were to saunter in with golden curls all over me? They wouldn't have it at any price. The Drones is what I would call a pretty broad-minded club, but they simply wouldn't have it. 'You can't do that there 'ere' about summed up what the attitude of the committee would be.

Little wonder, then, that I was in no frame of mind to frisk and frolic with this debonair dentist.

'Never mind about the penalties of Fame, B. K. Burwash,' I said urgently. 'We can discuss all that later. What I wish to do now is issue a statement. A frightful thing has happened, and unless prompt steps are taken through the proper channels, there is going to be a nasty stink kicked up. I may say I happen to know the ringleaders.'

'Just lean back and relax.'

'I won't lean back and relax. I want to issue a statement.'

And I was about to do so, when the door opened and a woman came in. She seemed a bit shirty. She was pshawing and tchahing as she entered.

'All this fuss!' she said. 'I've no patience with them. As if the child wasn't conceited enough already.'

She was a tall, rangy light-heavyweight, severe of aspect. She looked as if she might be an important official on the staff of some well-known female convict establishment. That this was not so was proved by the fact that B. K. Burwash addressed her as Miss Brinkmeyer, and I divined that this must be the woman the kid Cooley had said he disliked.

'I think the little man is feeling all right now, Miss Brinkmeyer,' said B. K. Burwash.

She greeted these kindly words with a snorting sniff indicative of disgust and contempt. I could see why the kid Cooley didn't like this woman. I didn't like her myself. She lacked that indefinable something which we know as charm.

'Of course he's feeling all right. Why wouldn't he be?'

B. K. Burwash said that he always felt a certain anxiety after giving gas. This seemed to stir her up further.

'Pah! Stuff and nonsense! Gas, indeed. When I was a child nobody ever gave me gas. When I was a child, my father used to tie a string to me and fasten it to the barn door and slam it. And it didn't get into the papers, either. All this fuss about a tiny little tooth, which wouldn't ever have started aching if he hadn't been eating candy on the sly, though knowing perfectly well what Clause B. (2) in his contract says. I intend to get to the bottom of this candy business. Somebody is bootlegging it to him, and I mean to find out who it is. He's as artful as a barrel-load of monkeys —'

I was conscious of a growing annoyance. I had fallen into a reverie and was once more endeavouring to grapple with the problems confronting me, and her voice interrupted my meditations. It was a harsh, rasping voice, in its timbre not unlike a sawmill.

I shushed her down with a gesture.

'Don't talk so much,' I said curtly.

'What did you say?'

'I said "Don't talk so much". How can I think with all this gabble going on? For heaven's sake, woman, put a sock in it and let me concentrate.'

This got a fair snicker out of B. K. Burwash, though I hadn't intended to strike the humorous note. It caused Miss Brinkmeyer to pinken and breathe heavily.

'I'd like to put you across my knee and give you a good spanking.'

I raised a hand.

'No horse-play, if you please,' I said distantly.

And then something occurred to me, and the whole situation seemed to brighten. I had just remembered what the kid Cooley had said when sketching out his plans for what he was going to do when he was big enough.

Well, goodness knew he was big enough for anything now. My branch of the family has always run to beef a bit, myself not least. When I boxed for Cambridge, I weighed fourteen stone in the nude.

I gave a hearty chuckle, the first I had felt like emitting for some considerable time.

'Woman,' I said, 'you would do better, instead of threatening violence to others, to look out for yourself. You don't know it, but you are in a very sticky spot. The avenger is on your track. When the blow will fall, we cannot say, but some day, in some place, you are going to get a poke in the snoot. This is official.'

B. K. Burwash became graver. He seemed troubled.

'I hope I did not overdo that gas,' he mused. 'I don't like this. It sounds like delirium. The little fellow's manner has been strange ever since he came to.'

La Brinkmeyer scouted this theory.

'Stuff and nonsense! He isn't delirious. He's talking that way just to be aggravating.'

'You think so?'

'Of course. Have you ever had to look after a sassy, swollen-headed, wisecracking child star who thinks he's everybody just because a lot of fool women crowd to see him on the screen and say doesn't he look cute and sweet and innocent?'

B. K. Burwash said no, he had not had this experience.

'Well, I've been doing it for a year, and I know his ways.'

This seemed to reassure the dubious dentist.

'You feel, then, that there is no cause for anxiety?'

'Of course there isn't.'

'You relieve me. I was afraid he was not quite himself.'

'He's himself, worse luck.'

'Ha!' I exclaimed, smiling a bit, for this struck me as

quaint. Ironical, you might say. 'Funny you should say that. Because myself, in a nutshell, is precisely what I'm bally well not.'

It seemed an admirable opportunity to issue that statement. The topic could not have been more neatly introduced.

'Madam,' I began, 'and you, B. K. Burwash, prepare yourselves for a bit of a surprise. Unless I am very much mistaken, this is going to make you sit up a trifle.'

'Oh, be quiet.'

'The poet Shakespeare has well said that there are more things in heaven and earth than are dreamed of in our philosophy. One of these has just broken loose in this very room. You will doubtless be interested to learn that owing to an unforeseen crossing of the wires in the fourth dimension —'

'Stop this nonsense and come along.'

'But I wish to issue a statement. Briefly, then, owing, as I say, to funny work in the fourth dimension . . . mark you, I call it the fourth, but it may quite easily be the fifth . . . I'm a bit shaky on dimensions —'

'You'll be shaky if I start shaking you, as I shall in a minute, I know I shall. I've no patience with you. Will you come *along*! '

I came along. And if you feel that this was weak of me, I can only say that the Albert Memorial would have come along in precisely the same manner, had Miss Beulah Brinkmeyer attached herself to its wrist and pulled. I left the chair like a cork emerging from a bottle under the ministrations of a sinewy butler.

'Oh, all right,' I said, resigning myself to the inev. 'Pip-pip, Burwash.'

As a matter of fact, I was not sorry I had been interrupted in the issuing of my statement, for Reason had suddenly returned to her throne and I perceived that I had been on the point of making an ass of myself.

I mean to say, the one lesson one learns from these stories about coves getting switched into other coves' bodies is that on such occasions statements are no good. No use whatever. Just a waste of breath. The chaps in the stories always try to make them, and nobody ever believes a word. I resolved that from now on I would be cold and taciturn and refrain from all attempts to put myself right with the public. However irksome it might be to remain silent on a topic concerning which I had so much to say, a complete reserve was, I saw, the wiser policy.

Contenting myself, accordingly, with a word of warning to the effect that if she shook me I should be sick, I accompanied Miss Brinkmeyer to the door. My demeanour as I did so was not jaunty, for I was, I must confess, apprehensive and ill at ease. I was asking myself how I was going to render supportable a life spent in the society of this decidedly frightful old geezer. In comparing her to Simon Legree, the Cooley child had shown himself an astute judge of character. She seemed also to possess many of the less agreeable qualities of the late Captain Bligh of the *Bounty*.

In the street a sumptuous automobile awaited us, and presently we were rolling along, she sniffing at intervals as if my company gave her the pip and self leaning back against the cushions with a meditative frown. And after a while the car turned in at a drive gate and pulled up in front of a large white house.

Chapter 8

CHEZ BRINKMEYER – at which I gathered that we had now arrived – was evidently one of the stately homes of Hollywood. The eye detected spacious lawns, tennis courts, swimming-pools, pergolas, bougainvillea, three gardeners, an iron deer, a ping-pong porch, and other indications of wealth. If further proof was required that its proprietor had got the stuff in sackfuls, it was supplied by the fact that the butler, who had opened the door in response to the chauffeur's tooting, was an English butler. You don't run to an English butler in Hollywood unless you are a pretty prominent nib. The small fry have to rub along with Japanese and Filipinos.

The sight of this one did much to put new heart into me. He was like a breath from home, a large, moonfaced, gooseberry-eyed man of the fine old family butler brand and, drinking him in, I lost some of that feeling I had had of having fallen among savages. With him around, I felt, the agony of associating with Miss Brinkmeyer would be greatly diminished.

However, I wasn't allowed much opportunity of feasting the eyes upon him at the moment, because my companion – or keeper or jailer or whatever she was – got hold of my hand again and whisked me in at a brisk pace, eventually fetching up in a long, low-ceilinged sort of drawing-room with French windows opening on a patio.

Its only occupant was a stout, billowy bloke with horn-rimmed spectacles. From the fact that he was wallowing on a sofa as if the place belonged to him, I took it that it did belong to him – that he was, in a word, my host, the Mr Brinkmeyer under whose personal eye I was now to reside.

Once more, the kid Cooley had shown himself a shrewd

64

judge. He had told me this man was a pretty good sort of old stiff, and it was apparent from a glance that this was the case. I liked Mr Brinkmeyer's looks. Of course, after having been with his sister all this time, I was in no frame of mind to be fussy about other people's looks – practically anything would have seemed good to me just then, I mean – but he appeared to me kindly.

Of this kindliness he gave evidence with his opening words.

'Ah, here you are,' he said. 'Everything go off all right? Is he feeling quite well?'

Miss Brinkmeyer clicked her tongue.

'Now, for goodness' sake, don't you start. Of course he's feeling quite well. The way everybody talks, you'd think the child had been having a leg amputated or something. I've no patience with all this fuss.'

'Did he make a fuss?'

'I'm talking about the newspaper men. And all those fool women. Pah! Like a lot of hens.'

'They fussed over him?'

'Yes. In the most disgusting way.'

'Great publicity,' suggested Mr Brinkmeyer, in a deferential sort of way.

Miss Brinkmeyer sniffed.

'Very bad for him.'

'But good for the box-office.'

'I don't care. It makes me sick. Simply encouraging him. As if his head wasn't swollen enough already.'

Mr Brinkmeyer was examining me through his horn-rimmed glasses like a benevolent owl.

'It's not so swollen as it was.'

'Eh?'

'I say the swelling seems to have gone.'

'Yes, thank goodness.'

Hoping to establish an atmosphere of bonhomie and goodwill, I said it was kind of her to be pleased. She told me to be quiet.

'No, he doesn't look like he'd gotten the mumps any more,' she continued. 'He'll be back to normalcy, I guess, in time for unveiling that statue.'

'Yes,' said Mr Brinkmeyer. It seemed to me that he spoke rather gloomily. 'Yes, I guess he will.'

Pursuing my policy of trying to put everybody at their ease, I asked what statue. She told me to be quiet.

'And we won't have to cancel those Michigan Mothers.'

'What Michigan Mothers?'

For the third time she told me to be quiet. Not an easy woman to keep up a conversation with.

'If he'd been looking like a hubbard squash, we'd have had to put them off, and goodness knows what they'd have said, after coming all this way. But the swelling's practically gone already, and he's sure to be all right tomorrow.' She mused a bit, and added: 'As right as he ever is, the little toad.'

I could not pass this.

'I consider that highly offensive,' I said.

For the fourth time she told me to be quiet. Then, attaching herself to my wrist in the old familiar way, she lugged me out and up the stairs to a bedroom on the first floor. Pushing me in, she told me to lie down and go to sleep.

I could scarcely believe that I had heard her aright.

'Sleep?'

'You've got to have your afternoon sleep, haven't you?'

'But, dash it —'

'Oh, be quiet,' she said – making five in all. She then buzzed off, locking the door behind her.

I must say I laughed a shade mirthlessly. Sleep! That struck me as pretty good. Sleep, I mean to say, what? As if I had time for any rot like that. The immediate task confronting me, as I saw it, was to examine the situation and, if possible, ascertain what the hell was to be done about it. Because something would have to be done, and that with the minimum of delay. Avenues would have to be explored and stones not left unturned. What I had got to do was not sleep, but ponder.

I sat down on the bed and started in.

I don't know how long I pondered, but it was a fairish time, and I might have stuck at it indefinitely without getting a bite had I not in the course of my pondering risen from the bed and walked over to the window. The moment I got to the window, things suddenly clarified. I saw now what I ought to have seen at once, that my first move, before taking any other steps, must be to establish contact with the kid Cooley and call a conference.

I didn't suppose that he would be able to suggest any practical solution of our little difficulty – not being an Egyptian sorcerer, I mean – but at least he could give me a few pointers which might be of use to me in this new life of mine. And the best chance I had of getting together with him, it seemed to me, was to go to my bungalow at the Garden of the Hesperides, and see if he had turned up there. I had told him that that was where I lived, and if he remembered my words he would presumably repair thither sooner or later.

We Havershots are men of action, even when we have been turned into kids with golden curls smelling, I now perceived, of a rather offensive brand of brilliantine. There came over me a yearning to be out and about. I felt cramped and confined in this bedroom. Stifled is the word. A couple of feet below the window there was the roof of a sort of outhouse, and from this roof to the ground was a simple drop. Thirty seconds later I was down in the garden, and thirty seconds after that out of it and speeding for the old home.

I don't know if I had actually expected to find the kid at the bungalow. At any rate, he wasn't there. The place was empty. Wherever Joey Cooley was, he was not thinking things over quietly in an arm-chair at the Garden of the Hesperides.

67

This being so, there seemed nothing to do but to wait. So I sat down in the arm-chair myself and began to brood again.

Now, with all the wealth of material for brooding with which these recent disturbing happenings had provided me, it should, one would have thought, have been easy enough for me to keep my mind from straying from the main issue. But no. It strayed like the dickens. Before I had been sitting two minutes, I had switched right off from the items on the agenda paper and was meditating with a sort of hideous tenseness on ice-cream, doughnuts, pumpkin pie, custard pie, layer cake, chocolate cake, fudge, peanut clusters, and all-day suckers. I couldn't seem to get away from them. With a terrific effort I would wrench my mind away from ice-cream, and – bingo! – in a flash I would be thinking of doughnuts. And no sooner had I thrust the vision of doughnuts from me than along would come the pumpkin pie and the all-day suckers.

It was a totally new experience for me. I hadn't thought – in an emotional way – of this type of foodstuff for years and years. But now fudge and chocolate cake seemed to be dancing sarabands before my eyes, and I felt that I would have given anything for a good whack at them. Not since the distant days of my first private school had I been conscious of such a devastating hunger. Peckish is not the word. I felt like a homeless tapeworm.

It came over me in a wave what a perfect ass I had been in my previous experience as Reginald, Lord Havershot, not to have laid in a stock of these things against some possible emergency like this. I ought to have told myself, I reflected, that you never know when you may not be going to be turned into a kid of twelve, and that, such an occurrence being always on the cards, it is simply loony not to have a little something handy in the ice-box.

I was, in fact, beginning to feel pretty censorious about my former self, for I can't stand those woollen-headed, thriftless fellows who never think of the morrow, when I was brought up short by the sound of footsteps approaching the front door.

'Reggie,' someone called.

I recognized the voice. It was that of my Cousin Egremont. I remembered that he had said he was coming to pay me a visit in order to sample my cellar, and I might have known he would not let the grass grow under his feet.

'Reggie, old bird. Are you in, Reggie?'

Well, you know how it is. There are moments when you don't want to meet people. You just don't feel in the mood. I was, as I had told Ann Bannister, extremely fond of old Eggy, and in the past – as, for example, on the occasion of that New Year's Eve party of which he had spoken – I had often been glad of his company; but now I found myself shrinking from it. I felt that he would be surprised at finding a golden-haired child where he had expected to find a carroty-haired cousin, and there would be all sorts of tedious questionings and probings, and I simply wasn't equal to it.

So, to avoid the distasteful encounter, I just slid noiselessly from the chair and ducked down behind it, hoping that when he came in and saw nobody in the room he would go away again.

A fat chance, of course. I should have known his psychology better. Eggy isn't the sort of chap who goes away from rooms in which there is Scotch whisky just because they are empty. Let the fixings be there, and he does not worry about missing hosts. He came right in and made for the sideboard like a homing pigeon. I couldn't see him, but I heard a musical plashing, then a gollup, then another musical plashing, then another gollup, then a third musical plashing, and I could read his actions like a book. He had had a couple quick, and was now preparing to have another at his leisure.

Over this one he seemed disposed to linger a bit. The first fierce thirst was slaked, and he could now dally, so to speak and, as it were, roll the stuff round his tongue. I heard him wander across the room, and the crackle of a match and a wisp of smoke rising to the ceiling showed that he had found my cigars. A moment later, there happened what I might have known would happen. He came over to the arm-chair and sank into it with a luxurious whoof. It was the only comfortable chair in the room, so naturally he had made a bee-line for it.

So there we were – he plainly all set for a cosy afternoon, and I crouching up against the wall, a bally prisoner. If I had been the Naval Treaty in a safe-deposit box at the Admiralty, I couldn't have been more securely tucked away.

It was one of those situations which make a chap wrinkle the brow and wonder how to act for the best, and I was engaged in doing this when there was a knocking at the front door.

Apparently someone stood without.

Chapter 9

'COME in,' called Eggy.

I couldn't see, of course, who it was who entered in response to this invitation, but from the fact that he now rose I gathered that the new arrival must be a girl of sorts. You don't get old Eggy hoisting himself out of arm-chairs just to greet the male sex. The voice that spoke told me I was right. It was a crisp, authoritative voice, but definitely female.

'Good afternoon,' it said.

'Good afternoon,' said Eggy.

'Are you the owner of this bungalow?'

'Oh, no.'

'You seem to be making yourself at home.'

'Oh, that's all right. It belongs to a chap called Havershot, and I'm his flesh and blood. Havershot's. He's my cousin.'

'I see.'

'And on his behalf – I feel sure he would spring to the task, if he were here – may I offer you a spot?'

'A what?'

'A snifter. I can recommend the Scotch.'

'Are you suggesting that I should drink liquor?'

'That's the idea.'

'Well, let me tell you, Mr Man, —'

'– ering.'

'Pardon?'

'The name is Mannering.'

'Oh? Well, let me tell you, Mr Mannering, that I don't drink liquor. I have come here collecting subscriptions for the Temple of the New Dawn.'

'The – what was that again?'

'Haven't you ever heard of the Temple of the New Dawn?'

'Not that I remember.'

'Haven't you ever heard of Sister Lora Luella Stott?'

'No. Who is she?'

'She is the woman who is leading California out of the swamp of alcohol.'

'Good God!' I could tell by Eggy's voice that he was interested. 'Is there a swamp of alcohol in these parts? What an amazing country America is. Talk about every modern convenience. Do you mean you can simply go there and *lap*?'

'I was speaking figuratively.'

'I knew there was a catch,' said Eggy, disappointed.

'Sister Lora Luella is converting California to true temperance.'

'How perfectly frightful.'

There was a silence. From her next words, I fancied that the female must have been examining Eggy with a certain intentness, for she said:

'My! You look terrible.'

Eggy said there was no need to be personal. She said yes, there was.

'You're all twitchy, and your eyes are like a fish's. And your skin!'

'It's the best I've got,' said Eggy, a bit stiffly, it seemed to me.

'Yes, and it's the best you'll always have, so long as you go on steeping yourself in that foul stuff. Do you know what that is you're drinking?'

'White Thistle.'

'Black ruin. Shall I tell you what Sister Lora Luella Stott would do if she were here?'

'What?'

'She would dash the glass from your hand.'

'Oh?' said Eggy, and I'm not sure it wasn't 'Ho?' 'She would, would she?'

'That's what she'd do. And she would be right. Even a poor human wreck like you is worth saving.'

'Poor human wreck?'

'That was what I said.'

'Ho?' said Eggy, quite distinctly this time.

There was another silence.

'Tell me,' said Eggy at length, and there was hauteur in his voice. 'Just tell me this, Miss —'

'Prescott.'

'Just tell me this, Miss Prescott. Are you by any chance under the impression – have you allowed yourself to run away with the foolish notion – are you really such a poor judge of form as to imagine that I am stinko?'

'If by "stinko" you mean —'

'I mean stinko. Listen,' said Eggy, with a certain quiet pride. 'British Constitution. Truly rural. The Leith police dismisseth us. She stood at the door of Burgess's fish-sauce shop in Ethelbertha Street, Oswaldtwistle, welcoming him in. Now what?'

I must say I couldn't have found an answer to that, but the female did.

'Pshaw!' Very educational for the kiddies, no doubt, but that doesn't mean a thing. All those silly shibboleths.'

'I can say that, too. Silly shibboleths. There. Ethelbertha Oswaldtwistle stood at the door of Burgess's fish-sauce shop, dismissing the Leith police with silly shibboleths. You hear? As clear as a bell. And you cast innuendos on my sobriety.'

'Pshaw!' said the female, continuing. 'The mere fact that you can say all that makes it all the worse. It means that you have passed the stage where your tongue goes back on you and are headed straight for the danger-line. I know what I'm talking about. My father used to drink till he saw the light, and he prided himself on being able to say anything at any time of the day or night, no matter how swacked he might be, without tripping over a syllable. I always remember what the doctor said to him. "That's only a wayside station," the doc. said. "You're an express and you don't stop at the wayside stations. But, oh boy! Wait till you hit that terminus."'

'Terminus?'

'He meant when he would begin to see things —'

'Don't talk about seeing things!'

'– and hear voices —'

'And don't,' said Eggy, 'talk about hearing voices!'

'That's just what I am going to talk about. Somebody's got to do something to snap you out of it. I'm being your best friend, really. You ought to be thanking me on your knees for warning you. Yes, sir, unless you pull up mighty quick, you're slated to get yours. I know the symptoms. What made Pop see the light was meeting a pink rabbit that asked him for a match, and something like that's going to happen to you if you don't take a brace on yourself. So think it over. Well, I mustn't stay here all afternoon, talking to you. I've my subscriptions to collect. How do you feel about a small donation to the cause?'

'Pshaw!' said Eggy, rather cleverly coming back at her with her own stuff.

'Well, I wasn't counting on it,' said the female. 'But you just remember what I've told you.'

She apparently popped off at this point, for the armchair gave a scrunch as Eggy dropped into it again. I could hear him breathing heavily.

Now, during this conversation, though I had been listening attentively to every word, I suppose what they call my subconscious mind must have been putting in a lot of solid work without my knowing it. Because when I turned to my personal affairs once more, I found that my whole mental outlook had changed. I had switched completely round from my former view of things and now saw that in avoiding Eggy I had been making a strategic error.

That frightful hunger for doughnuts and the rest of the outfit was still gnawing me, and I now perceived that something constructive might be done about it. Eggy, instead of being a pest, might prove a life-saver. He wasn't a millionaire, of course, but he had a comfortable income and would surely, I felt, be good for the price of an all-day sucker, if properly approached. I rose, accordingly, with the intention of making a touch.

74

Mark you, I can see now, looking back, that the moment was ill-chosen. But this didn't occur to me at the time. All I was thinking about was getting the needful. And so, as I say, I rose.

The prospect whom I was planning to contact, as they call it in America, was leaning back in the arm-chair, still breathing in that rather stertorous manner, and my head came up just behind his. I was thus nicely placed for addressing my remarks to his left ear.

'Eggy,' I said.

I remember once, when a kid – from what motive I cannot recall, but no doubt just in a spirit of clean fun – hiding in a sort of alcove on the main staircase at Biddleford Castle and saying 'Boo!' to a butler who was coming up with a tray containing a decanter, a syphon, and glasses. Biddleford is popularly supposed to be haunted by a Wailing Lady, and the first time the butler touched ground was when he came up against a tiger-skin rug in the hall two flights down. And I had always looked on this as the high spot in emotional expression until, as I have related, I rose quietly from behind the arm-chair and said: 'Eggy.'

The old boy's reaction wasn't quite so immediate as the butler's had been. The latter had got off the mark instantly, as if he had had the wings of a dove, but Eggy for perhaps six seconds just sat in a frozen kind of way, staring straight in front of him without moving a muscle. Then his head came slowly round and our eyes met.

This was the point at which he really buckled down to it. It was now that after a leisurely start he showed a genuine flash of speed. One piercing scream escaped his lips, and it was still ringing in the air when I found myself alone. Despite the fact that he had been lying back in an arm-chair when the idea of moving occurred to him, Egremont Mannering was through the front door in – I should say – considerably under a second and a quarter. He was just a blur and a whizzing noise.

I hurried to the window and peered cautiously out. I

was curious to see where the dear old chap had landed. At the rate at which he had been travelling, it seemed incredible that he could still be in California, but to my surprise there he was, only a few yards away. I suppose he must have braked very quickly.

With him was a girl in beige, and when she spoke I knew that this must be our recent caller. Presumably she had been starting to walk away, when that fearful yell had brought her back to get the news bulletin. Eggy was clutching at her arm, like a drowning man at a straw.

I must say the girl's appearance surprised me a bit. From the tone of her voice and the general trend of her conversation I had somehow got the impression of somebody of the Beulah Brinkmeyer type, but she was quite pretty in, I admit, a rather austere kind of way. She looked like a vicar's daughter who plays hockey and ticks off the villagers when they want to marry their deceased wives' sisters.

'Now what?' she said.

Eggy continued to clutch at her arm.

'Woof!' he said. 'In there!'

'What's in there?'

'A ghastly imp's in there. It poked its head over the back of my chair – absolutely cheek by jowl – and said: "Eggy, old top, I've come for you, Eggy!"'

'It did.'

'You bet it did. "I've come for you, Eggy, old top," it said. Dashed familiar. I'd never met the little bounder in my life.'

'You're sure it wasn't a pink rabbit?'

'No, no, no. It was an imp. Do you think I don't know an imp when I see one?'

'What sort of imp?'

'The very worst type. I disliked it at first sight.'

The girl pursed her lips.

'Well, I warned you.'

'Yes, but how was I to know it was going to happen to me right away like that? It was the awful suddenness of the thing that jarred me. This cad of an imp just appeared. Without a word of warning.'

'What did you expect it to do? Forward a letter of introduction?'

' "I've come for you, Eggy," it said. In a sort of hideous, leering way. "Yoo-hoo, Eggy," it said. "I've come for you, old sport." What ought I to do, do you think?'

'Shall I tell you what you ought to do?'

'That's what I want to know. It said: "Pip-pip, Eggy...." '

'There's only one thing to do. Come with me and put yourself in Sister Lora Luella Stott's hands.'

'Is she good about imps?'

'Imps are what she's best at.'

'And has she a cellar?'

'A what?'

'Well, naturally I need a bracer. And I need it quick. It's no use my going to this Stott if she isn't likely to set 'em up.'

The girl was staring at him incredulously.

'You don't mean you're thinking of drinking liquor after what has happened?'

'I never needed a snifter more in my life. Drink liquor? Of course I'm going to drink liquor. I'm going to suck it up in a bucket.'

'You aren't going to swear off?'

It was Eggy's turn to stare incredulously. The girl had spoken as if she couldn't believe her ears, and now he spoke as if he couldn't believe his.

'Swear *off*? At a moment like this? When every nerve in my body has been wrenched from its moorings and tied in knots? What a perfectly fantastic idea! I can't understand an intelligent girl like you entertaining it. Have you overlooked the fact that all this has left me very, very shaken? My ganglions are vibrating like a jelly in a high wind. I don't believe you realize the sheer horror of the thing. "Eggy," it said, just like that, "here I am, Eggy, old bird...." '

77

She gave a sort of despairing gesture, like a vicar's daughter who has discovered Erastianism in the village.

'Well, go your own way. Act just as you please. It's your funeral. . . .'

'I do hate that expression.'

'But when you want it – and you're going to want it pretty soon and mighty bad – remember that there is always a warm welcome waiting for you at the Temple of the New Dawn. No human flotsam and jetsam is so degraded that it cannot find a haven there.'

She walked off, leaving Eggy flat. He, after looking at the bungalow in a hesitating sort of way, as if wondering if it would be safe to go back there and have another go at the Scotch, decided that it wasn't, and tottered off over the horizon to get his bracer elsewhere. And I, having given the Cooley kid another quarter of an hour to turn up, pushed off myself. And presently, after an easy climb on to the outhouse roof, I was back in the bedroom once more, feeling hollower than ever.

Only just in time, as it turned out, for scarcely had I sat down on the bed when a key turned in the lock and there was Miss Brinkmeyer.

'Have you had your sleep?' she asked.

The way this woman harped on sleep annoyed me.

'No,' I said. 'I haven't.'

'Why not?'

'I was too hungry.'

'Well, my goodness, if you were hungry, why didn't you ring the bell? I'll send you up your supper.'

She withdrew, and after a bit a footman of sorts appeared – a Filipino, apparently, by the look of him. And conceive my emotion when I observed that on the tray which he carried there was nothing but a few dry biscuits, a glass of milk, and a saucerful of foul prunes.

Well, I tried to reason with the man, pointing out the merits of chump chops and steak puddings, but all he would say was 'Excuse, yes', and 'Very good, hullo', and 'No, perhaps, also', and a lot of rot like that, so eventually

I dismissed him with a weary gesture. I then cleaned up the contents of the tray and sank into a reverie.

The shades of evening fell. And after they had been falling for quite some little while I heard footsteps coming along the corridor. A moment later the door opened and Ann Bannister came in.

Chapter 10

ANN was looking marvellous. The sight of her cheerful face, to one who when the door began to open had been expecting to see the Brinkmeyer, was like manna in the wilderness. It warmed the cockles of the heart, and I don't mind telling you that they were in need of a spot of warming. Those prunes had tested me sorely.

She smiled at me like one old pal at another.

'Well, Joseph,' she said. 'How are you feeling?'

'Extremely hollow,' I replied.

'But otherwise all right?'

'Oh, quite.'

'No pain where the little toofy-peg used to be?'

'Not a bit, thanks.'

'That's good. Well, sir, you had a great send-off.'

'Eh?'

'All those newspaper boys and girls.'

'Oh, yes.'

'By the way, I gave them the stuff they wanted. It was your press agent's job, really, but he was down fussing over those Michigan Mothers, so I took it upon myself to step into the breach before they tore you asunder. I told them they might quote you as saying that the President had your full support. Was that right?'

'Oh, quite.'

'Good. I wasn't sure how you stood politically. And then they wanted to know what your views were on the future of the screen, and I said you wished to go on record as stating that in your opinion the future of the screen was safe in the hands of men like T. P. Brinkmeyer. It struck me that it wouldn't hurt, giving old B. a boost. You like him, and it will please Miss Brinkmeyer – who, if you recall, has not been any too friendly since you put the Mexican horned toad in her bed.'

'What!'

'How do you mean – what?'

'I didn't put a Mexican horned toad in Miss Brinkmeyer's bed, did I?'

'Surely you haven't forgotten that? Of course you did,
and very amusing it all was, though Miss Brinkmeyer, perhaps, did not laugh as heartily as some.'

I chewed the lip quite a bit. You wouldn't be far out in
saying that I was appalled. I could see that in assuming
the identity of this blasted child I had walked into quite a
spot. If ever there was a child with a past, he was it, and I
didn't wonder that he was a shade unpopular in certain
quarters. The thing that astonished me was how he had
managed to escape unscathed all this time.

I had had no notion that this apparently peaceful home
was, in reality, such a maelstrom of warring passions. The
bally kid was plainly a regular Public Enemy, and I was
not surprised that when Miss Brinkmeyer grabbed my
wrist and pulled she did it with the air of one who wished
it was my neck. I don't say I felt exactly in sympathy with
La B., for she was not a woman who invited sympathy, but
I did see her point of view. I could follow her mental processes.

'I thought it might soften her a little if you gave the old
boy a build-up. You approve?'

'Oh, absolutely,' I replied. I was all for anything that
would help the situation in that quarter.

'Well, then they asked for a message to the people of
America, and I said something about keeping up courage
because Prosperity was just around the corner. Not good,
but the best I could do on the spur of the moment. And
"Prosperity Just Around Corner, Says Joey Cooley" won't
look too bad in the headlines.'

'Far from it.'

'And then I called up the head office of the Perfecto
Prune Corporation and told them that you attributed the
wonderful way you had come through to the fact that you
ate Perfecto Prunes at every meal.'

This hit me very hard.

'*Every* meal?'

'Well, don't you?'

'Do I?' I said, still shaken.

She raised an eyebrow.

'I can't make you out to-night, Joseph. Your manner is strange. You seem all woozy. First you forget about putting the horned toad in Miss Brinkmeyer's bed, which was certainly last week's high spot, and now you show a shaky grip of the prune situation. I don't believe you've ever really come properly out from under that gas. The effects still linger. What you need is a good rest. You'd better hurry into bed.'

'Bed? At this time of day?'

'It's your regular time. Don't tell me you've forgotten that, too. Come along. I'll give you your bath.'

You might have expected that, after all I had gone through, I would have been hardened to shocks by this time, but such was not the case. At these frightful words the room seemed to swim about me and I gaped at her as through a mist. Although she had told me that she was Joey Cooley's governess-companion-nursemaid, it had never occurred to me that their relations were of this peculiar intimacy. My essential modesty rose in passionate revolt.

'No!' I cried.

'Don't be silly.'

'No! Never!'

'You've got to have a bath.'

'Not in your presence.'

She seemed a bit nonplussed. No doubt a situation of this tenseness had not arisen before.

'You can have your toy duck in the water.'

I waved the suggestion aside.

'It is useless to tempt me with bribes,' I said firmly. 'I will not be tubbed by you.'

'Oh, come along.'

'No, no, a thousand times no!'

Matters appeared to have reached a deadlock. She gazed at me imploringly. I met her gaze with undiminished determination. The door opened. Miss Brinkmeyer entered.

'It's time you had —'

'Now, don't you begin.'

'— your bath,' she concluded.

'That's what I've been telling him,' said Ann.

'Then why isn't he having it?'

Ann hesitated. I could see that she did not wish to make trouble for me with the big white chieftainess, and I honoured her for the kindly thought. I helped her out.

'I don't want to,' I said.

'Want to?' The Brinkmeyer came through with one of her well-known snorts. 'It isn't a question of what you want, it's a question —'

'Of modesty,' I thundered, cutting her short. 'The whole matter is one of principle. One has one's code. To a bath, *quâ* bath,' I said, borrowing some of old Horace Plimsoll's stuff, 'I have no objection whatever. In fact, I should enjoy one. But when I am asked to countenance turning the thing into a sort of Babylonian orgy —'

The Brinkmeyer looked at Ann.

'What is he talking about?'

'I don't understand. He's funny to-night.'

'He doesn't amuse *me*.'

'Strange, I mean.'

'Nothing strange about it,' snorted the Brinkmeyer. 'That's what that fool of a dentist said. Tried to make me believe it was delirium. I told him the child was just being a pest, the way he always is. And that's what he's being now.'

I delivered my ultimatum. I was civil but adamant.

'I will take my bath, but I cross that bathroom threshold alone.'

'Yes, and splash your hand around in the water and come out pretending you've had it.'

I treated the slur with the silent contempt it deserved. I grabbed my pyjamas and nipped into the bathroom, locking the door behind me. Swift, decisive action while they're still gabbling – that's the only way to handle women. They are helpless in face of the *fait accompli*.

I fancy that the Brinkmeyer shouted a good many things, all probably in derogatory vein, through the door, but the rush of the water mercifully drowned her voice. I drew a piping-hot tub and sank into it luxuriantly. I could now hear what the Brinkmeyer was saying – something about scrubbing behind the ears – but I ignored her. One does not discuss these things with women. I found the toy duck, and it surprised me what pleasure I derived from sporting with it. And what with that and what with the soothing effects of a good long soak, I came out some twenty minutes later with my nervous system much restored. My feeling of *bien être* was completed by the discovery that the Brinkmeyer was no longer with us. Worsted by my superior generalship, she had withdrawn, no doubt in discomfiture. Only Ann remained to tuck me up.

This she did in a motherly manner which, I confess, occasioned me some surprise. I had always been fond of Ann – indeed, as we have seen, there had been a time when I had loved her – but in my dealings with her I had been conscious right along of – I won't say a hardness exactly but a sort of bright, cocksure, stand-no-nonsense bossiness, such as so many self-supporting American girls have, and this I had always considered a defect. She had lacked that sweet, soft, tender gentleness which had so drawn me to April June. But now she might have stepped straight into that poem about 'A ministering angel, thou', and no questions asked. As I say, it surprised me.

She assembled the blankets about my person, rallying me affably as she did so.

'You are a nut, young Joseph. What's the matter with you to-night?'

'I'm all right.'

'Just one of your humorous efforts, I suppose. You're

84

a funny old bird, aren't you? One of these days, though, if you go on joshing Miss Brinkmeyer, she'll haul off and paste you one. I'm surprised she didn't do it just now.'

These words had rather a sobering effect. I recognized their truth. Now that I looked back on the recent scene, I recalled that I had noticed her hand quiver once or twice, as if itching for the slosh.

'H'm,' I said.

'Yes, I'd be careful, if I were you. Restrain that love of fun of yours. The trouble with you, my Joseph, is that your sense of comedy is too keen. Anything for a laugh is your motto. Well, good night, old cut-up.'

'Good night.'

'Comfy?'

'Fine, thanks.'

'Better get to sleep as quick as you can. You've a busy day to-morrow.' She gave me what seemed to me a significant glance – why, I didn't know. 'Very busy, eh?'

'Oh, rather,' I said, not wishing to betray ig.

'It's all fixed for to-morrow evening.'

'Oh, yes?'

'Yes. Well, good night.'

She kissed me on top of the head and pushed off, leaving me to lie there in thoughtful mood. One of the major catches of having been changed into little Joey Cooley, I perceived, was that, until I began to get the hang of things, I wasn't going to be able to understand what people were talking about half the time. A dashed nuisance, of course, but one that had to be faced.

I lay there, gazing pensively at the open window, which had turned into a dark-blue oblong with a couple of stars in it. And, as I gazed, these stars suddenly disappeared. Some substantial body had inserted itself between them and me, and I could hear the slither of a leg coming over the sill.

I switched on the light. A figure was standing in the room. It was the figure of a beefy bird in a quiet grey suit, its lower limbs finished off with powder-blue socks matching the neat tie and melting, as it were, into tasteful suède shoes. In fact, to cut a long story short, the third Earl of Havershot in person.

'Attaboy!' said this figure in a satisfied tone of voice. 'Here we are at last.'

Chapter 11

THE first thing I noticed about this new and revised edition of little Joey Cooley was that he didn't appear to be at all disturbed by what had occurred. The recent switch seemed to have made little or no impression on him. He was absolutely calm and quite collected. Insouciant would about describe his demeanour. He strolled across to the bed and sat down on it as if he hadn't a care in the world.

I suppose the fact of the matter is that in Hollywood you get to learn to take the rough with the smooth, and after you've lived there for a time nothing rattles you – not even waking up and finding yourself in someone else's body. You simply say: 'Ah, someone else's body, eh? Well, well!' and carry on. His opening remarks did not deal with the switch, but with my supper menu.

'Prunes!' he said, eyeing the stones with a slight shudder. 'It would be prunes. I don't suppose there's a kid alive that's eaten more prunes than I have. Well, buddy, you're welcome to them.'

And adding something in a low voice about spinach, he produced from his breast pocket a rather tired-looking ice-cream cone and flicked a bit of dust off it.

The spectacle affected me profoundly. Every fibre in my being seemed to call out for that cone.

'Hi! Give me a lick!' I cried, in a voice vibrant with emotion.

He passed it over without hesitation. If he had been Sir Philip Sidney with the wounded soldier, he couldn't have been nippier.

'Sure,' he said agreeably. 'You can have it all. It's a funny thing, but I don't seem to like ice-cream cones so much as I used to. I could eat my weight in them once, but now they don't kind of have any fascination for me.

And it's the same with chocolate cake and fudge and pumpkin pie and doughnuts and —'

I cut him short with a passionate cry.

'Stop it!'

'Eh?'

'Don't mention those things to me. Do you think I am made of marble?'

'Oh, sorry.'

There was a silence. I finished the cone.

'Gee! You look a scream,' he said.

'So do you look a scream,' I retorted.

'I guess we both look screams,' he went on amiably. 'How do you suppose all this happened? Quite a surprise to me, it was. I woke up in the wrong room with a strange dentist pushing a glass at me and telling me to rinse, and then I found that I was somebody else, and I looked in the mirror and saw that it was you. Handed me a big laugh, that did.'

'I don't see anything funny about it.'

'Maybe you're right. But it tickled me at the time. Hello, I says to myself, there's a mistake somewhere. Have you any idea how the thing was worked?'

I advanced my theory that there had been a mix-up in the fourth dimension. He seemed to think well of it.

'Yessir, that's just about what it must have been, I guess. You never know what's going to happen to you next under this Administration, do you?'

'Well, it doesn't matter how it happened. The point is that it is all most irregular and I want to know what the dickens we're going to do about it?'

'Don't seem to me there's anything we can do about it.'

'We could issue statements.'

'What, tell people you're me and I'm you. Sure we could, if you don't mind being put in the booby-hatch.'

'You think that would be the upshot?'

'Well, wouldn't it?'

'I suppose it would,' I said, having mused. 'Yes, I see what you mean.'

There was no question about it that he was right. A clear, shrewd thinker, this kid. The loony-bin is inevitably the portion of those who go about the place telling that kind of story. I saw now that it would not, as I had at one time supposed, be merely a matter of incredulity and let it go at that on the part of one's audience. Strait waistcoats would be called for and padded cells dusted off.

'Besides,' he said, 'I've no kick coming. I call this a good break for me. I like it.'

In spite of the fact that I was in his debt for that ice-cream cone, I found his manner jarring upon me not a little. A dashed sight too smug, was my verdict.

'You do, do you?'

'Sure. I've always wanted to be big, and I am big. Swell! The way I look at it, everything's jakesey-jooksey.'

My annoyance increased. His airy nonchalance gave me the pip. The young blighter appeared to have no thought except for self.

'Jakesey-jooksey, eh?'

'Jakesey-jooksey is right.'

'For you, yes.'

'Well, it's me I'm thinking about.'

'Then think about me for a bit.'

'You?'

'Yes, me. If you want to know my views, I'm extremely sick about the whole bally business. I have a very definite feeling that I have been handed the sticky end of the deal. There I was, buzzing along perfectly happy as a member of the British peerage, eating well, sleeping well, nice income from rents and so on, and just got my golf handicap down to single figures. And what ensues? All of a sudden, without being consulted, I'm changed into a child who has to look slippy in order not to be bathed by females and whose social position seems to be that of some malefactor doing a five-year stretch at Dartmoor or somewhere. Ordered hither, ordered thither ... lugged into cars, lugged out of them ... hauled upstairs, bunged into bedrooms. ...'

He gave me an enquiring look.

'I see you've met the old girl.'

'I have.'

'Did she get hold of your wrist and pull?'

'She did.'

'She used to get hold of my wrist and pull. Full of energy, that dame. I think she eats a lot of yeast.'

'It isn't just energy. There was animus behind it.'

'Eh?'

'I say her actions were inspired by animus. It is patent that she hates your gizzard.'

'Well, yes, we've never been really buddies.'

'And why not?'

'I don't know.'

'I do. Because you didn't conciliate her. Because you never bothered to exercise tact and suavity. A little more geniality on your part, a little more of the pull-together spirit, and she might have been a second mother to you. To take a simple instance, did you ever bring her a red apple?'

'No.'

'You see!'

'What would I do that for?'

'To conciliate her. It's a well-known method. Ask any of the nibs at the nearest kindergarten. It would have been the easiest of tasks to bring her a red apple. You could have done it on your head. Instead of which,' I said bitterly, 'you go about the place putting Mexican horned toads in her bed.'

He blushed a little.

'Why, yes.'

'There you are.'

'But that's nothing. What's a Mexican horned toad or so among friends?'

'Tchah!'

'I'm sorry.'

'Too late to be sorry now. You've soured her nature.'

'Well, she soured mine. All those prunes and spinach.'

'Tchah!' I said again. I was pretty shirty.

We fell into another silence. He shuffled his feet. I stared bleakly before me.

'Well, there it is,' he said, at length. He looked at my wrist watch. 'Say, I guess I'll have to be moving along in a minute. Before I go, let's get one or two things straightened out. Havershot you said your name was, didn't you?'

'Yes.'

'How do you spell it?'

'You will find a card-case in that coat.'

He fetched out the card-case.

'Gee!' he said. 'Are you one of those English Oils?'

'I am. Or, rather, I was.'

'I always thought they were string-bean sort of guys without any chins. That's the way they are in the pictures.'

'I used to go in for games, sports, and pastimes to a goodish extent, thus developing the thews and sinews.'

'Kind of an athlete, eh?'

'Precisely. And that's what makes me so particularly sick about all this. Look at that arm,' I said, exhibiting it.

'What's wrong with it?'

'What's wrong with it! What future have I got with an arm like that? As far as boxing and football are concerned, it rules me out completely. While as for cricket, can I ever become a fast bowler again? I doubt if an arm like this will be capable of even slow, leg-theory stuff. It is the arm of one of Nature's long-stops. Its limit is a place somewhere down among the dregs of a house second eleven.'

'I don't know what you're talking about.'

'I'm talking about what's going to happen to me in a few years, when I go to school. Do you think I like the prospect of being a frightful little weed who will probably sing alto in the choir and for the privilege of kicking whose trouser seat the better element will fight like wolves?'

'Well, say, listen,' he rejoined hotly, 'do you think I

like the prospect of going about for the rest of my life with a face like this?'

'We will not discuss my face.'

'No. Better hush it up, I guess. Golly, what a map!'

'Please!'

'Well, you started it.'

There was a rather stiff silence. We were both piqued. He looked at the watch again.

'I got to be going,' he said. 'I've a call to make down at Malibu. Got to see my press agent.'

'What for?'

'Oh, just to say hello.'

'You can't say hello to press agents looking like that.'

'Oh, yes, that's all right. He'll understand. Say, there's another thing I just thought of. Where do I go nights?'

'I beg your pardon?'

'Well, I've got to sleep somewhere, haven't I? Where were you living?'

'I told you. I have a bungalow at the Garden of the Hesperides.'

'That's all right, then. Well, anything you want to know?'

I thought for a moment. There were, of course, a hundred questions I wanted to ask, but I couldn't think of them. Then something occurred to me.

'What's all this about unveiling a statue?'

'Oh, that's just a statue of old Brinkmeyer.'

'I see.'

So they were shoving up a statue to the old boy, were they? Well, I had no objection. No doubt a thoroughly well-deserved honour. Whether a man who looked like a captive balloon was wise to allow statues of himself to be exhibited was, of course, a question to be decided by himself alone.

'Do I unveil it?'

'Of course you don't. Anything else?'

'They were saying something about some Michigan Mothers.'

'That's a deputation that's come over from Detroit. You receive them.'

'Admirers, are they?'

'That's right. The Michigan branch of the Joey Cooley Faithful Fan Club.'

'They come to pay their respects, as it were?'

'That's the idea. And you receive them.'

'Oh, well, I don't suppose I shall mind that.'

He seized the opening. It was plainly his desire to cheer and encourage.

'Sure you won't. You aren't going to mind anything. You mustn't believe all that stuff I was telling you in the waiting-room. I was feeling kind of down, on account that tooth of mine was giving me the devil. You'll find this a pretty soft racket you've dropped into. You've got about the biggest following of anyone in pictures. Wait till you see the fan mail. And it's sort of fun acting up in front of the camera. Yessir, I think you're going to like it. Well, I must be scramming. Pleased to have met you.'

He moved to the window and shoved a leg over the sill.

'Oh, say, look,' he said, pausing. 'About Ma Brinkmeyer I almost forgot to tell you. If you ever want another horned toad, you get it from the gardener with the squint and the wart on his nose. He's always around the place. Just tell him it's for putting in Miss Brinkmeyer's bed, and he won't charge you anything.'

He disappeared, to pop up again a moment later.

'Oh, say, look,' he said, 'there's something I ought to warn you about. I'll give you a ring to-morrow.'

I sat up, a-quiver.'

'Warn me about?'

'Yay. I haven't time to tell you now, but there's something you've got to watch out for. I'll phone you in the morning.'

He disappeared once more, and I lay back, still a-quiver.

I hadn't liked those last words. A sinister ring they had seemed to me to have.

However, I wasn't able to brood on them long. Nature took its toll of the tired frame. Before I knew where I was, my eyes were closing, and I was asleep.

My first day as Joey Cooley had ended.

Chapter 12

I SUPPOSE everybody's had the experience at one time or another of waking up after a nightmare in which they were chased by leopards or chewed by cannibals or some such thing and drawing a deep breath and saying to themselves: 'Phew! Good egg! It was only a dream, after all.' A dashed agreeable sensation it is, too.

That's how it was with me next morning when, opening my eyes to another day, I reviewed the recent events. It was as if a great weight had rolled off me. For about five seconds, the relief was amazing. 'Well, well,' I felt, 'how very droll, to be sure. Positively bizarre.' And then suddenly it all went phut.

It was catching sight of the sleeve of my pyjama jacket that first made me think a bit. It so happens that in the matter of pyjamas I've always been a trifle on the choosy side. I'm not one of those fellows who just charge into a hosier's and grab anything. They have to be silk for me, and a nice lively pattern, too. And this sleeve, it would have been plain to the most vapid and irreflective observer, was constructed of some foul patent health-conserving wool. It was, moreover, a light, bilious green in colour, like my cousin Egremont at breakfast-time.

'Hullo!' I said to myself. 'What, what?'

And then I saw a beastly little hand protruding from the end of the sleeve, and the truth came home to me. I didn't have to hop out of bed and look in the glass. That half-portion of a hand told its own story. It informed me absolutely officially that what I had been kidding myself was a dream had been no dream at all. I really had become this blasted Cooley child, complete to the last button, and what I had once more to ask myself was: What would the harvest be?

The shock was so severe that I just lay there on my

back, staring at the ceiling. It was as if I had walked into a right swing while boxing with the village blacksmith.

However, I was not allowed much time for chewing the bitter cud. The kid Cooley's day apparently started early. I don't suppose I had been groaning in spirit more than about ten minutes or so when some kind of a secretary hove alongside with a fountain-pen and about a gross of photographs for me to sign. She was followed by a masseur. Then a facial rubber blew in to tune up my features. And after him a hairdresser, who attended to my curls.

And I was lying there, a bit used up, wondering whether the next item on the programme would be a chiropodist or somebody to put me through a course of rhythmical breathing, when the door opened and the butler manifested himself.

'Good morning, sir,' he said.

'Good morning,' I replied. I was glad to see him. As on the previous day, I found him consoling. The sight of that smooth, round face and spreading waistcoat had a restorative effect. 'Come in and take a seat,' I said hospitably, for I had long since become reconciled to the fact of my bedroom being a sort of meeting-place of the nations. 'Or are you just passing through?'

'I have brought your breakfast, sir.'

This had the effect of bucking me up still more, for breakfast in bed is always breakfast in bed, until he went out and reappeared with the tray, and I perceived that all it contained was milk, some stuff that looked like sawdust, and a further consignment of those blighted prunes. A nice bit of news to have to break to a stomach which had been thinking in terms of scrambled eggs and kidneys.

'Hey!' I cried.

'Sir?'

'What's all this?'

'It is your customary breakfast, sir.'

'Hell!' I said, with feeling. 'Well, all right. Better than nothing, I suppose.'

96

He regarded me with kindly sympathy as I dug into the sawdust.

'It's hard, sir, isn't it.'

'Pretty foul.'

'They tell me it's to keep your weight down.'

'Oh, I suppose they've got some sort of story.'

'It is what is called a balanced diet. But it is not pleasant to be compelled to abet this, if I may so describe it, Spartan regimen. I know what young gentlemen's appetites are.'

'Me, too.'

'I know just how you must feel, sir. You may be a highly important figure in the world of motion pictures, but you are only a small boy, after all, aren't you?'

'And not likely to get larger on this muck.'

'If I had my way, I'd let you eat what you wanted. You're only young once.'

'Twice?'

'Sir?'

'Nothing.'

'What you would enjoy, I dare say, would be a nice plate of sausages.'

'Please!'

'They're having them downstairs. Sausages and buckwheat cakes.'

'Would you torture me, butler?'

'No, sir, it's only that I was thinking that if you could pay me some small honorarium to compensate me for the risk of losing my place, I might contrive to smuggle some up.'

The prunes turned to ashes in my mouth. Not that it altered the taste of them much.

'I haven't any money.'

'None at all, sir?'

'Not a penny.'

He sighed.

'Well, there you are, you see. That's how it goes.'

I finished the prunes in silence, and dipped into the

milk. I was musing on this matter of money. There, I saw, lay the nub of my troubles. No cash.

'Could you lend me a bit?'

'No, sir.'

I swigged milk morosely. He sighed again.

'There is a great deal of sorrow in the world, sir.'

'Quite.'

'Look at me.'

I did, pretty sharply. His words astounded me.

'Why, there's nothing wrong with you, dash it. You're all right.'

'Far from it, sir.'

'Don't talk drip, butler. I expect you breakfasted till your eyes bulged.'

'I made a hearty breakfast, yes, sir. But is breakfast everything?'

'I see what you mean. There's lunch, too. And dinner.'

'There's the heartache of the exile, sir. There's the yearning to be away from it all. There's the dull despair of living the shallow, glittering life of this tinsel town where tragedy lies hid behind a thousand false smiles.'

'Oh, is there?' I said aloofly.

I was in no mood to listen to other people's hard-luck stories. I declined to allow this butler to sob on my shoulder. He appeared to be looking to me to hold his hand and be the little mother, and I wasn't going to do it.

'I dare say you are wondering how I come to be here, sir.'

'No, I'm not.'

'It's a long story.'

'Save it for the winter evenings.'

'Very good, sir. Ah, Hollywood, Hollywood,' said the butler, who seemed not to like the place. 'Bright city of sorrows, where fame deceives and temptation lurks, where souls are shrivelled in the furnace of desire, whose streets are bathed with the shamed tears of betrayed maidens.'

'Keep it clean.'

'Hollywood! Home of mean glories and spangled

wretchedness, where the deathless fire burns for the out-spread wings of the guileless moth and beauty is broken on sin's cruel wheel. If you have finished with the tray, sir, I will take it.'

He popped off sombrely. And as there didn't seem to be any more callers coming – one of those slack periods which occur, no doubt, in the busiest lives – I got out of bed and donned the frilly shirt and knickerbockers and went downstairs to see how things were coming along with the Brinkmeyer family.

They had apparently been breakfasting out in the patio, for there was a white-clothed table in the middle by the goldfish pond. It bore the remains of a meal, and it was with a rush of emotion that I perceived that on a dish in the centre there was lying a derelict sausage. Sated with pleasure, these gorgers hadn't been able quite to make the grade. They had left of their abundance this admirable sausage.

The goldfish were looking up expectantly, obviously hoping for their cut, but my need was greater than theirs. I ate the unclaimed. The goldfish made faces like Leslie Henson and withdrew. And I picked up the morning paper which was lying on the table. I had a not unnatural curiosity to see what it said of yesterday's doings. As I had taken over little Joey Cooley as a going concern with all the goodwill and fixtures, his notices were my notices.

If this journal was a reliable indication of the trend of critical thought, I had had a good press. In spite of the heaviness of my heart and the emptiness of my stomach, I could not but feel gratified to see that I had practically ousted the rest of the world's news from the front page. There was the usual announcement that the President – that old Good Time Charley, bless his heart – was planning to spend another billion dollars of other people's money on something or other, but except for that the only non-Cooley item was a paragraph tucked away in the south-east corner to the effect that the unveiling of the statue of T. P. Brinkmeyer, head of the Brinkmeyer-Magnifico

Motion Picture Corporation, would take place to-day at six p.m. on the Brinkmeyer-Magnifico lot.

I had just begun to turn the pages to see if there was further material inside, hunting absently the while among the dishes in case there might be another sausage somewhere, when Mr Brinkmeyer in person came drifting through the French windows, clad in a dressing-gown and looking more like a captive balloon than ever.

His manner, it seemed to me, was that of a captive balloon with something on its mind. His eyes had a sort of haunted look. He wandered about the patio, followed by the cord of his dressing-gown, rubbing his hands nervously.

' 'Morning,' he said.

'Good morning.'

'Nice weather.'

'Beautiful.'

He gave a sort of giggling groan.

'Well, young man, to-day's the day.'

'Yes,' I said. I took it that he was alluding to this statue business. 'Quite a binge it will be, no doubt.'

'And I wish it was over!'

He gave another of those groans, and I thought a word of encouragement might help. I could see that he was one of those men who shrink from public functions and beanos.

'Tails up, Brinkmeyer,' I said.

'What's that?'

'I said: "Tails up, Brinkmeyer." You mustn't be nervous.'

'But I am. You know what?'

'What?'

'She says I've got to wear my cutaway coat and a stiff collar.'

'You'll be the belle of the ball.'

'And a gardenia, she says. And spats. I shall feel like a sissy.'

He took another turn about the patio.

'Spats!' he said, looking at me piteously.

I was beginning to be a bit fed up with this business of every bally person I met wanting me to kiss the place and make it well. I liked this old buster, but I had troubles of my own.

'You could scarcely expect to turn up in sneakers and a sweater, my good fellow,' I said – rather unkindly, perhaps, but, as I say, I was annoyed.

'Yay, I know. But spats!'

'Better men than you have worn spats.'

He continued to circulate.

'You know what? Half the trouble in this world comes of people getting ambitious. They don't know when they're well off.'

'Shrewdly put, Brinkmeyer.'

This observation seemed to arrest him. He paused in his patio-prowling and gave me one of his owl-like looks.

'What's that?'

'I said: "Shrewdly put, Brinkmeyer." There is much in what you say.'

'You're talking kind of funny this morning,' he said. Then his mind seemed to skid back to what was on it. 'Listen. I got too ambitious.'

'Yes?'

'There I was, perfectly happy in the cloak and suit business, and I ought to have stuck to it. But, no. Nothing would do but I had to go into the pictures. And look at me now. President of the organization, worth every cent of twenty million dollars . . .'

An idea struck me.

'You couldn't lend me a bit, could you?'

'. . . And what does it all amount to? Here I am, got to stand up there in spats, with everybody staring at me, looking like a comic valentine. I might have known it would happen. It's always the way. You get on just the least little bit in this world, and first thing you know they're putting up statues to you. The moment your back's turned. I ought to have stuck to the cloak and suit business.'

I forgot my own troubles. All this was moving me. It occurred to me how little the outside world knew of the discontent that seethed in practically every bosom you met in Hollywood. The casual observer saw these bosoms going about the place and envied them, assuming that, being well provided with the stuff, they must be happy. And all the time discontent seethed. In my own little circle, April June wanted to be a wife and mother. Joey Cooley wanted to be back in Chillicothe, Ohio, eating fried chicken, southern style. The butler wasn't any too pleased with things. And this Brinkmeyer sighed for the cloak and suit business. A bit poignant.

'Those were the days! All friends together like a lot of kids. . . . Matching fabrics, joshing the buyers. . . .'

I think he would have spoken further on the matter, for his manner seemed to indicate that there was much on his chest, but at this moment Miss Brinkmeyer came out of the house, and he bit back the words that were rising to his lips. He looked sheepish. I, too, as always in the presence of this female, was conscious of a certain embarrassment. We stood there shuffling our feet. It was as if we had been a couple of the lads at the dear old school surprised by the head master while enjoying a quiet smoke in a corner of the cricket field.

'Ah, my dear,' said old Brinkmeyer, 'I was just having a chat with little Cooley here.'

'Oh?' said Miss Brinkmeyer.

She seemed to be feeling that there was no accounting for tastes. The look she gave me was austere. That horned toad evidently still rankled in all its pristine freshness. It was plain that she saw no reason to revise her opinion that I was just an off-scouring of the underworld.

'About that statue.'

'What about it?'

'Oh, we were just talking about it. Exchanging views.'

'Well, I hope he quite understands what he has to do. We don't want him muddling everything up.'

I started visibly.

'Good Lord!' I said. 'I'm not mixed up in this statue jamboree, am I?'

I was much exercised. Ever since I had ceased to be Reginald, Lord Havershot, people seemed to have been springing something new on me all the time. I wondered if any child had ever led a fuller life than this kid Cooley. Never an idle moment, I meant to say. If not doing so-and-so, busily occupied with such-and-such.

Miss Brinkmeyer threw her hands heavenwards. One noted the touch of fever.

'Well, of all the ... Don't tell me you've forgotten, after the way you've been rehearsed in every word and move. ...'

I saw that suavity was the note.

'Oh, no, rather not. I'm pretty sure I've got the idea. But you know how it is. So many things on one's mind, don't you know. Just barely possible I may have forgotten a spot or two of the procedure. I'll tell you what. Run over the main points on the programme, and I'll see if I'm clear.'

She swallowed once or twice. Still a bit overwrought, she struck me as.

'The ceremony begins at six sharp.'

'Yes. I know that.'

'While the speeches are going on —'

'Do I make a speech?'

'No, you do *not*, and don't let me catch you trying to. While the speeches are going on, you stand at the back.'

'I can do that all right. Well within my scope.'

'After the speeches comes the unveiling. The moment Mr Hays has unveiled the statue, you run forward with the nosegay and give it to Mr Brinkmeyer.'

I frowned a quick frown.

'Did you say nosegay?'

'Nosegay was what I said.'

'Gosh!'

'For goodness' sake, it's quite simple, isn't it?'

Simple, yes. But what I was feeling was what a priceless pair of asses we should look. I mean, nosegays! And I could see that old Brinkmeyer saw eye to eye with me in this matter. He didn't like the cutaway coat. He didn't like the gardenia. He didn't like the spats. Add a golden-haired child leaping at him with nosegays, and you had something that might well make a man of retiring disposition wish he was back in the cloak and suit business.

I shot him a sympathetic glance, which seemed to be appreciated.

'And as you hand him the nosegay, you say: "Pitty f'owers for 'oo, Mithter B'inkmeyer".'

Well, that didn't seem so bad. Not a frightfully attractive layout, of course, but might have been considerably worse. I might have had to address the multitude at length. Unaccustomed though I was to public speaking, I felt pretty sure I shouldn't blow up in a short, snappy gag like that.

I nodded intelligently.

'I see. Yes, I get that. "Pretty flowers for you, Mr Brinkmeyer."'

She did the bending and stretching exercises once more. She seemed to be registering despair. Her whole demeanour was that of one unable to cope.

'For goodness gracious sake! Are you really dumb, or are you just trying to be aggravating? Haven't I told you a hundred times? Not "pretty" – "pitty". Not "flowers" – "f'owers". Not "you" – " 'oo". And not "Mr Brinkmeyer" – "Mithter B'inkmeyer". Will you please get the line right! We've had conference after conference ... all the highest-paid authors in the organization working on the thing ... and you go and mess it up. You say "Pitty f'owers for 'oo, Mithter B'inkmeyer". And, remember, not a syllable more. No wisecracks.'

'Right ho.'

'About my spats, for instance,' said Mr Brinkmeyer.

'Right ho.'

'And don't giggle. Smile, but not giggle.'

'Right ho.'

'And then hold it.'

'The nosegay?'

'The picture.'

This puzzled me.

'What picture? You didn't mention any picture.'

She wandered off on to a side-issue.

'Do you want a good box on the ear?'

'No.'

'Then don't try to be funny. After business with nose-gay, speak the line and hold the picture.'

'She means "Don't cut",' explained Mr Brinkmeyer.

'Exactly. Hold it. Wait for the kiss.'

I shook from ringlets to toenails.

'Kiss?'

'That's where I kiss you,' said Mr Brinkmeyer, in an odd, strangled voice, like one speaking from the tomb. Behind their glasses his eyes looked hunted and haggard.

I was still quivering.

'You kiss me?'

'Of course he kisses you. Haven't you been told that over and over and over? Can't you understand plain English? He – kisses – you. It will make a very pretty and appealing picture.'

I was just seeking for words in which to make plain how little it appealed to me, when the footman who had brought me my supper on the previous evening appeared.

'Excuse yes possibly,' he said.

'Well, what is it?'

'Chap at door,' said the footman, becoming clearer.

Miss Brinkmeyer nodded.

'It must be your new elocution teacher,' she said, starting to move towards the exit. 'I think you and the child had better have a run through, Theodore. He's such a lunkhead that he probably hasn't got it even now. You can use the coffee-pot as a nosegay.'

'No need to do the kiss?' said Mr Brinkmeyer, rather pleadingly. 'Just walk the kiss, eh?'

'Certainly. I don't suppose you want to kiss the little insect more than is absolutely necessary,' said Miss Brinkmeyer, and with these offensive words took her departure. I waited till she had disappeared, then fixed Mr Brinkmeyer with a steely eye.

'Brinkmeyer,' I said, in a low, hard voice, 'was this your idea?'

He disclaimed the charge vehemently.

'Sweet suffering soup-spoons, no! Given a free hand, I wouldn't touch you with a pair of tongs.'

It was exactly how I felt.

'Same here,' I said. 'I wouldn't touch *you* with a pair of tongs.'

We gazed at each other with something like affection. Twin souls.

'How would it be if we just shook hands?' I suggested. 'Or you could pat me on the back.'

'No. I've got to kiss you. She says I must. Well, it'll all be over this time to-morrow. There's that. But I wish I'd stuck to the cloak and suit business.'

I was still much moved. I felt that the responsibility should be fixed.

'If it wasn't your idea, whose was it?'

He scowled.

'It was that press agent guy of yours – that Booch – who thought it up. He said it would mean publicity of the right sort, darn him. And Beulah said it was a great notion. Gee! I'm glad that fellow got poked in the snoot. A mystery, they call it. The mystery to me is why nobody ever thought of doing it before.'

I started. The words had touched a cord in my mind.

'Poked in the snoot? Did somebody do that to him?'

'Did they! Haven't you read the paper?'

'Not that bit.'

'Lookut!' said Mr Brinkmeyer, diving for the periodical and opening it at the middle page. His face had lost its drawn look. He had become virtually gay and practically bobbish.

I took the paper, and headlines met my eye.

As follows:

STRANGE OCCURRENCE AT MALIBU
MYSTERY FIEND SMITES TWO
'POKED US IN SNOOT,' SAY VICTIMS

The report beneath these headlines ran thus:

It will be no use Love sending a gift of roses to Cosmo Booch, noted press agent, or Dikran Marsupial, ace director, for some little time to come, because they won't be able to smell 'em. Both are home at this writing with swollen noses, the result of an encounter with what appears to have been a first-class fiend.

As Faust once remarked, there are moments when a fellow needs a fiend, but neither Cosmo Booch, ace press agent, nor Dikran Marsupial, noted director, needed this one when he descended on the former's cosy little cottage beside the sad sea waves of Malibu. They were playing checkers and did not require a third.

AN EYE-WITNESS

As to what it was all about, your correspondent has to confess himself a trifle fogged. Cosmo, questioned over the telephone at a late hour last night, was incoherent. So was Dikran. Each made odd spluttering noises, but contributed little or nothing to ye corr.'s enlightenment. Fortunately, there turns out to have been an eye-witness in the shape – if you can call it a shape – he would do well to knock off starchy foods – of George G. Frampton, well-known and popular member of the Hollywood Writers' Club.

FIEND GIVES GEORGE ELBOW

George G. Frampton, as all the world knows, is attached to the commercial side of the *Screen Beautiful* (ace motion-picture magazine), and it was in the course of one of his whirlwind drives for subscriptions, advertisements, or what have you that he found himself at Malibu. He was, indeed, on the point of calling upon Mr Booch to take up the matter of a half-page in the Special Number, when he was interested to find himself thrust to one side by a fiend.

LEAPED FENCE

George knows very few fiends, and this one, he says, was a complete stranger to him. He describes him as of powerful physique, and gorilla-esque features, and states that he was dressed in a quiet grey suit with suède shoes, as worn by the better class of fiend. He leaped the low fence which separates the Booch domain from the waterfront and proceeded to the porch.

IN A FLASH

It all happened, says George, who can turn a phrase as well as the next man, in a flash. The fiend leaped on to the porch and immediately dispelled any notion that might have been lurking in the minds of the checker players that here was a mere kibitzer who had come to breathe down the backs of their necks and offer advice, by pasting Cosmo Booch squarely on the schnozzle. And while Cosmo was calling on the Supreme Court to have this declared unconstitutional, he did precisely the same to Mr Marsupial. He then left by the front or carriage entrance.

MENTALLY UNBALANCED?

The whole affair is wrapped in mystery. All your correspondent could get from the two victims was the statement: 'He poked us in the snoot.' They were unable to offer any explanation. They had never seen their assailant before, nor – this is our guess – do they want to see him again. All they want is something to reduce the swelling. Another facet of the mystery is – Why, if he was going to punch anybody, did not the fiend punch George G. Frampton? The fact that, being in a position to poke George in the snoot, he did not do so opens up a disquieting line of thought. Is the locality haunted by a mentally unbalanced fiend?

We are watching developments closely.

Mr Brinkmeyer, who had been reading over my shoulder, seemed a bit querulous.

'I can't see what they want to call him a fiend for,' he said. 'Why fiend? Sounds kind of a good scout to me.

Stepped right up and let him have it. I'd like to meet that fellow.'

'So would I,' I said, and I meant it. I wished to get in touch with little Joey Cooley without delay, and reason with him.

For I had read this excerpt, as you may suppose, with mixed feelings. While the broad, basic fact that the man responsible for me getting kissed by the President of the Brinkmeyer-Magnifico Motion Picture Corporation had got it on the nose was far from displeasing, I could not disguise it from myself that the thing cut both ways.

However much your soul may have gone into someone else's body, you see, you can't help feeling a sort of responsibility for the body that used to be yours before someone else's soul went into it. You don't want the new tenant damaging its prestige and lowering it socially.

If this sort of thing was to continue, it seemed to me a mere question of time before the escutcheon of the Havershots would be blotted by the circumstance of the head of the family getting bunged into a dungeon cell for thirty days without the option.

I felt very strongly that this child Cooley must be talked to like a father. Some older and wiser head must buttonhole him and counsel prudence and restraint.

As I reached this conclusion, the footman entered.

'Telephone perhaps possibly,' he said.

'For me?' said Mr Brinkmeyer.

'No, thank you, please. For the young juvenile.'

'That's right,' I said. 'I was expecting a call. Lead me to the instrument.'

Chapter 13

THE telephone was in a sort of booth place along the hall. I closed the door carefully to ensure privacy, and flung myself on it, making eager hunting noises.

'Hullo,' I said. 'Hullo. Hullo.'

It was plain the moment he gave tongue that the child was in the pink. There was a merry ring in his voice.

'Hello? Is that you?'

'Yes.'

'This is the hundred and fiftieth Duke of Havershot.'

'Not Duke. Earl. And third, you ass.'

'Well, how's everything? Have you had breakfast?'

'Yes.'

'How were the prunes?'

'Damn the prunes!'

He chuckled fruitily.

'You'll have to learn to love them, buddy. Guess what I had for breakfast?'

'I decline to guess what you had for breakfast.'

'Well, believe me, it was good. Say, listen, have you seen the paper?'

'Yes.'

'Read about the Malibu Horror?'

'Yes.'

'Rather a good notice, I thought. Say, listen, did you ever do any boxing?'

'Yes.'

'I thought you must have. My timing was nice.'

'It was, was it?'

'Yessir. I seemed to be getting a lot of steam behind the punch. Well, I'm much obliged. I got those two bozoes a couple of beauts! You'd ought to have seen it. Bam. ... Wham! ... and down they went. I near died laughing.'

It seemed to me that it was time to squelch this kid. Too

bally exuberant altogether. He appeared to be under the impression that this was the maddest, merriest day of all the glad new year – a view in which he was vastly mistaken.

I spoke with considerable acerbity.

'Well, you've gone and landed yourself in a nice posish. A dashed nice posish, I don't think.'

'Says which?'

'What the hell do you mean, says which?'

'I mean, why?'

'Do you realize that you are a fugitive from justice?'

'What of it?'

'You won't be so dashed airy when the hands of the gendarmes fall upon your shoulder and they shove you in chokey for assault on the person.'

He laughed jovially. Getting more exuberant all the time.

'Oh, that's all right.'

'You think so, do you?'

'Sure. Those two ginks had never seen me before. You never met them, did you?'

'No.'

'Well, then.'

'But suppose you run into them again.'

'They won't recognize me.'

'Of course they will.'

'No, they won't. Not after I've shaved off this moustache.'

I uttered a quavering cry.

'You aren't going to shave off my moustache?'

I spoke with feeling, for I loved the little thing. It had been my constant companion for years. I had tended it in sickness and in health, raising it with unremitting care from a sort of half-baked or Hitler smudge to its present robust and dapper condition. More like a son than a moustache it had always been to me.

He appeared to be not without decent instincts, for

there was a marked touch of remorse in his voice as he replied.

'Got to,' he said regretfully. 'It's going to make all the difference.'

'It took me years to grow it.'

'I know, I know. It's a shame. Say, listen, I'll tell you what I'll do to meet you. You can cut off my curls.'

'Oh, right ho. Thanks.'

'Don't mention it.'

This gentleman's agreement concluded, he dismissed the subject and turned to one which he evidently considered of greater import.

'Well, that's that. Now I want to talk about this statue thing.'

His words brought back the bleak future that lay before me.

'Yes, by Jove. You never told me I'd got to be kissed by old Brinkmeyer.'

This seemed to amuse him. I heard him snicker.

'That's what you're worrying about, is it?'

'Of course it is.' A sudden tremor seized me. 'You don't mean there's anything else, do you?'

He snickered again. A sinister snicker.

'You betcher. You don't know the half of it. If being kissed by old Brinkmeyer was all the trouble that was ahead of you, you could go singing about the house. It's the statue.'

'Eh?'

'Yessir. That's what you want to watch out for. That statue.'

'Watch out for it?'

'Yay.'

'What do you mean?'

I put the question a bit acidly, for he seemed to me to be talking drivel, and it annoyed me. I mean, how the dickens do you watch out for a statue?

'You've got to take steps.'

'What steps?'

'Immedjut steps. You got to act promptly. What you want to do is hustle round to the studio right away. . . . No, you can't go right away, because you've an elocution lesson. . . . I guess you won't be able to fit it in this morning. . . . But first thing this afternoon . . .'

'What on earth are you talking about?'

'I was just wondering. . . . No, this afternoon's no good, either. There's those Michigan Mothers. Gee! I guess you'll just have to let it go. Too bad.'

I was conscious of a sudden qualm about those Michigan Mothers. I don't know why. Probably because the way things were being sprung on me in this new life of mine had made me suspicious of dirty work on all sides.

'Listen,' I said. 'When you say I've got to receive these bally Mothers, what do I have to do?'

'Oh, nothing. They just kiss you.'

'What!'

'That's all. But, of course, it's going to cut into your time. I don't see when you're going to be able to get at that statue, quite.'

I ignored this babble of statues. My mind was wrestling with this frightful thing.

'They *kiss* me?'

'That's right. They form a line and march past, kissing you.'

'How many of them?'

'Oh, just a handful. This is only a branch lodge. I wouldn't say there'd be more than five hundred.'

'Five hundred!'

'Six at the outside. But, as I was saying, it'll take time. I don't see how you'll be able to attend to that statue.'

'But, look here, do you mean to say I've got to be kissed by Mr Brinkmeyer *and* six hundred Michigan Mothers?'

'It's a shame, because a couple of minutes with a sponge and some carbolic or sump'n' would prob'ly fix it. Well, I guess your best plan is stout denial. After all, they can't *know* it was you. Yes, take it by and large, seems to me

113

that's the best thing. Just good little old stout denial. I've known it to work.'

It came to me as through a mist that he was saying something.

'What's that?'

'I'm telling you. You won't have time to sponge it off, so I say – stick to stout denial.'

'Sponge what off?'

'I'm telling you. I say they can't *know* it was you.'

'Know it was me what?'

'They may suspect, but they can't be certain.'

'Certain of what?'

'It might have been anyone. Just put that to them. Get tough. Say "Why me, huh? How do you know it was me? It might have been anyone". Ask 'em to prove it.'

'Prove what?'

'I'm telling you. About this statue.'

'What about it?'

'Day before yesterday,' said this ghastly kid, at last getting down to the stark facts, 'I went and painted a red nose on it.'

You can't reel much in a small telephone-booth, but I reeled as far as the conditions would permit.

'You painted a red nose on it?'

'Yessir.'

'Why?'

'It seemed a good idea at the time.'

'But, good Lord . . .'

'Well, darn it, if there's a statue going to be unveiled and you suddenly find a pot of paint lying around on one of the sets, you don't want to waste it,' said the kid – reasoning, I had to admit, not unsoundly.

But though I could follow the psychology, it didn't make things any better for me. I was still shaken to the core.

'But what will happen when they see it?'

'Ah!'

'Hell's foundations will quiver.'

'There'll be a fuss,' he conceded. 'Yessir, there'll be a fuss, right enough. They'll start running around in circles yelling their heads off. But if you stick to stout denial you'll have 'em baffled.'

'I shall not have 'em baffled. They won't be baffled for a single ruddy instant. What's the use of stout denial? Do you think I haven't been you long enough to know that your name in this vicinity is mud? Miss Brinkmeyer will leap to the truth. She will immediately see all. A fat lot of good it will be denying it to her, stoutly or not stoutly.'

'Well, I don't see what else you can do.'

'You don't, eh?'

'No, sir, not now you haven't time to hustle along with a sponge of carbolic or sump'n'. Nothing to be done about it.'

I resented this supine attitude.

'There's a dashed lot to be done about it.'

'Such as —?'

Well, there, of course, he rather had me. Then a great idea struck me. I saw daylight.

'I'm going to get out of this.'

'What, away from it all?'

'Yes.'

'Where to?'

I felt better. The whole scheme was beginning to shape itself.

'Well, look here, you will be going back to England shortly.'

'Why?'

'Of course you will. You live there.'

'I never thought of that.'

'You've got to look after the estate.'

'Gosh! Have I got an estate?'

'Of course you've got an estate. And a social position and so on. Not to mention tenantry and what not. You'll have to be there to attend to things.'

'I couldn't do it!'

'What!'

'No, sir. I couldn't do it in a thousand years. Look after an estate, what I mean, and maybe get the Bronx cheer from all that tenantry. I shan't go near England.'

'You will. And you'll be all right, because I shall be at your side, to advise and counsel. I shall sneak away from here and join you on the boat. You'll have to adopt me or something – old Plimsoll can tell us the procedure – and then I can live with you at Biddleford and in due season go to Eton and after that to Cambridge, and run the estate for you, and eventually be the prop of your declining years. You won't have to do a thing except just loll back and watch your arteries harden.'

'That's the idea, is it?'

'And a jolly good idea.'

'I see.'

'And, of course, in order to get away, I shall require money. You must, therefore, send round immediately by bearer in a plain sealed envelope a few hundred dollars, enough to pay my fare to — Hullo! Hullo! Are you there?'

He wasn't. At the first mention of parting with the stuff he had hung up.

I came out of the booth – I might say distraught. Yes, I will say distraught, because distraught was just what I was. I could see no happy ending. Actions speak louder than words, and from the fact that this foul child had bunged the receiver back on its hook the moment we started to go into committee of supply, it was clear that he had definitely declared himself out of the financial end. He was resolved to stick to his cash like glue and not let me have a penny of it.

And cash from some source I must secure with the minimum of delay. The storm clouds were gathering. Ere long the lightning must strike. After what the kid had told me about the statue, it did not need a razorlike intelligence to show me that things were hotting up, and that flight was the only course.

To remain here would mean not only being subjected to a deluge of kisses from Mr Brinkmeyer and the Michigan Mothers – this I might, by biting the bullet and summoning up all my iron fortitude have endured – but shame and exposure in the matter of the statue's red nose. That was the rub. For following swiftly on that shame and exposure would come the reckoning with Miss Brinkmeyer – a woman who already had been restrained from clipping me on the earhole only by the exercise of willpower beyond the ordinary. No amount of will-power could prevent her taking action now. I could not but feel that on an occasion like this it would probably run to a Grade A spanking with the back of a hair brush.

Yes, unquestionably I had got to get the stuff.

But, equally unquestionably, there didn't appear to be a single damned source from which I could do so.

There was Eggy, of course. He, no doubt, if informed of the position of affairs, and made to understand that only a temporary loan from him stood between a fondly loved cousin and the back of Miss Brinkmeyer's hairbrush, would let me have a bit. But how was I to establish contact with him? I hadn't a notion where he was living. And my movements were so restricted that I was not in a position to go wandering from party to party till I hit on one where he was gate-crashing.

Besides, I had to have money now, immediately. In another few hours it would be too late.

It was hopeless. There was nothing to be done. It was an unpleasant conclusion to be forced to come to, but there was no getting away from it, I was stymied. I would have to stay where I was and accept what the future might bring, merely trusting that when the worst happened a telephone directory or a stout bath towel placed in the interior of my knickerbockers would do something to ease the strain.

Musing thus, I came abreast of the drawing-room. This drawing-room hadn't a door, just an archway with curtains across it. And suddenly, as I was about to pass by, from the other side of these curtains there proceeded a voice.

'Oh, yes,' it said. 'Oh, quite.'

I halted, spellbound. The speaker was Eggy.

Chapter 14

I THOUGHT for a second that I must have imagined it. I mean, it seemed too good to be true that the one chap I wanted to see should have popped up out of a trap like this so exactly at the psychological moment. I couldn't have been more surprised if I had been Aladdin just after rubbing the lamp.

To make sure, I crept to the curtains and peeped through.

It was Eggy all right. He was sitting on the edge of a chair, sucking the knob of his stick. Opposite him sat Miss Brinkmeyer. Her back was towards me, but I could see Eggy's face clear enough. It was, as always at this time of day, greenish, though not unpleasantly so. He is one of those fellows with clean-cut, patrician features whom green rather suits.

Miss Brinkmeyer was speaking.

'I'm glad you agree with me,' she said, and there was an unwonted chumminess in her manner, as if she were getting together with a kindred soul. 'As a teacher of elocution, you should know.'

The mystery was solved. Putting two and two together, I was enabled to follow the run of the scenario. I remembered that Ann had told me that she had got Eggy a job. The kid Cooley had mentioned that I had an elocution lesson this morning. And when the footman had announced his arrival just now, Miss Brinkmeyer had said: 'What ho, the elocution teacher', or words to that effect.

All quite simple, of course, and I wasn't a bit surprised to find Eggy operating in this capacity. Since the talkies came in, you can't heave a brick in Hollywood without beaning an English elocution teacher. The place is full of Britons on the make, and if they can't get jobs on the screen, they work the elocution-teaching racket. References and qualifications are not asked for. So long as you're English, you are welcomed into the home. I am told that there are English elocution teachers making good money in Hollywood who haven't even got roofs to their mouths.

'Nothing,' said Miss Brinkmeyer, continuing, 'is more important in talking pictures than a good accent. Looks, acting, personality ... they don't mean a thing if you've got a voice like a bad dream.'

'True.'

'Like this child has. Have you ever seen him on the screen?'

'Well, no. What with one thing and another —'

'There you are. And you come from England.'

'Yes.'

'London?'

'Yes.'

'Lived there right along, I guess?'

'Oh, rather.'

'And you've never seen a Cooley picture. That's what I mean. Mr Brinkmeyer will have it that the little boll-weevil's voice is all right, because look what he grossed last time in Kansas City or wherever it may be, and all stuff like that. But what I tell Mr Brinkmeyer is that America isn't everything.'

'Quite.'

'You can't afford to neglect Great Britain and the Dominions. Look how he flops in London, I tell Mr Brinkmeyer. And now you bear me out by saying you've never so much as seen him.'

'Ah.'

'I guess pretty nearly nobody has over there, judging by the returns. And why? Because he's got an Ohio accent you could turn handsprings on.'

'Tut.'

'And what I tell Mr Brinkmeyer is that it's got to be sandpapered around the edges as soon as ever it can be, or we'll be losing out on him.'

'Quite.'

'Of course, naturally we don't want him to have one of those regular English accents. But there's a sort of in-between way of talking that goes everywhere. Like Ronald Colman and people.'

'Ah.'

'And that's what I want you to teach him.'

'Quite.'

'Of course, I don't know what your methods are. Miss Bannister just said you were the most celebrated teacher of elocution in London and had trained all the announcers of the British Broadcasting Corporation. . . .'

This seemed to startle old Eggy a bit. He didn't quite swallow his stick, but very nearly.

'Did she?' he said, having drawn it to the surface again.

'Sure. She said you were particularly good at ironing out their Lancashire accents. That's what gave me the idea that you might be able to cope with this Ohio affliction this child has got.'

'Oh, quite. We must see what we can do. . . . Er – Miss Bannister all right this morning?'

It was the first thing he had said that hadn't gone well. Miss Brinkmeyer drew herself up with a good spot of chill on. I couldn't think what she had got against Ann, but it was plain she didn't like her.

'I haven't seen Miss Bannister this morning.'

'No?'

'When I do, I shall have something to say to her.'

'Why, is anything up?'

'I would prefer not to discuss it.'

'Oh, quite.'

A bit of a lull followed. The jarring note had been struck, and it had knocked the conversation temporarily endways. Miss Brinkmeyer sat with folded arms. Eggy sucked his stick.

Miss Brinkmeyer was the first to come out of the silence.

'Well, as I was saying, I don't know what your methods

are. I haven't a notion how you experts start on this kind of proposition —'

Eggy perked up.

'I'll tell you,' he said. 'Methods differ. There are various schools of thought. Some have one system, some another. I, personally, like to begin by taking a good stiff Scotch and soda —'

'What!'

'Or, better, two Scotch and sodas. This keys up the brain and puts one in the vein to instruct. So if you have Scotch in the house —'

'We have not.'

'Then make it rye,' said Eggy, full of resource.

Miss Brinkmeyer eyed him coldly.

'We have no liquor of any description.'

'None?'

'None.'

'Oh?' said Eggy, and I suppose that was about all a chap who had had such a setback to his dreams and visions could have been expected to say.

'Mr Brinkmeyer and I are regular attendants at the Temple of the New Dawn.'

'Oh?' said Eggy. He took another suck at his stick, as if trying to extract what poor refreshment he could from that.

'Yes. I had some little difficulty in persuading Mr Brinkmeyer to become a disciple, but eventually I succeeded, and he now sits under Sister Stott.'

Eggy removed the stick from his mouth, squared his shoulders, cleared his throat, and spoke in a firm, resonant voice.

'He sits under Sister Stott.'

'That's what I said — he sits under Sister Stott.'

'I mean, I can say it.'

'I don't understand you.'

'Pretty good, don't you think?'

'What is good?'

'Being able to say it.'

It seemed to seep through into Eggy's mind that an explanation would be in order.

'I was only thinking of something that happened yesterday. I met a girl who talked the most subversive rot. I had been rattling off things like "British constitution" and "The Leith police dismisseth us" without an effort, and she tried to make me believe that being able to say things didn't affect the issue. She scared me a bit, I confess, but to-day I can see through her specious arguments. Perfectly absurd, I mean, to pretend that a fellow is not absolutely all right if he can say things like "British constitution" and "The Leith police dismisseth us", not to mention such a complex and intricate sentence as "He sits under Stister Stott" . . . or, rather, he stits . . . Wait,' said Eggy, marshalling his forces. 'We mustn't allow ourselves to become confused. This is a perfectly straight, clean-cut issue. Putting the thing in a nutshell, then, he stots . . .'

He paused. A rather worried look came into his face. And then just as he was starting to have another go at it, his voice died away in a sort of whistling sigh. The stick, slipping from his nerveless grasp, clattered to the floor. He sat rigid in his chair, his Adam's apple going up and down very slowly. He had caught sight of me peering through the curtains.

I couldn't see Miss Brinkmeyer's face, but I imagine it wore an enquiring look. One of those odd looks. Her voice sounded odd.

'Is something the matter, Mr Mannering?'

The green of Eggy's face had shaded away to a delicate white. I had come through the curtains and was standing there giving him an encouraging smile. I wanted to put the old chap at his ease.

'No,' he said. 'Oh, no. No, thanks.'

'You seem unwell.'

Eggy swallowed once or twice.

'No, not a bit, thanks. Never better.'

He removed his eyes from mine with a powerful effort. 'If only it wouldn't grin!'

'Grin?'

'I can't see why it has to grin.'

'I beg your pardon?'

'Nothing,' said Eggy. 'Nothing. Only there's something so sort of ghastly and gloating about it. Pink rabbits, now, must be quite different.'

It semed to be beginning to dawn on Miss Brinkmeyer that she had run up against something rather hot.

'Would you like a glass of water?'

'Eh? No. No, thanks.'

There was a silence.

'I say,' said Eggy, 'tell me about this Temple, will you. It attracts me. This girl I was speaking of mentioned it yesterday, and I liked the sound of it. One of these Cure establishments, is it? I mean, take the case of a fellow – let's call him A – who's been hitting it up a bit. Do they take him in and make him over?'

'That is just what they do.'

'Even if he is a bit far gone?'

'No wreck is too far gone for Sister Stott to save.'

'I have an idea I'll join up. I'm practically a teetotaller already, of course, but I've been having a bit of imp trouble lately. Nothing serious, but annoying. Where do I find this Temple?'

'It's out at Culver City.'

'Do you have to be proposed and seconded and all that?'

'You just walk in. All are welcome.'

'That's good.'

'But we haven't time to talk about that now.'

'No, no. Quite.'

'I want to warn you about this child. Be firm with him.'

'Oh, rather.'

'Stand no nonsense from him. He'll try to put something over on you if he thinks he can.'

'A tough egg, what?'

'As tough as they come. I should describe him as a kind of human hydrophobia skunk.'

I wasn't going to stand this sort of thing. Constructive criticism, yes. Vulgar abuse, no.

I stepped forward.

'I heard that remark,' I said coldly.

Miss Brinkmeyer turned.

'Oh, you're there, are you?'

'Good God!' said Eggy. 'Can you see it, too?'

'I beg your pardon?'

'Can you see an imp standing over there?'

'Imp is right. This is the Cooley child.'

'It is?'

'Certainly.'

'Phew!' said Eggy, sinking back in his chair and beginning to mop his brow.

Miss Brinkmeyer gave me one of her unpleasant looks. 'Your hair's all out of curl. Why can't you keep it tidy. This is Mr Mannering, who is going to grapple with that accent of yours. Say "How do you do, Mr Mannering".'

I was perfectly willing to meet her over so small a point.

'How do you do, Mr Mannering?' I said.

'How do you do?' said Eggy. 'I think I've met your astral body.'

'Well, you've heard him speak now,' said Miss Brinkmeyer, rising. 'I'll leave you to it. I have to see the cook. Do what you can about that voice of his. Get that Ohio twang out of it, if you have to use an axe.'

For some moments after she had gone, Eggy sat plying the handkerchief and heaving like a troubled ocean. Presently he put the handkerchief away.

'Golly, what a relief!' he said. 'You gave me a nice shock, my lad, I can tell you. You ought to do something about that astral body of yours – keep it on the chain or something. You may not know it, but yesterday it got loose somehow and came and breathed in my left ear, not only causing me alarm and despondency but putting me on an entirely wrong track and leading me to take a completely mistaken view of the state of affairs. Of course, it's all right now. I see that the whole thing —'

I stood wrapped in thought. Now that I had succeeded in getting him alone, I was wondering how best to approach the rather delicate matter in hand.

'I see now that the whole thing was a perfectly natural psychic phenomenon. A perfectly natural psychic phenomenon,' he repeated, as if the words did him good. 'I don't say I understand it – probably our minds are not meant to understand these things – but I expect it's happening all over the place all the time. And that girl tried to kid me that I was breaking up! It just shows how you ought never to listen to people. They mean well, but they talk rot. Do you realize that if we hadn't met like this, so that I was able to see that the whole thing was a perfectly natural psychic phenomenon, I should by this time have been a bally teetotaller? I assure you. My mind was made up. I was fully resolved to go to that Temple of whatever it is and sign on for the duration.'

I continued to muse. My position, I could see, would require careful explanation. It would be necessary, of course, to issue a statement, and this would have to be done in just the right way.

I had little doubt that in the end I would be able to get the salient data across to him. Eggy, though jumpy, is not at all a sceptical chap. To take but one instance, he believes everything the racing experts in the morning papers write. He would, I fancied, make a receptive audience.

But, of course, the preliminary *pourparlers* would have to be done just so.

His voice took on a peevish note.

'What an ass that girl was. Suppose her father did see a pink rabbit. Suppose it did ask him for a match. What of it? These things are entirely a matter of the individual. What will cause one man to see pink rabbits will have no effect whatsoever on another who is made of sterner stuff. It's a question of constitution and, I fancy, of glands. I've got a magnificent constitution and my glands are top-hole, so I have nothing to worry about. But I mustn't go gassing on like this all the morning. Probably boring you stiff. Besides, I'm supposed to teach you elocution.

'Well, I've heard your voice, laddie, and I agree with the old girl that something's got to be done about it. It wants massage or amputation or something along those lines. It's that "*ow*" that seems to be the main snag. The way you said "How do you do?" sounded like a banjo with stomach trouble. Suppose we start by treating that. Repeat this after me. "How now, brown cow ..."'

I came to a decision. It was no good beating about the bush. I must lay my cards on the table. Explanations might be necessary later, but first of all I must get straight down to what old Plimsoll calls the *res*.

'Listen,' I said, 'I've got something to say to you.'

'Exactly. "How now, brown cow." Come on, laddie, all together now. Repeat after me: "How now, brown cow, do not frown beneath the bough".'

I refused to be diverted from my purpose in order to humour him with any such drivel.

'I must begin by mentioning,' I said, 'that I am your cousin, Reggie Havershot.'

Eggy had been repeating 'How now, brown cow' in an inviting and encouraging manner, but this stopped him like a bullet. He blinked several times.

'Did you say something then?' he asked in a low, rather hollow voice.

'I said that I was your cousin Reggie Havershot. It's quite simple,' I went on reassuringly. 'My soul got into the wrong body.'

There was silence for a moment. He seemed to be drinking it in. Then just as I thought he had begun to grasp the gist, he heaved a long, shuddering sort of sigh and with a gesture of sad resignation stooped and picked up his hat and stick.

'This is the end,' he said. 'I give up. If anyone asks for me, I shall be at the Temple of the New Dawn. Address letters care of Sister Stott.'

He passed through the curtains with a bowed head.

'Hi! Wait a minute!' I cried and, legging it after him, collided with some solid body. For an instant everything went black, and it was not long before I discovered the reason for this. I was standing with my face embedded in a human stomach.

I backed a bit, and looked up. It was the butler in whose midriff I had been parking myself.

Chapter 15

'OOF!' he said, massaging the wound. 'Woof!'

Had I been my usual courteous self, I should no doubt have paused to apologize and condole, for there was no question that I had caught the man a stinker. His face was a vivid mauve and his gooseberry eyes were watering freely. But I had no time now for doing the civil thing to butlers. I wanted to overtake Eggy and go on with my statement.

With this end in view, I hared for the front door, only to find that he was nowhere in sight. He had gone, leaving not a rack behind.

It was in sombre mood that I returned to the hall. The butler was still there, looking somewhat restored. The purple flush had left his face, and he had ceased to knead his waistcoat. He was leaning against the wall, puffing gently. Nature and a robust constitution had apparently pulled him through.

I gave him a bleak look. I found it hard to forgive him for his untimely intrusion. But for encountering him in the fairway, I should have been able to resume my chat with Eggy, amplifying the statement I had made with corroborative detail, as old Plimsoll would say. And owing to being delayed, I had lost him. He had vanished beyond recall, like the dew off a rose. Blast all butting-in butlers was the way I felt about it.

'Sir,' said this one, as I floated by.

I gave him another bleak look. His conversation was the last thing I desired. I wanted to brood.

'Might I have a word with you, sir?'

I went on floating by.

'I have had an idea, sir. With reference to the matter we were speaking of over your breakfast-tray.'

I continued to pass along.

'This matter of money, sir.'

This checked me. No other word in the language would have done it. I stopped, looked, and listened.

'You mean you've thought of a way by which I can collect a bit of capital?'

'Yes, sir. I fancy I have found the solution to our problem.'

I goggled. He did not look a remarkably intelligent man. And yet, if credence was to be given to his words, he had succeeded where many a fine thinker would have failed.

'You have?'

'Yes, sir.'

'You mean that on reflection you find that you can advance me a trifle?'

'No, sir.'

'Then what *do* you mean?'

He became a bit conspiratorial. He looked this way, and he looked that. He peeped into the drawing-room and he peered up the stairs.

'It came to me as I was cleaning the silver, sir.'

'What did?'

'This idea, sir. I have often found that my brain is at its nimblest when I am cleaning the silver. It is as though the regular rhythmical motion assisted thought. His lordship frequently used to say —'

'Never mind about his lordship. What's your idea?'

He repeated the Secret Society stuff. 'Are we alone and unobserved?' his manner seemed to say. He lowered his voice to a whisper.

'The tooth, sir!'

I did not follow him.

'What's the truth?'

'Not truth, sir – tooth, sir.'

'Tooth?'

'Yes, sir. What crossed my mind, as I cleaned the silver, was the tooth. It came to me all of a sudden.'

I could make nothing of this. His words were the words

of a plastered butler. But surely no butler could be plastered at so early an hour as this. Even Eggy hardly ever was.

'Whose tooth?'

'Yours, sir.' A look of anxiety came into his face. 'You have the tooth, sir?'

I continued to grope.

'I had a tooth out yesterday.'

'Yes, sir. That's the one I mean. Did the dentist give it to you, sir?'

'How do you mean, give it to me? He took it from me.'

'Yes, sir, but when I was a small lad and had a tooth extracted the dentist would always give it to me to keep among my knick-knacks. And I was hoping —'

I shook my head.

'No. Nothing of that sort oc —' I paused. A sudden recollection had come to me. 'Yes, he did, by Jove. I've got it here in a cardboard box.'

I felt in my pocket, and pulled the thing out. The butler uttered an ecstatic 'Ha!'

'Then all is well, sir,' he said in a relieved voice, like a butler who has had a weight taken off his mind.

I still didn't get it.

'Why?'

He became the Black Hander once more. He looked this way and he looked that. He peeped hither and peered thither. Then he lowered his voice to such a whisper that I couldn't hear a damn word.

'Speak up,' I said sharply.

He stooped and placed his lips to my ear.

'There's gold in that thar tooth!'

'Gold? Filling, do you mean?'

'Money, sir.'

'What!'

'Yes, sir. That was what suddenly came to me as I was cleaning the silver. One moment, my mind was a blank, as you might say. The next, I'd got it. I was polishing the cup Mr Brinkmeyer won in the Motion Picture Magnates'

Annual Golf Tournament at the time, and it just fell from my hands. "Puncture my vitals!" I said . . .'

'Eh?'

' "Puncture my vitals", sir. It was a favourite expression of his lordship's in moments of excitement. "Puncture my vitals!" I said. "The tooth!" '

'Meaning what?'

'Think, sir, think! Reflect what a position you hold in the public esteem, sir. You are the Idol of American Motherhood. And the fans are inordinately desirous of obtaining souvenirs of their favourites, I can assure you. I have known large sums to change hands for one of Mr Fred Astaire's trouser buttons, very large sums indeed. And the human appeal of a trouser button cannot be compared with that of a tooth.'

I quivered. I had got his meaning at last.

'You think this tooth could be sold?'

'Over the counter, sir, over the counter.'

I quivered again. The man was beginning to inflame me.

'Who would buy it?'

'Anybody, sir. Any of the big collectors. But that would take time. My idea would be to approach one of these motion-picture magazines. The *Screen Beautiful* suggests itself. I should be vastly surprised if they didn't give two thousand dollars for it!'

'What!'

'Yes, sir, and they'd get their money back a dozen times over.'

'They would?'

'Certainly they would, sir. What would happen is, they'd run a competition for their readers. A dollar to enter the contest and the Cooley tooth to go to whoever did whatever it was – like it might be naming the twelve most popular stars in their correct order, or something like that.'

My head was buzzing. I felt as if I had backed an outsider in the Grand National and seen it skip over the last fence three lengths in front of the field.

'Two thousand dollars?'

'More, sir. Five, if you had a good agent.'

'Do you know a good agent?'

'What I would suggest, sir, is that you employed me to handle the deal for you.'

'Would you?'

'I should be proud and happy to do so, sir. For the customary agent's commission.'

'What would that be?'

'Fifty per cent, sir.'

'Fifty? I know an author chap whose agent sells his stuff for ten.'

'Literary productions, yes, sir, but not teeth. Teeth come higher.'

'Fifty's much too much. Dash it, it's my tooth.'

'But you are not in a position to trade.'

'I know, but —'

'You need somebody who knows how to talk terms.'

'Do you know how to talk terms?'

He laughed indulgently.

'You would not ask that, sir, if you had ever seen me negotiating for my commission with the local tradesmen.'

I stood musing. The conversation might have reached a deadlock, had he not made a gesture.

'Well, well, sir, we will not haggle. Shall we say twenty?'

This seemed more reasonable.

'Right ho.'

'Though twenty per cent on the transaction will not make me a rich man. However, it shall be as you say. Might I have the box, sir, and perhaps a line in your handwriting, guaranteeing authenticity. These magazine editors have become very suspicious of late, ever since Film Fancies was took in by a Clark Gable undervest which proved to be spurious. I have a fountain-pen, sir. Perhaps you would just write a few words on the box.'

'Something like "Authorized tooth of J. Cooley. None other is g nuine"?'

'That v ould do admirably, sir. Thank you, sir. Thank you, sir. I will take it to the magazine office directly luncheon is concluded. Until then I fear that my official duties will confine me to the premises.'

Some hours later, I was pacing beside the swimming-pool, humming a gay air. Luncheon was over. So were my troubles. The future, once so dark, seemed bathed in a golden glow.

The smooth, efficient way in which this excellent butler had taken charge was enough to show me that I could have placed my affairs in no better hands. He might have been selling teeth on commission all his life. He had rung up the *Screen Beautiful*, arranged for an interview, settled that the money, when a figure had been arrived at, was to be paid in small bills, and had gone off to the office to close the deal.

I had had a rotten lunch, at which the spinach *motif* had been almost farcically stressed, but despite the aching void within me I felt a new child. I was all buoyancy and optimism. Even if this butler proved to be less of a spell-binder than I took him to be and only managed to get a couple of thousand, that would be ample for my purpose. And something in his calm, purposeful face and quiet, confident manner seemed to tell me that he would extract the top price.

And so, as I say, I hummed a gay air, and would no doubt have continued to hum it for some little time, had not my attention been attracted by an intermittent low whistling which appeared to proceed from a clump of bushes across the lawn. I supposed, at first, that it was merely some local bird doing its stuff, but a few moments later a female voice spoke.

'Hey! Joseph!'

Ann's voice. I went across to see what she wanted.

Chapter 16

THE bushes were so thick that I couldn't see her at first. Then her face came into view and I noted that she, like the recent butler, had gone all conspiratorial. One of her eyes was closed in a significant wink, and attached to her lips was a finger. She was also wiggling her nose warningly, and when she spoke, it was in a croupy whisper.

'S'h!' she said.

'Eh?'

'Secrecy and silence!'

'How do you mean?'

'Where's Miss Brinkmeyer?'

'I don't know. Why?'

'There is dark work afoot, young Joseph. Speak low, for the very walls have ears. I've got a pork pie for you.'

'What!'

I don't know when I've been so profoundly moved. At that moment, my devotion to April June very nearly transferred itself to this girl before me. It was as if I were getting on to her hidden depths for the first time. I spoke in a trembling voice.

'You've got it on you?'

'It's in the house.'

'What size pork pie?'

'A big one.'

'Gosh!'

'Not so loud. Are you sure Miss Brinkmeyer's nowhere around?'

'I haven't seen her.'

'I'll bet she pops up . . . There!'

From the direction of the house there had come a rasping voice, and, turning, I perceived the neighbourhood curse hanging out of an upstairs window. She was regarding me in a nosey and offensive manner.

'What are you doing there?' she asked, plainly of the opinion that whatever it might be it was something I ought not to be doing. Even at this distance one sensed the lack of trust and simple faith.

It was a moment for swift and constructive thought.

'I am watching a beetle,' I said.

'A what?'

'There is a beetle here. I am watching it.'

'You are not bringing beetles into the house.'

I raised my eyebrows. Wasted on her at that range, of course.

'It is not my intention to bring it into the house. I am merely observing its habits.'

'Oh? Well, don't get yourself all mussed up.'

She disappeared, and Ann bobbed up once more like a wood-nymph.

'You see. Your every movement is watched. Conveying pork pies to you, young Joseph, is like carrying despatches through the enemy's lines. I was going to tell you to slip in here and await my return, but it isn't safe. I forgot she could see us from her bedroom window. I'll tell you what. Stroll casually along and nip into the bathing-hut. I'll join you there.'

It was, as may be supposed, with no little chagrin that I walked off. Every minute that separated me from that pie was like an hour. I made for the bathing-hut, chafing.

There was a gardener inside, cleaning it out with a mop.

'Good afternoon, sir,' he said.

The purity of his enunciation surprised me a bit, for he looked Japanese and I should have expected something that sounded more like a buffalo pulling its foot out of a swamp. However, I was not at leisure to go into this, for I wanted to get him out of here with the greatest possible despatch.

'Are you going to be long?' I said.

'You wish to sit in this hut, sir?'

'Yes.'

'I have just finished. There, I think that will do.'

He did a couple of dabs with his mop and came out. As he passed me, I saw that he had a squint and a wart on his nose, and I divined that this must be the man of whom Joey Cooley had spoken. I felt very much inclined to take up the matter of horned toads with him. The window from which Miss Brinkmeyer had spoken was next but one to my bedroom, numbering off from the right, so that I now knew where to go in order to deposit horned toads where they would do most good. And after the way she had butted in just now, upsetting my schemes, she needed a sharp lesson.

However, I resisted the urge, and went into the hut. And presently Ann appeared.

I sprang to my feet eagerly, but my dreams were not yet to come true. All she was carrying was what Miss Brinkmeyer would have called a nosegay of roses. I stared at it dully.

'I'm sorry,' said Ann, noting my perturbation and reading its cause aright. 'You'll have to wait a little longer. I was just coming out of the hall, when Miss Brinkmeyer came downstairs. I had to cache the stuff hurriedly in an Oriental vase. I'll get it as soon as the coast's clear, so don't look so shattered.'

I tried not to look shattered, but the disappointment had been severe and it was difficult to wear the mask.

'And, anyway, here's something that will make you laugh,' said Ann. 'You see these roses. Who do you think sent them?'

I shrugged my shoulders moodily. It did not seem to me to matter who had sent them. Roses as a substitute for pork pie left me very tepid.

'Who?'

'April June.'

My lethargy slipped from me like a garment.

'What!'

'Yes. I thought that would hand you a giggle.'

It hadn't handed me a giggle at all. She had got the

wrong angle entirely. I was profoundly touched. The thought of April June finding time in the midst of her busy life to send flowers to a sick—or tolerably sick—child made me glow all over. It even made me forget the hunger that gnawed me.

There seemed to me something so beautifully characteristic about the kindly act. That gentle heart, I felt, had functioned so absolutely in accordance with the form book. All the old devotion came sweeping back over me.

'Yes, she has sent you roses. Conscience, I suppose.'

'Conscience?' I said coldly, for she had spoken in a nasty dry way which I didn't at all like. I found myself eyeing her askance. The warmth of emotion which her offer of a pork pie had aroused in me was fading. I began to feel that I had been wrong about her hidden depths. A shallow girl, I now considered. 'Conscience?' I said. 'What do you mean?'

'I suppose she felt she owed you something, after horning in on your big scene like that and trying to steal your publicity the way she did. I'm sure I don't know what the girl needs a press agent for. There isn't one in the business who can teach her anything about sneaking the spotlight.'

'I don't understand you.'

She laughed.

'Hasn't anyone told you about that? Yesterday, when you were under the gas, the door suddenly burst open and April June rushed in. "Where is my little pal?" she cried, clasping her hands and acting all over the lot. "I want my little pal" – directing, as she spoke, a meaning glance at the newspaper boys, who snapped her in six positions – including bending over you and kissing your unconscious brow. Somebody then led her gently away, shaking with sobs. Oh, horse-feathers!'

I gave her another cold look. The expression which she had used was new to me, but one could gather its trend. Her ribald and offensive tone jarred upon me indescribably.

'I consider her behaviour little short of angelic,' I said.

'What!'

'Certainly. There is no other word for it. How many girls in her position would have bothered to take time off in order to come and kiss brows?'

She stared.

'Are you trying to kid me?'

'I am not.'

'You mean you really don't think April June is a pill?'

The first time I had heard this monstrous word applied to the woman I loved – by Joey Cooley over the *National Geographic Magazine* – I had, it will be remembered, choked down my indignation and extended the olive branch. But now I was in no mood to overlook the slur.

'That is quite enough,' I said. 'Either cease to speak derogatorily of that divine woman, or leave my presence.'

She was plainly piqued. A sudden flush mantled her cheek. I could see that she burned, not with shame and remorse, but with resentment.

'Oh?' she said. 'Well, if that's the way you feel about it ... all right, then. Good-bye.'

'Good-bye.'

'And not a bit of that pork pie do you get. No, sir, not a sniff of it.'

I confess that I wavered. The thrust was a keen one. But I was strong. I waved a hand nonchalantly – or as nonchalantly as I could.'

'That is entirely your affair,' I said in a reserved manner.

She paused at the door. Her bearing betrayed irresolution. Her better self, it appeared, was not wholly dead.

'You'd like that pie.'

I vouchsafed no answer.

'And you know you think her a pill. You've told me so yourself.'

'I would prefer not to discuss the matter.'

'Oh, very well.'

She was gone. I sat there, brooding.

My thoughts were very bitter. Now that I was at leisure

to devote myself to concentrating on it exclusively once more, I realized all that that pork pie had meant to me. My whole policy was wrapped up in it. And the reflection that April June would never know what I had given up for her sake stung like a serpent's tooth.

Presently I rose and wandered out into the sunshine, tightening my belt in the hope of dulling the ache within me. I walked at random, too distrait to care where I was going, until an unwonted softness in the terrain caused me to look down, and I saw that I had strayed off the path on to a border, beyond which was the low wall which encircled the Brinkmeyer estate. And I was about to put myself into reverse, for I had little doubt that one got hell in this establishment for trampling on the flower-beds, when I was arrested by the sight of a head. It shot up over the wall and said 'Yah!' The apparition was so unexpected that I halted in my tracks and stood staring.

It was a red head, whose roundness and outstanding ears gave it a resemblance to one of those antique vases with handles on each side, and it belonged to a tough-looking boy with green eyes and spots on his face. He was eyeing me in a manner unmistakably hostile.

'Yah!' he said.

The lad was a complete stranger to me. But then, so was almost everybody else I met in this new world of mine. To Joey Cooley, I presumed, he would have been well known. From this aspect and tone of voice I deduced that this must be someone whom my predecessor had at one time or another offended by word or act.

My silence seemed to spur him on to further flights.

'Yah!' he said. 'Little Lord Fauntleroy!'

I was conscious of a rising resentment. At the outset, I had had no views about this young blister one way or the other, but now there was beginning to burgeon within me a very definite feeling that what he wanted was a good sock on the jaw. That epithet 'Little Lord Fauntleroy' had pierced the armour and struck home. Ever since my awakening in the chair of B. K. Burwash, those golden ringlets had been my hidden shame. And I have no doubt, so stirred was I, that I should have leaped the wall and attacked him with tooth and claw, had not I been brought up short by the sight of that miserably inadequate hand which had so depressed me earlier in the day. To try to sock anybody on the jaw with a hand like that would have been just labour chucked away. With a sigh, I realized that a pitched battle was out of the question.

I was obliged to fall back on words.

'Yah!' I said, feeling that there was no copyright in that very effective ejaculation. It wasn't too bright, of course, but it was something.

'Yah!' he replied.

'Yah!' I came back, as quick as a flash.

'Yah!' he riposted. 'Sissy! Pansy! Cake-eater!'

I began to fear that he was getting the better of the exchanges.

'Curly-top! You look like a girl.'

A happy recollection came to me of something which Barmy Fotheringay-Phipps of the Drones had once said to Oofy Prosser in my presence, on the occasion of Oofy declining to lend him ten bob till next Wednesday. It had made Oofy, I recalled, as shirty as dammit.

'You look like a spotted dog,' I said.

It was the right note. He winced and turned vermilion. I suppose a profusely spotted chap dislikes having it drawn to his attention what a profusely spotted chap he is.

'Come on out here,' he cried. 'I dare you.'

I did not reply. I was feeling my arm, to see if, after all, something could not be done about this. But the forearm was like a match-stick and the biceps like a pimple. Hopeless.

'I dare you! I double dare you!'

Suddenly, out of a clear sky, the solution came to me. I have said that I was standing on a flower-bed. This flower-bed, I now perceived, was adorned by a small tree, on which the genial Californian sun had brought out a great profusion of hard, nobbly oranges. It altered the whole aspect of affairs. Say it with oranges! The very thing.

To pluck one and let fly was with me the work of an instant. And conceive my gratification on discovering that Joey Cooley, whatever his shortcomings in the matter of physique, was an extraordinarily fine shot with an orange. David, having his unpleasantness with Goliath, could not have made better target practice. My missile took the lad squarely on the tip of the nose, and before he could recover from his natural surprise and consternation I had copped him again no less than thrice – one on the left eye, one on the right eye, and one on the chin, in the order named. I then plucked more fruit and resumed the barrage.

The thing was a walkover. It was the old story. Brains tell. The untutored savage jumps about howling threats and calling for dirty work at close quarters, and the canny scion of a more enlightened race just stays away and lets him have it at long range with his artillery, causing him to look a bit of an ass.

This red-headed stripling looked more than a bit of an ass. He stuck it out for another half-dozen oranges, and then decided to yield to my superior generalship. He legged it, and I got him on the back of the neck with a final effort.

Final, because as I poised myself for another pop my arm was gripped by an iron hand, and I found myself whirling in the air like a trout fly.

'For goodness gracious sake!' said Miss Brinkmeyer, seeming not a little moved. 'Can't I take my eyes off you for a single minute without your being up to some fool game? You've ruined my orange tree.'

I had not much breath with which to make a reasoned defence, and I think she did not hear what I said about military necessity. She lugged me to the house.

'You get off to your room this instant,' she said, among a number of other remarks of a deleterious nature, 'and don't you dare to leave it till it's time to go to the studio.'

I could not but feel that it was a poorish sort of homecoming for one who had conducted himself with such notable resource in a difficult situation and achieved so signal a victory, but there was nothing to be accomplished by arguing the point. It was evident that she would not be a good listener. I permitted her, therefore, to escort me to my room, and she went off, banging the door behind her. I lay down on the bed and gave myself up to thought.

I speculated as to the identity of the spotted lad, and wondered what was the source of his obvious distaste for Joey Cooley. Knowing Joey Cooley, I imagined that this measles case probably had a good deal of right on his side, but all the same I was glad that I had put it across him. My pride was involved. There are some remarks which one does not forgive, and if you have been forced to assume the identity of a kid with golden ringlets, 'Little Lord Fauntleroy' is one of them.

But it was only for a brief space that I was able to relive the recent scene and glory in my prowess. Abruptly, as if a button had been pressed, that agonizing desire for food began to assert itself once more.

I was still wrestling with it, when I heard footsteps outside the door and Ann came in.

'Here you are, you little mutt,' she said. 'I hadn't the heart to hold out on you.'

She thrust something into my hand. It was a large, succulent pork pie.

I had nothing to say. In these supreme moments one hasn't. I just raised the thing to my lips and dug my teeth into it.

And, as I did so, the door burst open, and there was Miss Brinkmeyer, looking like Lady Macbeth at her worst.

'Just as I suspected!' she cried. 'I knew someone was bootlegging the stuff to him, and I had an idea it was you all the time. Miss Bannister, you're fired!'

I stood at the crossroads. Two alternatives presented themselves before me. I could stop eating and plead for Ann with all the eloquence at my disposal, or I could keep on pitching in, so as to wolf as much as possible before the pie was wrested from my grasp.

I chose the nobler course. I pleaded.

Not a damn bit of use, of course. I might just as well have remained silent and devoted my energies to getting mine while the going was good. The verdict was in, and there was no appeal. Acting from the best and kindliest motives, my benefactor had got the boot.

I was told to be quiet. I was shaken. I was depied. Ann popped off. The Brinkmeyer popped off. I was alone.

With a moody oath, I began to pace the floor. This took me near the window. Being near the window, I glanced out of it. And there, snipping a bush that stood beside the outhouse, was the gardener with the squint and the wart on his nose.

I paused, rigid. The sight of him had opened up a new line of thought.

A moment later, I was on the outhouse roof, attracting his attention with a guarded 'Hoy!'

Chapter 17

THE line of thought which the sight of this squint-cum-warted gardener had opened up was, briefly, as follows. I had Joey Cooley's assurance that the honest fellow had Mexican horned toads in his possession, and was prepared to supply them gratis with no cover charge, provided that their destination was Miss Brinkmeyer's bed. And what had suddenly occurred to me, as these ideas do, was that there was no reason now why I should not avail myself of his services.

There could be no question that La Brinkmeyer badly needed a horned toad in her bed. If ever a woman had asked for one, she was that woman. And it now struck me that the only objection to allotting her one – the fear of an aftermath or bitter reckoning – had been removed. That whole aspect of the matter could be dismissed, because when the storm burst I shouldn't be there. As soon as the butler returned with the cash and put me in funds, I proposed to absent myself. Establishing contact with the reptile, therefore, and grabbing her hair-brush and hastening to get in touch with me, Miss Brinkmeyer would find that my room was empty and my bed had not been slept in.

So I nipped on to the outhouse roof and called 'Hoy!' and the gardener came civilly up to ascertain my wishes.

I found that by lying on my stomach and shoving my head out I was able to conduct the conversation in a cautious undertone.

I came to the point at once. It was no time for beating about the bush.

'I say,' I said. 'I want a horned toad.'

He seemed interested.

'For the usual purpose?'

'Yes.'

'You desire quick delivery?'

'Immediate.'

He sighed.

'I am sorry to say I am all out of horned toads at the moment.'

'Oh, dash it.'

'I could do you frogs,' he said, on a more hopeful note.

I considered this.

'Yes, frogs will be all right. If slithery.'

'The ones I have are very slithery. If you will wait, I will fetch them at once.'

He went off, to return a few minutes later with a covered basket, which he handed up to me, saying that he would be glad if I would let him have it back when I had finished with it, as it was the one in which one of his colleagues kept his lunch. I reassured him on this point, and sped off to do the necessary.

The discovery of Miss Brinkmeyer's gala costume laid out on the bed in her room, ready to be assumed for the evening's binge, caused me to make some slight alteration in my plans. I placed a frog in each boot and distributed the remainder among the various objects of lingerie. It seemed to me that the moral effect of this would be greater than if I inserted them between the sheets.

The gardener was waiting below when I reached the roof again. He said he hoped that all had gone well, and once more I was struck by the purity of his diction, so out of keeping with his Japanese exterior.

'You speak extraordinarily good English,' I said.

He seemed gratified by the tribute.

'Very kind of you to say so, I'm sure,' he replied with the suggestion of a simper. 'I fancy, however, that you are labouring under a slight misapprehension. You have probably been led by my make-up into supposing that I am of foreign extraction. This is not the case.'

'Aren't you a Jap?'

'Externally only. I came here in this rude disguise in the hope of attracting Mr Brinkmeyer's notice. Once on the spot, you see, there is always the possibility of being able to catch the boss's eye. B-M have a Japanese picture scheduled for production, and I am hoping for a small role.'

'Oh, I see.' I had been in Hollywood long enough to know that very few things there are what they appear to be. 'You're an actor?'

'I play character parts. And I am hoping that an occasion may arise which will enable me to run off some little scena which will impress Mr Brinkmeyer. But I realize now that I would have done better to join the indoor staff. They are in so much closer contact with Mr Brinkmeyer. I particularly envy Chaffinch.'

'Chaffinch?'

'The butler. He is very fortunately situated.'

'But he's not an actor?'

'Oh, yes, indeed. Virtually all the domestic staffs of the big motion-picture magnates are composed of character actors. It is the only way we can get at them. It is perfectly useless going to these casting offices. They just take your name, and there is an end of it. That's the trouble with Hollywood. The system is wrong.'

I was amazed.

'Well, I'm blowed! He took me in.'

'I expect so.'

'I could have sworn he was genuine. That stomach. Those bulging eyes.'

'Yes, he is quite the type.'

'And he talked about serving with his lordship and all that.'

'Atmosphere. He is a most conscientious artist.'

'Well, I'm — Golly!' I said, breaking off abruptly. A sudden frightful thought had come to me. 'Here, take this basket. I've got to make a phone call.'

I buzzed off and dashed down to the telephone-booth in the hall. It was no moment for speculating as to what I should say if Miss Brinkmeyer caught me at the instrument. I was a-twitter with apprehension, and I'll tell you why.

In entrusting to this Chaffinch the negotiations in the matter of the tooth, my whole policy had been based on the belief that he was the butler he pretended to be. The honesty of butlers is a byword. There is no class of the community more trustworthy. A real butler would perish rather than stoop to anything which might even remotely be described as funny business.

My acquaintance with actors of the minor type, on the other hand, had left me with a rooted conviction that they are hot. I may be prejudiced, allowing my outlook to be coloured by the fact that during my University days a member of the cast of *His Forgotten Bride,* playing the small towns, once took five quid off me in a pub at Newmarket at a game which he called Persian Monarchs, but that is how I feel. Ever since that occasion, I have said to myself: 'Reginald, avoid actors. They are mustard.'

And so, as I searched through the telephone directory for the number of the *Screen Beautiful,* nameless fears surged in my bosom. For the first time, it had struck me like a blow from a stuffed eel-skin that if this bally *Screen Beautiful* was housed within anything like a reasonable distance, Chaffinch should long since have returned from his mission. I had seen him start off directly after lunch, and it was now well past four o'clock.

And it wasn't as if he had walked. With my own eyes I had beheld him get into a taxi.

I found the number, and the awed manner in which my name was received at the office switchboard might have gratified me, had the circumstances been other than what they were. But this, unfortunately, they were jolly well not. Respect was no good to me. I wanted reassurance.

But I didn't get it. Two minutes later, the blow had fallen and I knew the worst. I was informed by the editor in person that five thousand dollars in small bills had been handed to my agent more than an hour and a half ago. And when, endeavouring to control my voice, which showed a disposition to wobble all over the scale, I asked how long it would take to do the point-to-point trip in a fleet taxi, I was told ten minutes. It was then, cutting short some rot at the other end about illustrated interviews and personal messages, that I hung up the receiver.

There was no possibility of mistake. The facts were plain. My innocence had been taken advantage of. Trusting blindly to this blighted Chaffinch, I had been done down, double-crossed and hornswoggled. No doubt this fiend in butler's shape was even now on his way east with the stuff in his jeans, gone beyond recall.

I had certainly not had good luck with this telephonebooth. Twice only had I entered it, and on both occasions I had come out distraught. I had writhed in agony the first time, and I writhed in agony now. The thought that there was no cash coming to me and that I must abandon my dreams of escape into a wider, freer world made me stagger like Eggy on his birthday.

And then, creeping softly into my mind, there came another thought. Madly confident of being able to make a speedy getaway from the danger zone, I had filled Miss Brinkmeyer's bedroom with frogs.

I wasted no more time in fruitless regret. I had come down those stairs pretty quick. I went up them even quicker. Unless those frogs were gathered and removed with all possible despatch, the imagination boggled at the thought of what would ensue. The issue was clearly defined. I had got to get them out before Miss Brinkmeyer discovered them, or I should be properly parked up against a fire-plug.

I don't know if you have ever tried to gather frogs. It is one of the most difficult forms of gathering there is. Rosebuds – easy. Nuts in May – simple. But to collect and assemble a platoon of lively young frogs against time is a task that calls for all that a man has of skill and address.

The situation was further complicated by the fact that I could not at the moment recall how many of the creatures

I had strewn. The gardener had given me of his plenty, and I had just scattered them carelessly, like a sower going forth sowing. I had not bothered to count. At the time, anything in the nature of a census would have seemed immaterial. It was only now, as I stood stroking my chin reflectively, and trying to remember whether the six I had in my pocket completed the muster-roll, that I appreciated the folly of being casual in matters of this kind.

I stood pondering with bent brows, and might have gone on pondering indefinitely, had not my meditations been interrupted by the dickens of an uproar in the garden below. Stirring things seemed to be in progress. Alarums, as the expression is, and excursions. What impressed itself chiefly on the ear was a shrill feminine squeaking.

Well, if the hour had been two in the morning, I should, of course, being in Hollywood, have taken no notice, merely assuming that one of the neighbours was giving a party. But as early as this it couldn't be a party. And, if not a party, I asked myself, what?

It took me but an instant to slide to the window and look out. I found myself gazing upon the spacious grounds and part of the marble swimming-pool, but unfortunately my view was a good bit obstructed by a pergola covered with vines. The squeals were proceeding from some point outside my range of vision. For the time being, therefore, this female squealer was to me simply a voice and nothing more. Cross-examined regarding her, all I could have said at this juncture was that she had good lungs.

The next moment, however, further data were supplied. Round the corner of the swimming-pool, moving well, came Miss Brinkmeyer, and close on her heels a figure dressed in a quiet grey suit. And as its lower limbs twinkled in the evening light, I saw that they were finished off with powder-blue socks and suède shoes.

I don't suppose it is given to many fellows to stand looking out of a first-floor window, watching themselves chivy a middle-aged lady round a swimming-pool. The experience, I can state authoritatively, is rummy.

It takes the breath a bit. And yet, mind you, distinctly diverting. My relations with Miss Brinkmeyer being what they were – she, I mean to say, since my arrival in this joint having shown me so consistently her darker, less lovable side – I found myself enjoying the spectacle wholeheartedly. So much so that my annoyance when the runners passed out of sight was considerable.

And when, a moment later, there came to my ears the squishy slosh of a heavy body falling into water, I cursed pretty freely. I had that sickening feeling of having missed something good which is always so rotten.

But on top of this came other thoughts, notably the reflection that if Miss Brinkmeyer had fallen into the pool, it would not be long before she was seeking her bedroom in order to change her clothes. I was still uncertain about those frogs, but it was plain that I could not remain and conduct further researches. I might have secured the full quota or I might not, but even if I hadn't, I must depart while the strategic railways in my rear were still open.

It had taken me some minutes to arrive at this conclusion, but once it had been arrived at I did not delay. My bedroom, as I have said, was next door but one. I nipped into it like a home-going rabbit.

It was only after I had reached it that my efforts to solve the frog problem were rewarded with success. I remembered now. There had been eight frogs originally. Six I had on my person. The other two I had placed in my hostess's boots, where they still remained.

Chapter 18

THE effect of this discovery was to put a bit of a crimp in the wholesome enjoyment I had been feeling at the thought of Miss Brinkmeyer falling into the swimming-pool. I could see that a difficult and complex situation had arisen. It was too late now to go back and collect these frogs: yet to do nothing and just let Nature take its course must infallibly lead to unpleasantness on a rather major scale. For this was not one of those occasions when mere formal apologies would serve.

It was, in short, not easy to see what to do for the best, and I was still wrinkling the brow and endeavouring to frame a practical policy, when the Filipino footman entered.

'Excuse yes, you come no, please undoubtedly,' he said.

Although, as I have indicated, I was in something of a doodah, curiosity for the moment overcame mental agitation.

'Tell me,' I said, 'do you talk like that because it's the only way you can, or are you another of these character actors who appear to be such common objects of the wayside in this house?'

He dropped the mask.

'Sure,' he said, in faultless American. 'You got me right, brother. I do comedy bits and homely pathos. One of these days, if I can catch the old buzzard alone and he can't duck, I'm going to uncork a rapid-fire dialect monologue with the tear behind the smile that'll make Mr Brinkmeyer sign on the dotted line quicker'n a chorus girl can eat caviare. We're most of us in the profesh downstairs.'

'So I am told. I say,' I said, for I was still hoping against hope, 'you haven't seen Chaffinch about anywhere, have you?'

'He's gone.'

'I know he's gone. I thought he might have come back.'

'No, he's quit. He phoned me from the station an hour ago and said he'd had an unexpected legacy from his rich uncle in Australia and was leaving for New York right away. Lucky stiff.'

I don't suppose I had really hoped much against hope, but I now ceased to hope against hope at all. In the light of this first-hand information, it would have been a fat lot of good trying to be optimistic. My intuition had not deceived me. The hound, as I had divined, had done a bunk with the syndicate's cash-box and was now far away. I uttered a soft moan and ran a fevered hand through my ringlets.

However, one of the advantages of being Joey Cooley was that you were never able to worry about anything long, because just as you started buckling down to it, something even worse was sure to happen and you had to switch off and begin worrying about that.

'Well, come on, kid,' said the footman. 'Snap into it.'

'I beg your pardon?'

'The old girl told me to fetch you along.'

This was the point where I stopped worrying about Chaffinch. My jaw dropped a couple of notches.

'She wants to see me?'

'That's the idea.'

'Did she say what about?'

'No.'

'The word "frogs" was not mentioned, by any chance?'

'Not that I know of.'

A faint hope began to stir that this might not be the hand of doom falling, after all. I proceeded to Miss Brinkmeyer's room, and found that she had taken to her bed, beside which Mr Brinkmeyer was standing. The clothes which had been lying on the bed had been put away, and so had the boots with their sinister contents. Where they had been put, I did not know, but it seemed pretty evident that the worst had not yet happened, and this so bucked me up that I became rather breezy.

'Well, well, well,' I said, tripping in, rubbing my hands and smiling a sympathetic smile. 'And how are we, how are we, ha, ha?'

Something squashy hit me in the face. The patient had thrown a hot-water bottle at me. I saw what had happened. I had been too breezy. There is always this danger.

'Will you stop grinning and giggling!' she cried.

Old Brinkmeyer, in his kindly way, tried to pour oil on the troubled waters.

'She's nervous,' he said apologetically. 'She's had a bad shock.'

'I'll bet she has,' I agreed, switching off the smile, as it didn't seem to have gone with a bang, but plugging away at the sympathy. 'Bound to tickle up the nervous system, getting bunged into swimming-pools. I said to myself when I saw what was happening —'

Miss Brinkmeyer, who after launching the bottle had sunk listlessly back against the pillows, sat up.

'Did you see it?'

'Oh, rather.'

'Would you be able to identify the scoundrel?'

'Fiend,' corrected Mr Brinkmeyer, who liked to get these things right. 'Must have been that fiend we've been reading about in the papers.'

'Would you be able to identify this fiend?'

'Oh, absolutely. Short, slight chap with delicate, handsome features.'

Miss Brinkmeyer snorted.

'He was nothing of the kind. He was enormous and looked like a gorilla.'

'I don't think so.'

'Tchah!' said Miss Brinkmeyer, with that warmth which she so often displayed in my society. 'The child's an idiot.'

Mr Brinkmeyer again essayed a spot of oil-pouring.

'Here's an idea,' he said. 'Could he have *been* a gorilla?'

'You're an idiot,' said Miss Brinkmeyer. 'Worse than the child is.'

'I was only thinking that they're doing a Darkest Africa picture down at M.G.M. —'

'Oh, go into your dance,' said Miss Brinkmeyer wearily.

'Well, one of the gorillas might have got loose,' urged Mr Brinkmeyer deferentially. 'Anyway, the cops'll be here soon. Maybe they'll find a clue.'

'Maybe they won't,' said Miss Brinkmeyer, who seemed to have little faith in the official force. 'Still, never mind that now. What I wanted to see you about was this: I've put those Michigan Mothers off.'

'What!' I cried. This was great news. 'Told them to buzz back to Michigan, eh? Splendid. You couldn't have done better.'

'Don't talk like an imbecile. Of course I have not told them to go back to Michigan. I've postponed the reception till to-morrow. I'm much too unstrung to meet them to-day.'

'And she can't come to the unveiling of the statue,' said Mr Brinkmeyer. 'Too bad, too bad.'

'I certainly can't. And I can only hope that you and the child between you will not mess the whole affair up. Well, that's all. Take him away,' she said to Mr Brinkmeyer, closing her eyes after a short, shuddering look at me and sinking wearily back on the pillows again. 'The sight of him seems to make me worse. It's that fatheaded stare of his, I think, principally. Take him back to his room and keep him there on ice till it's time to go to the studio.'

'Yes, my dear,' said Mr Brinkmeyer. 'Very good, my dear. And you try to get a nice, long sleep.'

He led me out. His manner, until the door had closed behind us, was the quiet, sober manner which one likes to see in a brother who tiptoes from a sister's sick-bed. Nothing could have been more correct. But out in the passage it relaxed a trifle, and when we had entered my room he beamed like the rising sun and slapped me on the back.

'Whoopee!' he said.

The slap had been so hearty that it had sent me reeling across the floor. I fetched up against a chest of drawers and turned enquiringly.

'I beg your pardon?'

'She's not coming to the statue.'

'So I gathered.'

'You know what this means?' said Mr Brinkmeyer, trying to slap me on the back again but missing by several inches owing to my adroit footwork. 'It means I'm not going to wear my cutaway coat and stiff collar.'

'Oh?'

'And I'm not going to wear a gardenia.'

'Oh?'

'And I'm not going to wear spats.'

I found his enthusiasm infectious.

'And the kiss,' I cried. 'We'll cut the kiss?'

'Sure.'

'Just exchange a couple of civil nods, eh?'

'That's right.'

'In fact, why not eliminate the whole unpleasant nosegay business altogether?'

But he was not, it appeared, prepared to follow me quite so far as that. He shook his head.

'No. I guess we'll have to keep the nosegay sequence. It's one of the things the sob-sisters are sure to write up, and if she doesn't see anything about it in the papers to-morrow, she'll ask questions.'

I saw that he was right. These presidents of important motion-picture corporations are no fools.

'Yes,' I conceded. 'That's true.'

'But no kiss.'

'No kiss.'

'And no stiff collar, no gardenia, and no spats. Whoopee!' said Mr Brinkmeyer once more, and on this cheerful note withdrew.

For some moments after he had left, I paced the floor in a state of no little exhilaration. The future, true, had not entirely lost its grim aspect. Those Michigan Mothers had merely been postponed, not cancelled: the statue's nose remained as red as ever: and two of my frogs were still at large. But I had been sufficiently schooled by adversity by this time to be thankful for anything in the shape of a bit of luck, and the thought that I was not going to be kissed in public by T. P. Brinkmeyer was enough to make me curvet about the room like one walking on air.

And I was still doing so when I was brought to a halt by the sight of a cupboard door opening cautiously. A moment later, a face appeared. A face which, despite the fact that its upper lip had recently been shaved, I had no difficulty in recognizing.

'Hello,' said the Cooley child, emerging. 'How's tricks?'

A wave of indignation passed through me. I had not forgotten his behaviour on the telephone.

'Never mind about tricks,' I said frostily. 'What the devil did you ring off for like that when I was talking to you on the phone? What about that money?'

'Money?'

'I told you I had to have money in order to get away.'

'Oh, you want money, do you?'

'Of course I want money. I explained the whole situation in the most limpid manner. If I don't get some in the next couple of hours, ruin stares me in the face.'

'I see. Well, I haven't any on me, but I'll go and send you some.'

I felt that I had misjudged this lad.

'You will?'

'Sure. Don't give the thing another thought. Say, did you hear all that out in the garden? Nice little bit of luck, finding her like that. I never expected I'd get such quick action. Matter of fact, I wasn't gunning for her at all, really. I came to get that notebook.' He broke off. 'Hello! Listen. That'll be the constabules.'

Voices had become audible below. One was Mr Brinkmeyer's, and mingling with it came the deep notes that always proceed from the throats of the gendarmerie. Once you've heard a traffic cop asking for your driving licence, you cannot fail to spot the timbre.

'You'd better leg it,' I advised.

He betrayed no alarm. His air was that of one who has the situation well in hand.

'No, sir,' he said. 'I'm safe enough here. This is the last place they'd think of looking. They probably imagine I'm a mile away by now. All they'll do is fuss around for a while, and then go and spread a drag-net and comb the city. Well, buddy, I'm sitting on top of the world. I'm having one swell time. Yessir! Those two guys yesterday, a couple of supervisors this morning, and now Ma Brinkmeyer. I'd call that a pretty good batting average. How's everything coming out at your end?'

It was pleasant to be able to pour out my troubles into an attentive ear. I told him about Chaffinch, and he was becomingly sympathetic. I told him about the frogs, and he said whatever might happen, I should have the consolation of knowing that I had done the fine, square thing. When I told him about Ann's dismissal, he dismissed the affair with a wave of the hand.

'She's all right. She's going to get some press-agent job. Say, I ought to put you wise about that, by the way.'

'She told me.'

'Oh, she did? Okay, then. Well, I hope she lands it, because she's one of the best, Ann is. She didn't say who she was going to be press agent for, but one of the big stars, I guess. So she'll be all right.'

I might have informed him that Ann's prospective employer was April June, but I thought it wiser to refrain. Experience had taught me that any mention of April June was likely to draw some distasteful crack from him, which could not fail to cast a blight on our newly formed intimacy. I did not wish to have to tick him off for some ill-judged speech, when it was so imperative that he be conciliated and given no excuse for changing his mind about that money. So I merely said: 'Oh, ah,' in a guarded manner, and turned to a subject which had a good deal of interest for me, viz., the mystery of the spotted boy.

'I say,' I said, 'I was out in the garden just now, and a boy with spots on his face popped up over the wall and said "Yah!" Who would he be? He seemed to know you.'

He considered.

'Spots?'

'Yes.'

'What sort of spots?'

'The ordinary kind. Spotty spots. And he had red hair.'

His face lightened.

'I guess I know who you mean. It must have been Orlando Flower.'

'Who's he?'

'Just one of these ham actors that's jealous of a fellow's screen genius. Pay no attention to him. He don't rate. We were in a picture together once, and he thinks I squared the cutting-room to snip out his best scenes. Did he say anything besides "Yah"?'

'He called me Little Lord Fauntleroy.'

'That was Orlando Flower all right. He always called me Little Lord Fauntleroy. You don't have to worry about him. I just used to sling oranges at the poor sap.'

'What an extraordinary coincidence! I slung oranges at him.'

'You couldn't have made a better move. Keep right on along those lines. It's what he needs.' He paused, and moved to the window, scanning the terrain below with a keen eye. 'Well, those cops seem to have beaten it. I guess I'll be scramming, too. But give me that notebook first.'

'Notebook?'

'Sure. I told you that's what I came for.'

'What notebook?'

'I told you about that, too. You remember? When we were in that waiting-room. The notebook where I used to write down folk's names that I was planning to give a poke in the snoot to.'

I viewed him with concern. My old fears about lowering

the Havershot prestige had become active again. Whatever his antecedents may have been, he was now the head of the family, and any shoving in prison cells that might happen to him would reflect upon the proud Havershot name. On his own showing, he had already rendered himself liable to the processes of the Law by aggravated assault on the persons of a press agent, a director, two supervisors and Miss Brinkmeyer, and here he was, contemplating fresh excesses.

'You don't want to go poking any more people in the snoot,' I urged.

'I do, too, want to go poking lots more people in the snoot,' he rejoined with some warmth. 'Where's the sense in having this lovely wallop of yours if I don't use it? There's a raft of guys down on that list, but I can't seem to remember them without the prompt copy. So come across.'

'But I don't know where your dashed notebook is.'

'It's in your hip pocket.'

'What, this hip pocket?'

'That's right. Reach for it, buddy.'

I reached, as desired, and found the thing. It was a rather dressy little brochure, tastefully bound in limp mauve leather with silver doves on it. He took it with marked gratification.

'Attaboy, Junior,' he said. 'Louella Parsons gave me that for a Christmas present,' he added, fondling it lovingly. 'She told me to write beautiful thoughts in it. And did I what! It's full of beautiful thoughts. Thanks,' he said. 'Good-bye.'

He made for the window.

'And you'll send that money by messenger right away?' I said. I didn't want any mistake about that.

He paused with one leg over the sill.

'Money?'

'That money you're going to let me have.'

He laughed heartily. In fact, he laughed like a ruddy hyaena.

'Say, listen,' he said. 'I was only kidding you when I told you I was going to give you that money.'

I reeled.

'What!'

'Sure. It was just a bit of phonus-bolonus. I was stringing you along so's I could get hold of that notebook. I'd be a fine sap giving you money. I want it all myself.' He paused. He had been turning the pages of the notebook, and now a sudden pleased smile came into his face. 'Well, for sobbing in the beer!' he said. 'If I'm not the goof! Fancy me forgetting her! Believe it or not, it had absolutely slipped my mind that the one person I've always wanted to poke in the snoot was April June.'

I reeled again. The child, the notebook, and the room seemed to swim about me. It was as if this frightful speech had been a fist that had smitten me on the third waistcoat button.

Until he spoke those dreadful words, my whole mind had been absorbed by the horror of his treachery in the matter of that money. It had not occurred to me that there might be still darker depths of infamy to which he could descend. Now, all thoughts of money left me. I uttered a strangled cry.

He was clicking his tongue in gentle self-reproach.

'Here I've been, wasting my time on all this small stuff, when I ought to have been giving her hers right away. Well, I'll be off and attend to it now.'

I found speech.

'No, no!'

'Eh?'

'You wouldn't do that?'

'I certainly would.'

'Are you a fiend?'

'You betcher I'm a fiend. See daily press.'

He trousered the notebook, shoved the other leg over the sill, and was gone.

A moment later, his head reappeared.

'Say, I knew there was something I wanted to tell you,' he said. 'Watch out for Tommy Murphy.'

He vanished again. There was a scrabbling noise and a thud. He had dropped to the ground and was off upon his hideous errand.

Chapter 19

I STOOD aghast. Then tottering to the bed, I sat aghast. What the little perisher had meant to convey by those parting words I had no idea, nor did I devote any time to trying to fathom their mystic significance. My mind was wholly occupied with the thought of the fearful predicament of the woman I loved. Contemplating the ghastly outrage which this young bounder was planning, I found everything swimming about me once more. My blood froze and my soul recoiled in horror.

And talking of souls, what beat me was how the dickens he came to have one like the one he'd got. In our first conversation, if you recollect, he had mentioned a mother who lived in Chillicothe, Ohio. Surely this mother must have taught him the difference between right and wrong and instilled into his infant bosom at least the rudiments of chivalry. The merest A B C of mothercraft, that, I should have supposed. I know, if I was a mother, the very first thing I would do would be to put the offspring straight about the homage and deference which the male owes to the more delicate sex and give him the low-down on the iniquity of pulling this James Cagney stuff.

But I soon abandoned this train of thought. It was no time for sitting weakly on beds and speculating about mothers. April, I saw, must be warned, and that without delay. She must be approached immediately and informed that if the Lord Havershot, for whom she had begun to entertain feelings deeper and warmer than those of ordinary friendship, called at her home and showed signs of trying to get within arm's reach, it was imperative that she cover up and sidestep. If possible, she must be given a few elementary lessons in the art of ducking and rolling away from the punch. Only thus could the shapeliest nose in Hollywood be saved from a brutal assault which might leave it slanting permanently sideways.

Two minutes later, I was in the telephone-booth, hunting feverishly through the J's in the directory.

Her name was not there. The numbers of famous stars, I should have remembered, are seldom recorded. It would be necessary for me, I perceived, to repair to her house in person. I left the booth with that end in view, and ran into Mr. Brinkmeyer in the hall.

The president of the Brinkmeyer-Magnifico Motion Picture Corporation had unmistakably gone about his task of scrapping the cutaway-coat-and-stiff-collar programme in a big way. He was loosely and comfortably dressed in a tweed suit which might have been built by Omar the Tent Maker, and his neck was draped in roomy flannel. No spats appeared above his violin-case shoes, nor was there a flower in his buttonhole.

There were, however, flowers in his hand, and these he now offered to me.

'Hello,' he said affably. 'I thought you were in your room. We'll have to be starting in a minute. I was just coming to give you this.'

I looked at it dully. Preoccupied.

'The nosegay,' he explained.

I took it in an absent manner, and he laughed merrily. I had never seen a sunnier motion-picture president.

'Gosh!' he said. 'You're all dolled up like a gangster's corpse, aren't you? You look like a dude waiting at a stage door. Gee! It kind of brings back the old days. When I was in the cloak and suit business, I used to wait at stage doors with bouquets. I remember once —'

I checked him with a gesture.

'The story of your life later, Brinkmeyer, if you don't mind,' I said. 'I can't stop now.'

'Eh?'

'Most important appointment. Matter of life and death.'

He stared. It was plain that he was fogged. His air was

that of a man who would appreciate a fuller explanation.

'Eh?' he said again.

I confess that I danced like a cat on hot bricks. I wouldn't have minded him staring and saying 'Eh?' but the trouble was that while doing so he remained rooted to the spot, and his physique was such that he blocked up the entire passage. There wasn't room to edge past him, and he was not one of those men you can brush aside. And unless I could speed without delay on my mission of mercy, April June's nose was not worth a moment's purchase.

What the upshot would have been, had the deadlock continued, I cannot say. But fortunately there now proceeded from upstairs, rending the air and causing the welkin to ring like billy-o, a female scream. I recognized it immediately for what it was – the heart cry of a woman who has just found a frog in her bedroom.

'Gosh!' said Mr Brinkmeyer, quivering all over as if he had heard the Last Trump.

He turned and began to mount the stairs. It would not be correct to say that he leaped up them, for I suppose a full thirty years must have passed since he had been able to leap up anything: but he got off the mark with a swiftness most commendable in a man of his waistline. And the obstacle between me and the front door having been removed, I nipped ahead pretty smartly myself, and before you could say 'Service and Co-operation' was out on the steps.

The car was waiting there, with the chauffeur sitting woodenly at the wheel. I tapped him on the arm.

'Take me immediately to Miss April June's house,' I said.

The chauffeur was a square, stocky man with a face like a suet pudding. It was a face that did not mislead the observer. Looking at it, you felt that there sat a slow-thinking man, and he was a slow-thinking man. He eyed me bulbously.

'How's that?'

'Take me at once to Miss April June's house.'

'Whose house?'

'Miss April June's.'

'You want to go to Miss April June's house?'

'Yes. At once.'

He sucked in his lips thoughtfully.

'You're going to the studio.'

'Yes. But —'

'The studio – that's where you're going.'

'Yes. But —'

'I was told to bring the car round to take you and Mr Brinkmeyer to the studio.'

'Yes, yes. But —'

'And you can't go to the studio till Mr Brinkmeyer's ready. But I'll tell you what I'll do, while we're waiting,' he said, stepping down from his seat. 'I'll recite you "Gunga Din". See? Then you go to the old man and you say: "That's a very remarkable chauffeur you've got, Mr Brinkmeyer. Seems to me like he's wasted, driving a car. You'd ought to use him in a picture." Lookut,' said the chauffeur. ' "Gunga Din", by the late Rudyard Kipling.'

I uttered a wordless protest, but you cannot stop 'Gunga Din' addicts with wordless protests. He drew a deep breath and raised one arm stiffly. The other he kept across his stomach, no doubt for purposes of self-defence. He looked more like a suet pudding than ever.

' "You may talk o' gin and beer —" '

' "I don't want to talk o' gin and beer".'

' "When you're quartered safe out 'ere —" '

'I want to go —'

' "An' you're sent to penny-fights an' Aldershot it".'

'Look here —'

' "But when it comes to water you will do your work on slaughter" – other way round, I mean to say – "an' you'll lick the bloomin' boots of 'im that's got it".'

He removed the arm that lay across his stomach and raised it – first, however, warily lowering the other and putting that across his stomach. I suppose all reciters learn to take these precautions.

' "Now in Injia's sunny clime . . ." ' Here he apparently noticed that I was a restless audience who was going to be difficult to hold, for he added: 'And so on and so forth,' as if feeling that it would be necessary to condense the thing a bit. ' "Was our regimental *bhisti*, Gunga Din",' he concluded hurriedly.

He paused for breath here, and I seized the opportunity to offer him ten dollars if he would take me to April June's.

You wouldn't have thought a gleam could have come into those eyes, but one did.

'Got it on you?'

'No.'

'I thought you hadn't. It was "Din! Din! Din! You limpin' lump o' brick-dust, Gunga Din! Hi! Slippy *hitherao*! Water, get it! *Panee lao* . . ." '

I abandoned the fruitless task. It was a long, long trail to April June's bijou residence on Linden Drive, and I had hoped not to be compelled to undertake it on foot, but I saw that there was no alternative. Leaving him babbling about "squidgy-nosed old idols", I sped out into the great open spaces.

And I hadn't gone more than a couple of hundred yards, by Jove, when I was arrested by a "Hey!" in my rear, and turned to see a figure in a grey suit and powder-blue socks, the whole terminating in tasteful suède shoes.

For one moment as I beheld him, I had the idea that the voice of conscience must have been whispering in this changeling's ear, causing him to abandon his foul project. Such, however, was not the case. His first words told me that his hat was still in the ring.

'Suddenly remembered,' he said, 'that I don't know April June's address. You can tell me, I guess. Where do I find this beasel, buddy?'

I eyed him with all the cold loathing at my disposal. I was revolted to the core. That he should expect me, who had told him that I loved this girl, to sit in with him on his loathsome programme of giving her a poke in the snoot struck me as being about as near the outer rim as you could get.

'You tell me,' he said, 'and I'll slip you that money you wanted.'

'No,' I said firmly. I did not waver for an instant. To my mind, the man who sells the woman he loves for gold is a bit of a tick, and I know other fellows who think the same. 'No, certainly not.'

'Ah, come on.'

'No. My lips are sealed.'

His brow darkened. I had never realized before what an ugly brute I looked when peeved. He so closely resembled a gorilla at this juncture that I should not have been surprised if he had suddenly started beating his chest, as I believe gorillas do when things aren't going too well. The spectacle was an intimidating one, but my chief emotion, oddly enough, was not alarm but a marked increase in the fervour of my love for April June. I felt that a girl who could contemplate matrimony with a chap with a face like that must be a girl in a million.

He clenched a fist and advanced a step.

'You'd best come clean.'

'I will do no such dashed thing.'

'Suppose I poke *you* in the snoot?'

'I defy you.'

'Tough, eh? What could you do if I did?'

'I could call for assistance,' I said quietly. I pointed down the road. 'You will observe that we are not alone. You see that boy standing over there by the lamp-post? One slosh from you, one yell from me, and off, no doubt, like the wind he will be bounding to fetch the police force.'

My words appeared to baffle him less than I had hoped and expected. About now, it seemed to me, he ought to be looking fairly thwarted, but he wasn't. He didn't look thwarted a dashed bit. In fact, I noted that he was smiling in a nasty way, as I have seen fellows smile at the bridge table when producing the unexpected trump.

'Friend of yours?'

'No. I have never seen him before. But I have little doubt that he has enough civic spirit to rally round in the event of any sloshing, even though not personally acquainted with the victim.'

'Husky-looking guy.'

I had not examined the boy closely up to this point, but I now did so, and I agreed with him. He appeared to be a lad, for his years, of considerable muscular development. Not that I could see what that had to do with it. I had never suggested that I expected physical aid from him.

'Yes,' I said. 'He seems robust.'

'I'll say he is. Listen, shall I tell you something?'

'Do.'

He smiled unpleasantly.

'I will,' he said. 'Before Joey Cooley became the Idol of American Motherhood, a kid named Tommy Murphy had the job. His pictures used to gross big. And then I came along, and he dropped right into the discard. Nobody needed him any more, and he didn't get his contract renewed, and it made him pretty sore. Yessir, good and sore it made him. Ever since then he's been going around saying he wants my blood and claiming he's going to get it. Well, sir, if that boy has tried to catch me once, he's tried a dozen times and, believe me, it's taken some mighty shifty foot work to hold him off.'

A cold hand seemed to clutch my vitals. I began to get the drift.

'That's Tommy Murphy over there by that lamp-post. He puts in most of his time waiting outside the house, hoping for the best. I guess he saw you come out and followed you.'

The cold hand tightened its clutch. It was plain that in assuming the outer envelope of this gifted child I had stepped straight into a bally jungle, full of sinister creatures that might pounce at any moment. I had had no idea, till I became one, that the life of a child star in Hollywood was one of such incessant peril. I was not surprised that my companion had dreamed so wistfully of getting away from it all and going back to Chillicothe, Ohio. Miss Brinkmeyer alone was enough to take the gilt off the gingerbread. Add Tommy Murphy and you had something which might fairly be called a bit above the odds.

'Now, if you'd have been nice and told me where April June lives, I'd have stuck around and seen you home. But now I won't. I'll just walk off and leave you to it. Unless you change your mind and slip me that address.'

Well, it was a pretty frightful posish for a lover to be placed in, you'll admit. I shot a swift glance at this Murphy. It merely served to confirm my former opinion. I had said he looked robust, and he was robust. He was one of those chunky, square sort of striplings. He might have been the son of that chauffeur. And now that I examined him more closely, it was easy to note the hostility in his eye. It would not be too much to say that he was glaring at me like a tiger at the day's steak.

The landscape seemed to flicker, and I flickered a bit myself. What with the peril in which I stood and the peril in which April June stood, I don't mind admitting that I was all of a dither.

But Love triumphed over Self.

'No,' I said. 'Positively no.'

'You mean that?'

'Definitely.'

He shrugged my shoulders.

'Okay. Have it your own way. Well, sir, I wouldn't be in your shoes for something. No, sir! Because it isn't only Tommy Murphy. As I was coming along, I saw Orlando Flower lurking around. I guess I'd call him kind of tougher than Tommy, really. Though I don't know. It's a close thing. So I wouldn't be in your shoes for something. Still, have it your own way.'

With another of those bally sneers of his, he pushed off, and I was left alone in the world.

Alone, that is to say, except for the blister Murphy, who now came heading in my direction at the rate of knots. His eyes were gleaming with a nasty light – glittering, in fact – or you might say glinting – and he was licking his lips.

He looked like a boy whose dreams have come true, and who has found the blue bird.

Chapter 20

EYEING this Murphy, as he halted before me and stood measuring his distance, I found it extraordinarily difficult to believe that he could ever have been the idol of American Motherhood. American Motherhood, I felt, must be an ass. The boy did not appear to me to possess a single lovable quality. He looked like something out of a gangster film. Not at all the sort of chap you would take to your club.

I backed a step. In fact, I backed several steps. And after I had finished backing about the eighth, the ground became more yielding under my feet, and I found that I was standing on grass. There is a regulation in Beverley Hills, you may or may not know, which compels the householder to shove his residence a certain distance away from the road and put a neat lawn in front of it, and at this crisis in my affairs I was dashed glad that this was so. It seemed only too evident that in the near future I was going to be called upon to do a good bit of falling, and anything that might tend to make this falling softer was so much gained.

Up to this point, I should mention, the proceedings had been conducted in silence, broken only by stertorous and menacing breathing on the part of the thug Murphy and a faint chattering of teeth from me. It now occurred to me that a little chit-chat might serve to ease the tension. This frequently happens. Get a conversation going, I mean to say, and before you know where you are you have discovered mutual tastes and are fraternizing.

Barmy Fotheringay-Phipps told me once that he was confronted on a certain occasion by a steely-eyed bloke who wanted two pounds six and eleven for goods supplied, and he managed to get him on to the subject of runners and betting for that afternoon's meeting at Hurst

Park, and ten minutes later he, the bloke, was standing him, Barmy, a pint of mild and bitter at a near-by hostelry, and he, Barmy, was touching him, the bloke, for five bob to be repaid without fail on the following Wednesday.

Well, I wasn't expecting quite such a happy issue as that, of course, for I'm not the silver-tongued orator Barmy is and never have been, but I thought it possible that some good might come of opening a conversation, so I backed another step and managed to dig up a kindly smile.

'Well, my little man,' I said, modelling my style on that of B. K. Burwash. 'What is it, my little man?'

I detected no softening in his demeanour. He continued to breathe heavily. There ensued a bit of conversational vacuum.

'I can't stop long,' I said, breaking a silence which threatened to become embarrassing. 'I have an engagement. Nice, meeting you.'

And, so saying, I endeavoured to edge round him. But he proved to be just as difficult a chap to edge round as Mr. Brinkmeyer. Dissimilar in physique, they both had that quality of seeming to block every avenue. When I edged to the right, he shifted to the left, and when I shifted to the left, he edged to the right, and there we were aziz again.

I tried once more.

'Are you fond of flowers? Would you like a nosegay?'

Apparently no. As I extended the nosegay, he knocked it out of my hand, and the sickening violence with which he did so added to my qualms. I stooped and picked it up, and had another shot.

'Do you want my autograph, my little man?' I said.

The moment the words were out of my mouth I realized that I had said the wrong thing. The last topic, of course, that I should have brought up was that of autographs. Altogether too painful and suggestive. There had been a time, no doubt, when this lad before me had had to write them for the fans till he got corns on the fingers, and since the advent on the silver screen of little Joey Cooley, the demand had been nil. In mentioning autographs, therefore, I was simply awakening sad memories of vanished glory – in a word, dropping salt into the exposed wound.

If I had not spotted this for myself, his reaction would have told me I had made a floater.

'Autograph!' he said, in an unpleasant, low, growling voice that seemed to proceed from the left corner of his mouth. His eyes glinted tigerishly, and once more I sought in vain for an explanation of how he had ever come to be regarded with esteem by the mothers of America.

He began to speak. He spoke well and fluently – as it turned out, much too fluently, for it was the fact that he postponed direct action in favour of this harangue that dished his plans and aims.

You've probably noticed how often the same thing happens in detective stories. There's always a bit, I mean to say, where the villain has got the hero tied up in a chair or lashed to a bed and is about to slip it across him with the blunt instrument. But instead of smacking into it, the poor ass will persist in talking. You feel like saying: 'Act, man, act! Don't waste valuable time taunting the chap', because you know that, if he does, somebody is sure to come along and break up the twosome. But he always does it, and it always lays him a stymie.

It was so on the present occasion. A cooler head than Tommy Murphy's would have seen that the right thing to do was to get down to fundamentals straight away. But no, he chose to stand there with his chin out, telling me what he proposed to accomplish when once he was ready to begin.

He said, still in that hoarse, unpleasant voice that seemed to suggest that he had ingrowing tonsils:

'Autograph, huh?'

He said:

'Autograph, huh?'

He said:

'Don't you worry about autographs.'

He said:

'That'll be all about autographs from you. Do you know what I'm going to do to you? I'm going to soak you good, in case anyone should ask you. Do you know what I'm going to do to you? I'm going to knock the stuffing clean out of you. I'm going to lay you out like a pickerel on ice. I'm going to fix you so's there ain't nobody's going to sit and say "Oh, isn't he cute?" because you won't have any face left to be cute with. Do you know what I'm going to do to you? I'm going —'

Here he broke off – not because he had finished, for he had evidently plenty more to say, but because the ground on which we were standing suddenly sort of exploded.

Concealed here and there about these Beverley Hills lawns, you see, are little metal thingummies with holes in them, by means of which they are watered. One twiddle of a tap and the whole thing becomes a fountain. And this was what had happened now. Unseen by us, some hidden Japanese hand had turned on the juice, and there we were, right in the thick of it.

Well, it wasn't so bad for me. Owing to my policy of steadily backing, I had reached a spot which, for the nonce, was comparatively dry. But the excrescence Murphy chanced to be standing immediately over one of the thingummies, with the result that he copped it right in the eyeball. Ironically enough, after what he had been saying, it soaked him good.

His attention was diverted. Nobody could fail to let his thought wander a bit if he suddenly received about a pint and a half of water in the face, and for an instant Tommy Murphy's thoughts wandered. He leapt like the high hills, and I became pretty brisk and strategic. While he was still in mid-air, I was off and away, legging it down the road. I recalled that it was by this method that the child Cooley had been enabled to save himself embarrassment on other occasions.

Until this moment, except for a little casual orangebunging, I had had no opportunity of trying out this new body of mine and seeing what it was good for. My mirror had told me it was ornamental, and I had already divined that it was not any too muscular. With a gush of thankful emotion, I now discovered that it could run like blazes. As a sprinter over the flat, I was in the highest class.

I headed down the street at a capital pace. Uncouth noises in my rear told me that the hunt was up, but I had little fear that I would be unable to shake off my pursuer's challenge. These solid, chunky kids are only selling platers, at the best.

My judgement of form had not misled me. Class told. I entered Linden Drive a leader by several lengths, and was drawing so far ahead that I should have been able to come home on a loose rein, when somebody barged into me and I went base over apex into a bush.

And when I had extricated myself from this bush and come right side up again, I found myself gazing into the bountifully spotted face of Orlando Flower.

My position, in short, was precisely that of an African explorer who, breezing away from a charging rhinoceros, discovers, just as he has begun to think that everything is jakesey-jukesey, that he is *vis-à-vis* with a man-eating puma.

*

Orlando Flower, like Tommy Murphy, proved to be in conversational mood. He stood over me, clenching and un-clenching his fists, but he, too, postponed action in favour of talk.

'Yah!' he said.

At our previous meeting, it will be recalled, I had countered his 'Yah!' with an equally vigorous 'Yah!' of my own. But on that occasion there had been a stout wall be-tween us, and with this obstacle removed I felt singularly little in the vein for back-chat. At this close range, there was something hideously disconcerting in the spectacle of those green eyes set close together among their encircling spots. Joey Cooley had confessed himself unable to decide whether this boy or Tommy Murphy was the tougher egg, and I experienced the same difficulty in arriving at a verdict. But of one thing I was certain. I was not equal to saying 'Yah!' to him.

I maintained an uneasy silence, accordingly, and he said 'Yah!' again. And as he did so, there was a hoarse cry from down the road, and Tommy Murphy approached at a lumbering gallop. He came up and stood puffing, having evidently found the going a bit gruelling. It was some moments before he was able to speak. When he did so, he said, 'Hey!'

The boy Flower seemed displeased at the interruption.

'Well?' he said, with some acidity.

'You lay off of him,' said Tommy Murphy.

'Who, me?' said Orlando Flower.

'Yay, you,' said Tommy Murphy.

Orlando Flower gave him an unpleasant look.

'Huh?' he said.

'Huh,' said Tommy Murphy.

'Huh?' said Orlando Flower.

'Huh,' said Tommy Murphy.

There was a pause.

'I saw him first,' said Tommy Murphy.

It was a good legal point, of course, but Orlando Flower had his answer.

'Oh, yeah?'

'Yeah.'

'I caught him, didn't I?'

'I saw him first, didn't I?'

'I caught him, didn't I?'

'I'm telling you I saw him first.'

'I'm telling you I caught him.'

'You lay off of him.'

'Who, me?'

'Yay, you.'

'Huh?'

'Huh.'

'Huh?'

'Huh.'

And having thus got back to where they had started, they paused again and stood sticking out their chins at one another, while I remained in the offing, holding the nosegay and experiencing mixed emotions.

Chief among these, of course, was a rather vivid apprehension. It was far from agreeable to have to stand and listen to this brace of thugs arguing and disputing as to which should have the privilege of dotting me. But mingled with this alarm was pique and wounded pride. The whole situation was extremely humiliating for an old Boxing Blue.

Presently the huh-ing broke out again.

'Huh,' said Orlando Flower.

'Huh,' said Tommy Murphy.

'Huh,' said Orlando Flower.

There was a moment's silence. Then Tommy Murphy spoke.

'Huh,' he said, like one who has just thought of a new and original repartee.

The psychology of these two young pustules was a sealed book to me. I could not follow their mental processes. There appeared to me to be absolutely nothing about this last 'Huh' that made it in any way different from the 'Huh's which had preceded it. But there must have been, because its effect on the boy Flower was immediate. Flushing beneath his spots, he flung himself on Tommy Murphy, and they came to the ground together in a clawing mass.

Well, I don't say I'm a particularly intelligent chap, but even an ass like that chauffeur who had recited 'Gunga Din' would have known what to do in a situation like this. Pausing only to kick them in the stomach, I picked up my feet and passed lightly on my way.

As I reached April's door and pressed the bell, I looked over my shoulder. The two combatants had separated and risen and were staring at me helplessly, baffled by my adroitness and resource. I don't suppose two growing boys have ever looked so silly.

I waved my hand derisively at them.

'Yah!' I said. 'I wasn't speaking to you,' I added to the butler who had opened the door and was regarding me with some surprise. 'Just chatting with a couple of acquaintances down the road.'

Chapter 21

THE butler, when I asked to see April June, seemed a bit doubtful about the advisability of ushering me in. April, he explained, was expecting a visitor and had told him to tell callers that she was not at home. Fortunately, he appeared to come to the conclusion that a half-portion like myself could hardly be counted as a caller, and presently I was seated in a chair in the living-room, endeavouring to catch up with my breath.

As I sat there, a wave of not unmanly sentiment poured over me. It was in this room that I had so often talked with April, bending an attentive ear as she spoke of her ideals and coming back with something informative about the English order of precedence and the right of Countesses to squash into dinner ahead of the wives of Viscounts. The whole atmosphere was redolent of her gentle presence, and I am not ashamed to say I sighed. In fact, when I reflected how hopeless now my love was, I came within a toucher of shedding tears.

My wistful melancholy was accentuated by the sight of my photograph standing in the place of honour on her writing-table. There were other photographs about the room, some female with 'Fondest love from Mae' and that sort of thing on them, others male and bearing legends like 'All the best from Basil', but the only one on the writing-table was mine, and I thrilled at the sight of it.

And when I say thrilled, I mean partly with gratification, of course, but quite a bit, in addition, with an icy horror at the thought of how easily, if she had reached the stage where she kept his photograph on her desk, the current Lord Havershot would have been able to get within punching distance of this girl. Had I not come to warn her to keep on her toes and watch his left hook, the worst must inevitably have occurred. I could see her, unapprised of his low designs, starting up with a pretty cry of delight as he entered the room and hurrying forward with her guard down to greet him. And then, as she stood there with the love-light shining in her eyes . . . socko!

A gruesome picture, and one well calculated to make a chap shudder. I should probably have shuddered even more than I did, had there not begun to steal into my consciousness at this juncture a rummy sensation which I could not at first analyse. Then I got on to it. It was suddenly borne in upon me that I was dying of thirst. What with the warmth of the day and the fact that I had so recently been taking vigorous outdoor exercise, the epiglottis seemed to have become composed of sandpaper. Already I was gasping painfully like a stranded fish, and it seemed to me that if I didn't climb outside something moist in about half a jiffy, I should expire in dreadful agonies.

And this thought had scarcely flitted into my mind when I noticed that all the materials for a modest binge were hospitably laid out on a table in the corner. There was the good old decanter, the jolly old syphon, the merry bucket of ice, and, in brief, the whole bag of tricks. They seemed to be beckoning to me, and I tottered across like a camel making for an oasis and started mixing.

Of course, I ought to have realized that, while this urge to have a couple of quick ones was Lord Havershot's, the capacity for absorbing the stuff would be little Joey Cooley's; but at the moment, I confess, it didn't occur to me. I filled a flagon and drained it at a gulp.

It didn't seem to taste as good as I had expected, so I had another to see if I really liked it. Then, refilling my glass and lighting a cigarette from the box on the table, I returned to my chair. And I had scarcely seated myself when I became aware of an odd sort of buzzing in the head, accompanied by an extraordinarily urgent desire to burst into song. It puzzled me a bit, for, except in my bath, I'm not much of a singer as a rule.

I was pleased to find that I was in exceptionally good

voice. No doubt I was not in a mood to be critical, but I must say my performance delighted me. The number which I had selected for rendition was that old and tried favourite, the 'Eton Boating Song', and it came out as smooth as silk, except that I noted a tendency on the part of the words to run into each other a little. In fact, after a while, I found that I got on better by substituting 'umpty-tumpty-tiddles' and 'tiddly-umpty-tums' for the existing libretto, and I was giving these out with a will, waving my glass and cigarette rhythmically as I sang, when a voice, speaking from behind me, said 'Good evening.'

I switched off in the middle of an 'umpty', and turned. I found that I had been joined by an elderly female.

'Oh, hullo,' I said.

'Good evening,' she said again. She seemed a kindly, amiable old soul, and I warmed to her immediately. What attracted me about her particularly was the fact that she had a face exactly like that of a horse of mine at home, of which I was extremely fond. It made me feel that I was among friends.

The instinct of the Havershots, on beholding the opposite sex enter a room in which they are seated, is, of course, to shoot up like a rocket. It occasioned me, therefore, no little embarrassment now to find that I was unable to do this. I had a couple of shots, but each time was compelled to sag back again. The old *preux chevalier* spirit was functioning on all six cylinders, but the legs seemed to have worked loose at the joints.

'I say, I'm awfully sorry,' I said, 'but I don't seem able to get up.'

'Please don't trouble.'

'Touch of sciatica, I expect.'

'No doubt.'

'Or lumbago.'

'Very likely,' she neighed graciously. 'My name is Pomona Wycherley.'

'How do you do? Mine is —'

182

'Oh, I don't need to be told your name, Mr Cooley. I'm one of your fans. Have you come to see Miss June?'

'Yes. I want to see her on a matter of —'

'And you have brought her those lovely flowers,' she said, eyeing the nosegay, which was lying by my chair looking a bit shopsoiled after its recent vicissitudes. 'How sweet!'

The idea of shoving the nosegay off on to April as a mark of my personal esteem had not occurred to me before, but I saw now that this would be an excellent scheme.

'You think she'll like them?'

'She's sure to. You seem very warm, Mr Cooley. Did you hurry here?'

'You bet I hurried. The fact is, I was rather beset by scoundrels. There was a boy named Tommy Murphy —'

'Oh, was Tommy Murphy chasing you?'

'You know about Tommy Murphy?'

'Oh, yes. It's all over Hollywood. I believe they have bets in some of the studios on whether or not he will catch you.'

'Extremely dubious taste.'

'He didn't catch you, I hope?'

'Temporarily only. I eluded him. I also eluded a kid named Orlando Flower. In fact, I eluded both of them. It took a bit of earnest sprinting, of course, and, as you say, it has left me warm.'

'So you mixed yourself a little drink?'

I blushed. Her words had brought home to me how remiss I was being.

'I say,' I said. 'Can I offer you a spot?'

'No, thank you.'

'Ah, come on.'

'No, thank you, really.'

'You're sure?'

'Quite, thanks. It's so early in the evening, isn't it?'

'Is it?' I said, surprised. 'The usual hour for a snort, surely?'

'You seem to speak as an expert. Do you often take what you call a snort at this time?'

'Oh, rather.'

'Fancy that. Whisky?'

'Whisky invariably.'

'And I see you smoke as well.'

'Oh, yes. In fact, rather better.'

'Always cigarettes?'

'Sometimes cigarettes. I prefer a pipe.'

'Well, well! At your age?'

I couldn't follow this – possibly because the buzzing sensation in my head had now become more pronounced. The keen edge of my mind seemed a bit blunted.

'My age?' I said. 'Why, dash it, I'm twenty-seven.'

'What!'

'Absolutely. Twenty-eight next March.'

'Well, well, well! I should never have thought it.'

'You wouldn't?'

'No.'

'You wouldn't have thought it?'

'I certainly would not.'

Why this should have struck me as so droll, I don't know, but it amused me enormously, and I burst into a hearty guffaw. I had just finished this guffaw and was taking aboard breath with which to start another, when the door opened and in came April, looking extraordinarily ultra in some filmy stuff, *Mousseline de soie*, I shouldn't wonder, or something along those lines. Anyway, it was filmy and suited her fragile loveliness like the dickens.

When I say she came in, she didn't right away. She stood framed in the doorway, gazing wistfully before her as if in some beautiful reverie. At this point, however, I unleashed the second guffaw, and it seemed to hit her like a bullet. She started as if she had stepped on a tin-tack.

'You!' she said, in an odd, explosive sort of way. 'What are you doing here?'

I took a sip of whisky and soda.

'I want to see you on a matter of vital importance,' I said gravely, and was annoyed to find that the sentence had come out as one word. 'I want to see you up-on a mat-ter of vit-al import-ance,' I added, spacing it out a bit this time.

'He has brought you a lovely bouquet,' said Miss Wycherley.

The nosegay didn't seem to go very big. I was not feeling strong enough to pick it up, but I shoved it forward with my foot and April looked at it in — it seemed to me — a rather distant manner. She appeared not too pleased about something. She swallowed once or twice, as if trying to overcome some powerful emotion.

'Well, you can't stay here,' she said at length, speaking with something of an effort. 'Miss Wycherley has come to interview me.'

This interested me.

'Are you an interviewer, old horse?' I said.

'Yes. I'm from the *Los Angeles Chronicle*. I wonder if I could take a photograph of you?'

'Charge ahead.'

'No, don't put your glass down. Just as you are. The cigarette in your mouth, I think. Yes, that's splendid.'

April drew a deep breath.

'Perhaps,' she said, 'you would prefer that I left you together?'

'Oh, don't go,' I urged hospitably.

'No, no,' said Miss Wycherley. 'I would like to interview you both. Such a wonderful chance, finding you both here like this.'

'Exactly,' I agreed. 'Two stones with one bird. Dashed good idea. Carry on,' I said, closing my eyes so that I could listen better.

The next thing I remember is opening my eyes and feeling considerably clearer in the bean. That strange, blurred sensation had passed. I take it that I must have dozed off for a moment or two. As I came to the surface, April was speaking.

'No,' she was saying in a low, sweet voice, 'I have never been one of those girls who think only of themselves and their career. To me the picture is everything. I work solely for its success, with no thought of personal advantage. In this last picture of mine, as you say, many girls might have objected to the way the director kept pushing little Joey Cooley here forward and giving him all the best shots.' Here she paused and flashed an affectionate glance in my direction. 'Oh, you're awake, are you? Yes, I'm talking about you, you cute little picture-stealer,' she said with a roguish smile that nearly made me fall at her feet then and there. 'He is a dreadful, dreadful little picture-stealer, isn't he?' she said.

'He certainly ran away with that one,' assented the horse-faced female.

'Don't I know it!' said April with a silvery little laugh. 'I could see from the start what the director was trying to do, of course, but I said to myself: "Mr Bulwinkle is a very experienced man. He knows best. If Mr Bulwinkle wishes me to efface myself for the good of the picture", I said to myself, "I am only too pleased". I felt that the success of the picture was the only thing that mattered. I don't know if you see what I mean?'

Miss Wycherley said she saw just what she meant, adding that it did her credit.

'Oh, no,' said April. 'It is just that I am an artist. If you are an artist, you cease to exist as an individual. You become just part of the picture.'

That about concluded her portion of the entertainment, for at this point Miss Wycherley, perceiving that the mists of sleep had rolled away, turned to me and wanted to know what I thought about things. And as it happens that I hold strong views on the films, I rather collared the conversation from now on. I told her what I thought was wrong with the pictures, threw out a few personal criticisms of the leading stars – mordant perhaps, but justified – and, in a word, generally hauled up my slacks. I welcomed this opportunity of voicing my views, because in the past, whenever I had tried to do it at the Drones, there had always been rather a disposition on the part of my audience to tell me to put a sock in it.

So for about ten minutes I delivered a closely reasoned address, and then Miss Wycherley got up and said it had all been most interesting and she was sure she had got some excellent material for to-morrow's paper, and that she must be getting back to the office to write it up. April conducted her to the front door and saw her off, while I, observing that one of my shoelaces had worked loose in the recent race for life, got out of my chair and started to tie it up.

And I was still in the stooping posture necessitated by this task, when I heard a soft footstep behind me. April had returned.

'Half a jiffy,' I said. 'I'm just —'

The words died in my throat. For even as I spoke them a jarring agony shot through my entire system and I whizzed forward and came up against the chesterfield. For an instant I had an idea that one of those earthquakes which are such a common feature of life in California must have broken loose. Then the hideous truth came home to me.

The woman I loved had kicked me in the pants.

Chapter 22

I ROSE to my feet with some of the emotions of a man who has just taken the Cornish Express in the small of the back. She was standing looking at me with her hands on her hips, grinding her teeth quietly, and I gazed back with reproach and amazement, like Julius Caesar at Brutus.

'I say!' I said.

To describe myself as astounded at what had occurred would be to paint but a feeble picture of the turmoil going on beneath my frilly shirt. I had lost my grip entirely. I found the situation one in which it was not easy to maintain a patrician calm.

To the idea that there was practically nothing that couldn't happen to the unfortunate bird who had been rash enough to take on the identity of little Joey Cooley I had become by this time, of course, pretty well accustomed. That T. Murphies and O. Flowers should be going about seeking to commit mayhem on my person I was able to accept as in the natural order of things. If it had been Miss Brinkmeyer who had thus booted me, I could have understood. I might even have sympathized. But this particular spot of bother had come as a complete surprise. When it came to April June catching me fruity ones on the seat of the bags, I was frankly unable to follow the run of what Mr Brinkmeyer would have called the sequence.

'I say, what?' I said.

In addition to being shaken to my foundations spiritually, I was in none too good shape physically. The wound was throbbing painfully, and I had to feel the top of my head to make sure that the spine had not come through. Not since early boyhood, a time when a certain exuberance in my manner had, I believe, rather invited this sort of thing, could I recall having stopped such a hot one.

'I say, dash it!' I said.

Yet even now my love was so deep that had she expressed anything in the nature of contrition or apology – pleaded that her foot had slipped, or something like that – I think I would have been willing to forgive and forget and make a fresh start.

But she didn't express anything of the dashed kind. She seemed to glory in her questionable conduct. There was unmistakable triumph and satisfaction in her demeanour.

'There!' she said. 'How did you like that? Laugh that off!'

But nothing was farther from my thoughts than merriment. I couldn't have laughed at that moment to please a dying aunt.

For I saw now what must have happened. The exacting conditions of life in Hollywood, with its ceaseless strain and gruelling work, had proved too much for this girl's frail strength. Brainstorms had ensued. Nervous breakdowns had bobbed up. In a word, crushed by the machine, she had gone temporarily off her onion.

My heart bled for her. I forgot my aching base.

'There, there,' I said, and was about to suggest a cup of hot tea and a good lie-down, when she continued:

'Maybe that will teach you not to go crawling to directors so that they will let you hog the camera!'

The scales fell from my eyes. I saw that my diagnosis had been wrong. The shocking truth hit me like a wet towel. This was no nervous breakdown caused by overwork. Incredible though it might seem after all she had been saying about the artist not caring a hoot for personal glory so long as the picture came out well, it was straight professional jealousy. It was the old Murphy-Flower stuff all over again, only a dashed sight more serious. Because in adjusting my little difficulties with Thomas and Orlando I had had plenty of room to manoeuvre in. Now, I was cooped up within four walls, and who could predict the upshot?

I have made it pretty clear, I think, in the course of this narrative, that what had so drawn me to April June had been her wistful gentleness. In her, as I have repeatedly suggested, I could have put my shirt on it that I had found a great white soul.

There was nothing wistful and gentle about her now. The soft blue eyes I had admired so much were hard and had begun to shoot out sparks. The skin I would have loved to touch was flushed, the mouth set in a rigid line, the fingers twitching. She seemed to me, in brief, to be exhibiting all the earmarks of one of those hammer murderesses you read about in the papers who biff husbands over the coconut and place the remains in a trunk: and with all possible swiftness I removed myself to the other side of the chesterfield and stood staring at her dumbly. And, as I did so, I realized for the first time how a hen must look to a worm.

She went on speaking in tones that bore no resemblance whatever to those which had so fascinated me at our first meeting. The stuff came out in a high, vibrating soprano that went through me like a bradawl.

'And maybe you'll know enough after this to keep away when I'm receiving the Press. I like your gall, coming butting in when a special representative of a leading daily paper is approaching me for my views on Art and the trend of public taste! You and your bouquets!' Here, baring her teeth unpleasantly, she kicked the nosegay. 'I've a good mind to make you eat it.'

I sidled a little farther behind the chesterfield. Less and less did I like the turn the conversation was taking.

'I did think I would be safe from you in my own home. But no. In you come oozing like oil.'

I would have explained here, if she had given me the opportunity, that I had had an excellent motive in so oozing, for I had come solely in order to save her from a fate which, if not exactly worse than death, would have been distinctly unpleasant. But she did not give me the opportunity.

'Trying to attract all the attention to yourself, as usual. Well, if you think you can get away with that, think again.

You can just throw hay on that idea. You expect me, do you, not only to act as a stooge for you in front of the camera, but to sit smiling in the background while you horn in and swipe my interview?'

Again I endeavoured to assure her that she was totally mistaken in her view of the situation, and once more she nipped in ahead of me.

'Of all the nerve! Of all the crust! Of all the — But what,' she cried, breaking off, 'is the sense of standing here talking about it?'

I felt the same myself. It seemed to me that nothing was to be gained by continuing the conference.

'Quite,' I said. 'Right ho. Then I'll be pushing, what?'

'You stay where you are.'

'But I thought you said —'

'Let me get at you!'

I could not accede to her request, which even she must have seen was unreasonable. With a swift movement of the hand she had possessed herself of a large, flat, heavy paper-knife, and the last thing I was prepared to do was to let her get at me.

'Now, listen,' I began.

I got no further, because, as I spoke, she suddenly came bounding round the side of the chesterfield, and I saw that it was no time for words. Acting swiftly, I did a backwards leap of about five feet six. It was the manoeuvre which is known in America as beating the gun. With equal promptitude she did a forwards leap of perhaps four feet seven. And I, hearing that paper-knife whistle past my knickerbockers, put in a sideways leap of possibly three feet eight. This saved me for the nonce, but I could not but note that my strategic position had now changed considerably for the worse. She had driven me from my line of prepared fortifications, and I was right out in the open with both flanks exposed.

The moment seemed ripe for another attempt at conciliation.

'All this is most unpleasant,' I urged.

'It'll get worse,' she assured me.

I begged her not to do anything she would be sorry for later. She thanked me for the thought, but protested that I was the one who was going to be sorry. She then began to advance again, stealthily this time, like a leopard of the jungle; and, as I backed warily, I found myself reflecting how completely a few minutes can alter one's whole mental outlook. Of the love for this girl which so short a while before had animated my bosom there remained not a trace. That paper-knife of hers had properly put a stopper on the tender passion. When I remembered that I had once yearned to walk up the aisle by her side, with the organ playing 'The Voice That Breathed O'er Eden', and the clergyman waiting to do his stuff, I marvelled at my fat-headedness.

But she didn't give me time for anything lengthy in the way of musing. She leaped forward, and things began to brisk up again. And it was not long before I saw that this was going to be quite a vigorous evening.

To describe these great emotional experiences in detail is always pretty difficult. One is not in the frame of mind, while they are in progress, to note and observe and store away the sequence of events in the memory. One's recollections tend to be blurred.

I can recall setting a cracking pace, but twice the paper-knife caught me on the spot best adapted for its receipt, once when I had become entangled in the standard lamp by the fireplace, and again when I tripped over a small chair, and both were biffs of unparalleled juiciness. Their effect was to bring out all that was best in me both as a flat racer and as a performer over the sticks, and I nipped away and took almost in my stride the piano on which in happier circumstances she had once played me old folk-songs. I found myself behind the chesterfield again.

And such was the lissomeness which peril had given me that I think that I might now have managed to reach the door and win my way to safety, had not an imperfect knowledge of local conditions caused me to make a fatal bloomer. She was coming up smartly on my right and like an ass, I thought that it would be quicker to go under the chesterfield instead of round it.

I have said that I had sat many a time in this room and knew it well, but when I did so I was referring to that part of it which met the eye. I had no acquaintance with the bits you couldn't see. And it was this that undid me. Thinking, as I say, to take a short cut by wriggling under the chesterfield and coming out on the other side – a manoeuvre, mind you, which would have been Napoleonic if it had come off, because it would have put me within nice easy distance of the door – I dropped to the ground. Only to discover, as I started to wriggle, that the bottom of the bally thing was not a foot from the floor. I got my head in, and then I stuck.

And before I could rise and make for more suitable cover, she was busy with the paper-knife.

It seemed to speak to my very soul. I remember, even in that supreme moment, wondering how the dickens a female of her slight build and apparently fragile physique could possibly get that wristy follow-through into her shots. I had always looked upon the head master of my first school as a very fine performer with the baton, but he was not in it with this slim, blue-eyed girl. I suppose it is all largely a matter of timing.

'There,' she said, at length.

I had got round the chesterfield now, and we stood regarding each other across it. The brisk exercise had brought a flush to her cheek and a sparkle to her eyes, and she had never looked more beautiful. Nevertheless, the ashes of my dead love showed no signs whatever of bursting into flame again. I rubbed the spot and eyed her sombrely. It gave me a certain moody satisfaction to think that she was not going to be warned of what awaited her when Reginald, Lord Havershot, at last found his way to her door.

'There,' she said again. 'That'll teach you. Now scram.'

Even had the word been unfamiliar to me, I would have

gathered from the gesture which accompanied it that I was being dismissed from her presence, and I was all for it. The quickest way out was the way for me. I made for the door forthwith.

And then, in spite of everything, my better self asserted itself.

'Listen,' I said. 'There's something —'

She waved the paper-knife imperiously.

'Go on. Get out of here.'

'Yes, but listen . . .'

'Scram,' she said haughtily. 'This means you.'

I sighed resignedly. I shrugged my shoulders. I think, though I am not sure, that I said: 'So be it.' Anyway, I started to move for the door again. And then something over by the window caught the corner of my eye, and I stopped.

There, with their noses pressed against the glass, were Tommy Murphy and Orlando Flower.

I stood congealed. I saw what had happened. From the fact of their standing side by side in apparent amity, it was evident that the state of friction which had existed between them existed no more. They must have talked things over after my departure and decided that the best results were to be obtained by calling a halt on cut-throat competition and pooling their resources. They had formed an alliance. A merger is, I believe, the technical term.

The faces disappeared. I knew what this meant. These two young blots had gone off to take up a commanding position outside the front door.

April June advanced a step.

'I told you to scram,' she said.

I still hesitated.

'But, I say,' I quavered, 'Tommy Murphy and Orlando Flower are out there.'

'What of it?'

'We're not on very chummy terms. In point of fact, they want to knock the stuffing out of me.'

'I hope they do.'

She hounded me to the front door, opened it, placed a firm hand on the small of my back, and shoved. Out into the night I shot, and as the door slammed behind me there was a whoop and a rush of feet, and with a sickening sense of doom I realized that I was for it. Only fleetness of foot could save me now, and I was no longer fleet of foot. Nothing slows up a runner like the sort of thing I had been going through. The limbs were stiff and in no sort of shape for sprinting.

The next moment eager hands had clutched at me, and with a stifled 'Play the game, you cads!' I was down.

And then, just as I was trying to bite the nearest ankle in the hope of accomplishing something, however trivial, before the sticky finish came, a miracle happened. A voice cried: 'Stop that, you little beasts!', I heard the musical ring of two well-smacked heads, followed by two anguished yelps, and my assailants had melted away into the dusk.

A hand seized my wrist and helped me to my feet, and I found myself gazing into the sympathetic eyes of Ann Bannister.

Chapter 23

A SNORT of generous indignation told me that Ann's fine nature was deeply stirred. And even in the gathering darkness I could see her eyes flashing.

'The little brutes,' she said. 'Did they hurt you, Joey dear?'

'Not a bit, thanks.'

'Sure?'

'Quite. They hadn't time. Owing,' I said, with genuine feeling in my voice, 'to your prompt action. You were magnificent.'

'I did move pretty quick. I thought they were going to massacre you. Who were they?'

'Tommy Murphy and Orlando Flower.'

'I'd like to boil them in oil.'

I, too, felt that a touch of boiling in oil would do the young hell-hounds good, and regretted that it was not within the sphere of practical politics. However, I pointed out the bright side.

'You must have made them sit up a bit with those buffets of yours,' I said. 'They sounded good ones.'

'They were. I nearly sprained my wrist. I don't know whether it's Tommy or Orlando, but one of them's got a head like concrete, darn him. Still, all's well that ends well. Hullo! I thought you told me they didn't hurt you?'

'No.'

'Then why are you limping?'

It was an embarrassing question. After the stand I had taken in our conversation that afternoon, championing April June's sweetness and gentleness against all counter-argument, it would have made me feel a bit of a chump to reveal what I might call the paper-knife side of her character. I feared the horse-laugh and the scornful 'I told you so.' The best of women cannot refrain from these.

'I'm a bit stiff,' I said. 'I've been sitting.'

'And sitting makes you stiff, does it? You octogenarians! It's always your joints that go back on you. What were you doing there, anyway? Had you been calling on April June?'

'I did look in for a moment.'

'Knowing that Tommy Murphy and that Flower boy were just lurking and waiting for their chance! Really, young Joseph, you ought to scrap that head of yours. It isn't worth the upkeep. What did you want to see April June about?'

Here, too, I was unable to reveal the true facts.

'I went to give her a nosegay.'

'A *what*?'

'Flowers, you know. A bouquet.'

She seemed bewildered.

'You didn't.'

'Yes, I did.'

'Well, this beats me. I simply can't understand you, Joseph. One of these strange, inscrutable personalities, if ever there was one. I've heard you say a hundred times that you think April June a pill. In my presence, you have many a time and oft alluded to her as a piece of cheese. And yet you brave fearful perils to bring her gifts of flowers. And when I ventured on a few criticisms of her this afternoon, you drew yourself up to your full height and bit my head off.'

Remorse gripped me.

'I'm sorry about that.'

'Oh, don't apologize. All I'm saying is that it's puzzling. By the way, how much of that pork pie did you manage to get away with? I left early, if you remember.'

'Not much. I'm frightfully sorry about that, too.'

'I bet you are.'

'I mean that you should have lost your job because of your kindly act.'

'Oh, that's all right. I wasn't looking on it as my life work, anyway. Don't give it a thought, Joey. By this time

197

to-morrow I expect to be your late hostess's press agent. I was coming to see her, to talk things over, and that's how I happened to be on the spot just now. I suppose I ought to go back, but I don't like to leave you alone. I shouldn't be surprised if Tommy and his little friend weren't still lurking in the shadows somewhere. They're like the hosts of Midian. They prowl and prowl around.'

Precisely the same thought had occurred to me. I begged her with a good deal of earnestness on no account to leave me alone.

'Yes, I think you need my stout right arm.' She mused for a moment. 'I'll tell you what let's do. Could you manage a soda?'

'I certainly could.'

'All right. Then if you don't mind me taking you a little out of your way, we'll go to the Beverley-Wilshire drugstore and I'll buy you one. I can phone her from there.'

I assured her that I did not mind how much out of my way she took me, and in another jiffy we were breezing along – she talking idly of this and that; I silent, for my soul was a mere hash of seething emotions.

And if you want to know why my soul was a mere hash of seething emotions, I'll tell you. It was because in the brief space of time which had elapsed since she had caught Tommy Murphy and Orlando Flower those two snorters on their respective earholes, love had been reborn within me. Yes, all the love which I had lavished on this girl two years ago and which I had supposed her crisp remarks at Cannes had put the bee on for good was working away at the old stand once more, as vigorously as ever.

Many things, no doubt, had contributed to this. Reaction from the meretricious spell of April June, for one. Her gallant behaviour in the late turn-up, for another. But chiefly, I think it was her gay, warm-hearted sympathy, her easy kindness, her wholesome, genial camaraderie. And, of course, that pork pie. Anyway, be that as it may, I loved her, I loved her, I loved her.

And a lot of use it was loving her, I felt bitterly, as I

champed a moody nut sundae at the drug store while she did her telephoning. Of all sad words of what-d'you-call-it and thingummy, the saddest are these – It might have been. If only I'd had the sense of realize right away that there could never be any other girl in the world for me, I wouldn't have fooled about eating ice-cream at that party of April June's, and I wouldn't have started the old tooth off, and I wouldn't have gone to I. J. Zizzbaum at the same time that little Joey Cooley was going to B. K. Burwash, and, in short, none of this business would have happened.

As it was, where did I get off? She was betrothed to my cousin Eggy, and, even if she hadn't been, I was in no possible shape to ask her to share my lot. All the old obstacles which I had recognized as standing between myself and April June stood just as formidably between myself and her. In what spirit, even if she had been free, would she receive a proposal of marriage from Joey Cooley?

Heigh-ho, about summed it up, and I was murmuring it to myself in a broken sort of way, when she came out of the telephone-booth and joined me in a second nut sundae.

'I've talked to her,' she said. 'Everything's set.'

I didn't know what she meant by this, but I said 'Oh, yes?' and plugged away at my sundae, finishing it as she began hers. She asked me if I would like another. I said I would, and she ordered it. A princely hostess.

'Well,' she said, resuming conversation, 'you've had a busy afternoon, haven't you?'

I laughed a trifle mirthlessly.

'I have, indeed.'

'How did everything go off?'

'I beg your pardon?'

'Mr Brinkmeyer's statue. The unveiling.'

I started as if she had bitten me in the leg. A lump of nut sundae fell from my nerveless spoon. Believe it or not, what with the pressure of other matters, I had clean forgotten all about that statue.

'Gosh!' I exclaimed.

'What's the matter?'

It was some moments before I could speak. Then, frankly and without evasion, I told her all. She listened with flattering attention, pursing the lips a bit when I came to the frog *motif*.

'You think Miss Brinkmeyer has found those frogs?' she said.

'If I can read the female voice aright,' I replied, 'I am dashed certain she has found them. And by this time she will have learned that I gave the unveiling ceremonies a miss, and it will have been reported to her that the statue, when unveiled, had a red nose. In short, if ever a bloke was in a hell of a jam, I am that bloke.'

'You mustn't say "Hell", Joey.'

'There are times,' I replied firmly, 'when one has jolly well got to say "Hell". And this is one of them.'

She seemed to see my point.

'Yes, you're certainly in a swivet.'

The word, I took it, was American for "soup". I nodded gloomily.

'Still, there's one thing. They'll have forgotten all about it to-morrow.'

'You think so?'

'Well, of course.'

Her optimism infected me.

'That's fine,' I said.

She rose.

'The best plan is for me to take you home now,' she said. 'Come along. Everything's going to be all right.'

I allowed her to escort me to the Brinkmeyer residence. And it was only after she had left me at the gate that I saw the flaw in her specious reasoning. True, when one took into consideration the speed with which life in Hollywood moved, it might quite well happen, as she predicted, that the morrow would bring oblivion. But what she had omitted to take into her calculations was what the dickens was going to happen to-night.

I found my thoughts straying in the direction of Miss Brinkmeyer. After all that had occurred, it seemed too much to hope that I should find her in sunny mood. In fact, the nearer I got to my destination, the more firmly convinced did I become that that hair-brush of hers must be regarded as a moral certainty.

It was, accordingly, in pensive mood that I shinned up on to the outhouse roof. And I hadn't set foot on it before I began to suspect the worst. There was a light in my bedroom, and I found the circumstance sinister.

Moving softly I crossed the roof, and peered in. It was as I had feared. That light indicated trouble. The blind had not been drawn, and I was enabled to get a clear view of the interior.

My inspection revealed Miss Brinkmeyer sitting bolt upright in a chair. Her face was stony, and yet one noted on it a certain wistful, yearning look, as if she were waiting for something. She wore a pink dressing-gown, and in her hand, tightly grasped, was a hair-brush.

That look was explained. The something for which she was waiting was me.

I tiptoed back across the roof and noiselessly descended into the garden. I could see that what the situation demanded was clear, hard, intensive thinking. And I was burning up the brain cells pretty earnestly, when all of a sudden I became aware of a bloke standing beside me.

'Hey,' he said.

'Hullo?' I said.

'Are you the Cooley kid?' he said.

'Yes,' I said.

'Pleased to meet you,' he said. A civil cove.

'Pleased to meet you,' I replied, not to be outdone in the courtesies.

'Right,' he said.

Something wet and sploshy came slapping over my face, and I smelt the smell of chloroform. And it was suddenly borne in upon me that, on top of everything else I had been through that day, I was now being kidnapped. It seemed to me to put the tin hat on things.

'Well, this is a nice bit of box-fruit!' I remember saying to myself as I passed out.

And I meant it.

Chapter 24

CHLOROFORM is a thing I don't happen to be frightfully well up on – all I know is what I read in the thrillers – but in ordinary circs, I imagine, it doesn't take the bloke on the receiving end very long to come out from under it. And had all this occurred in the afternoon's earlier stages, I have no doubt that I should have been up and about in no time, as good as new.

But it will be recalled that I had had rather a full day, of a nature to tax the constitution and sap the vitality and all that, and that I hadn't been any too robust to start with. The result was that, having gone off like a lamb, I stayed off like a lamb, taking no interest in the proceedings for a very considerable time. I have a sort of dim recollection of going along in a car and fetching up at a house and being carried in; but the first thing I really remember is waking up in bed and finding that it was next morning. Bright sunlight was streaming in at the window, one or two birds were doing a spot of community singing, and the distant sound of church bells told that it was Sunday.

There's nothing like a good sleep for putting one in form. Tired Nature's sweet restorer, somebody calls it, and he's not so far wrong. I was delighted to find that, except for a little stiffness about the curves, natural after that paper-knife episode, I felt quite myself again. I rose and went to the window and looked out.

The house stood at the bottom of a lane, at the end of which was a main road or sorts. The Ventura Boulevard I discovered that it was later. This was a part of the country I had not seen before, and I was examining it with interest, when I suddenly became aware of a scent of sausages and coffee so powerful and inviting that I sprang for my clothes and started making my simple toilet without further delay. A moment before, I had been speculating as to the chances of these birds who had kidnapped me cutting fingers and things off me and slipping them in the parcel post in order to encourage the Christmas spirit in whoever was supposed to kick in with my ransom; but it didn't seem to matter so much now. I mean to say, if they let me get at those sausages first, I wasn't disposed to be fussy about what they did afterwards.

I was nearly ready for the dash downstairs, when there was a bang on the door and a voice spoke.

'Hello, there,' it said.

'What ho,' I replied.

'How's it coming?'

'How's what coming?'

'How do you feel?'

'Hungry.'

'Okay. There's sausages and pancakes.'

'Pancakes?' I said, my voice trembling.

'Sure,' replied this unseen bloke. A matey desperado. 'You just slip on something loose and come and join the party.'

Two minutes later, I was in the living-room, taking my first look at the gang. They were seated round a table, on which was a dish of sausages so vast that the sight of it thrilled me like a bugle. It was plain that there was going to be no stint.

As these were the first kidnappers I had met, I drank them in with a natural curiosity. There were three of them, all wearing full-size beards which made them look like a group photograph of Victorian celebrities. I can't say that all this foliage made for *chic*, but I suppose fellows in their line of business are obliged to think more of the practical side of things than of appearances. In any case, things were not as bad as they might have been. The beards were false ones. I could see the elastic going over their ears. In other words, I had fallen among a band of criminals who were not wilful beavers, but had merely assumed the fungus for purposes of disguise.

It may be that this discovery prejudiced me in their favour, but I must say they seemed very decent coves. There appeared to be a distinct disposition to set the young guest at his ease. They introduced themselves as, respectively, George, Eddie, and Fred, hoped I had slept well, and invited me to seat myself at the table. George helped me to sausages, Eddie said that the pancakes would be along in a minute and that if the sausages were not fixed as I liked them I had only to say the word, and Fred made a civil apology about the chloroform.

'I'm sorry about that, kid,' he said. 'You're feeling all right after it, eh?'

'Never better,' I assured him. 'Never better.'

'Swell. You see, George and Eddie been giving me the razz on account of me slipping the sponge on you that way . . .'

'You shouldn't ought to have did it,' said George, shaking his head.

' 'Tisn't as if he'd of been likely to of squawked,' said Eddie.

'Yay, I know,' said Fred, 'but there's a right way and a wrong way of doing everything. A fellow's got his technique, hasn't he? The artist in a fellow's got to have expression, hasn't it?'

'That's enough,' said George, who appeared to be something in the nature of president of this organization, speaking with rather a frigid note of rebuke. 'You go and look after those pancakes.'

'Oh, shoot,' mumbled Fred — evidently dashed, poor chap. 'I don't see where a fellow's technique's got to be stifled.'

He shuffled off into the kitchen, and George seemed to think it necessary to make an apology for him.

'No hard feelings, I hope?' he said. 'Fred thinks too much about technique. It's his temperament. You gotta excuse it.'

I begged him not to give the matter another thought.

'Anyway,' said Eddie, 'I'll say this for him – he cooks a pancake that has to be tasted to be believed.'

And shortly afterwards Fred returned with a smoking platter, and I tested the statement and found it correct. I am not ashamed to confess that I pitched in till my insides creaked. It was only some little time later that I found myself in a position to listen to the breakfast-table conversation.

Like all other breakfast-table conversations taking place at that moment in the Hollywood zone, it dealt with the motion pictures. George, who was reading the Sunday paper while he stirred his coffee absently with the muzzle of his automatic, said he saw where this new Purity Drive seemed to be gaining ground. He read out a paragraph about there being a rumour that Mae West's next picture was going to be *Alice in Wonderland*.

Fred and Eddie said they were glad to hear it. Eddie said it was certainly time somebody came along and threw water on the flames of the tidal wave of licence which had been poisoning the public mind, and Fred said Yay, that was about the way he had always felt.

'This is going to be a break for you, kid,' said George. 'Your stuff's clean.'

'Ah,' said Fred.

'You'll find yourself on top of the heap.'

'Sure,' agreed Eddie. 'He'll reap his reward.'

'If,' said George, striking a warning note, 'they give him the right sorta story. Clean or not clean, you gotta have a strong, human, compelling story. These guys that do your stuff, kid, they don't seem to have good story sense.'

'Ah,' said Fred.

'You gotta watch out for that, kid,' said Eddie.

'It's the system that's wrong,' said George. 'I blame the studio heads.'

'The Moguls,' said Eddie.

'The Mandarins,' said Fred.

'The Hitlers and Mussolinis of the picture world,' said George. 'What do they do? They ship these assortments of New York playwrights and English novelists out here and leave it all to them. Outside talent don't get a chance.'

'Ah,' said Fred.

'Well, lookut,' said George. 'Some guy from outside grabs him a swell idea for a picture, and what happens? The more he submits it to the Script Department, the more they don't read it. I've got a whale of an idea at this very moment for a story for you, kid, but what's the use? They wouldn't so much as look as it.'

'Was that the one you were telling us about Tuesday?' asked Eddie.

'The one about Public Enemy Number Thirteen?' asked Fred.

'Sure, that's the one,' said George, 'and it's a pippin.'

'You bet it's a pippin,' said Eddie.

'That's just about what it is,' said Fred.

I finished my pancake.

'It's good, is it?' I said.

'I'll say it's good,' said George.

'I'll say it's good,' said Eddie.

'*I'll* say it's good,' said Fred.

'I expect it's good,' I said.

'Listen!' said George, in a sort of ecstasy. 'Listen, kid. Get a load of this, and see if it's not like mother makes. There's this gangster that's been made Public Enemy Number Thirteen – see – and he's superstitious – see – and he feels he won't never have any luck just so long as he's got this Thirteen hoodoo – see – so what does he do?'

'Get this, kid,' said Eddie.

'Get this, kid,' said Fred.

They were leaning forward, their beards twitching with excitement.

'He's too kind-hearted to go shooting up one of the Public Enemies that's higher on the list, though he knows that if he does that'll make him Public Enemy Number Twelve. . . .'

'I see it as a Lionel Barrymore part,' said Eddie.

'Warner Baxter,' said Fred.

'Bill Powell,' said George curtly, putting them both in their places. 'So he gets an idea for pulling a play that'll put the Government wise to how good he is, so's maybe they might even promote him to Number One or Two, and here's the idea. Him and his gang get on a liner that's carrying a lot of gold across to the other side, and they hold up the captain and the officers and take charge of the ship and steer for the coast of South America, and when they're there they're going to blow the boat up and escape into the interior with the gold. See?'

I didn't want to damp the chap, but I had to point out a flaw. I mean, after all, that's what these story conferences are for.

'I don't think you need be discouraged,' I said. 'I can see you've got an idea. But you haven't worked it out.'

George bridled.

'How do you mean? What's wrong with that ship sequence?'

'You get your comedy there,' said Eddie. 'You'd make the captain a comedy type. I see Charles Butterworth.'

'Joe Cawthorne,' said Fred.

'Edward Everett Horton,' said George.

'Where's your love interest?' I asked quietly.

The question plainly rattled them. George scratched his chin, Eddie and Fred their left cheek and head respectively.

'Love interest?' said George. He brightened. 'Well, how does this strike you? Coast of South America, girl swimming out to the anchored ship. The air is heavy with the exotic perfume of the tropics . . .'

'Flamingoes,' suggested Eddie deferentially.

'Sure,' said George. 'Flamingoes. The air is heavy with the exotic scent of the tropics and a cloud of pink flamingoes drifts lazily across the sky, and there's this here now prac'lly naked girl swimming out to —'

I shook my head.

'Too late,' I said. 'By the time you get to South America, you're in your fourth reel.'

George banged the table.

'Well, hell,' he said, 'never mind about the love interest. . . .'

'You've got to have the heart-throb,' I insisted.

'No, you haven't, not if your story's strong enough. Look at *All Quiet on the Western Front*.'

'Yeah,' said Eddie. 'And *Skippy*.'

'Yeah,' said Fred. 'And *The Lost Patrol*. How much do you think that one grossed?'

'I still maintain that you must have a love interest.'

'Don't you worry about love interest,' said George. 'Let's get on to where you blow in. These gangsters scuttle the ship – see – and they get off in the boat – see – same as in *Mutiny on the Bounty* – see – and, well, sir —'

'Well, sir —' said Eddie.

'Well, sir,' said George, 'supposing that in this boat there's a little bit of a golden-haired boy – cute . . .'

'Ah,' said Fred.

'Get the idea?' said George, rising. 'Is that good, or is it good? Hey, Fred, Eddie, come on over here. Squat down on this rug. Lookut, kid. The rug's the boat, and there's nobody in it but just the gangsters and you. See? And they fall for you.'

'They *love* you,' said Eddie.

'Ah,' said Fred.

'That's what they do,' said George. 'They love you. And there's only just so much food and water, so the gangsters push each other overboard so's you will have enough . . .'

'Until —' said Eddie.

'There's only —' said Fred.

'Until,' said George, 'there's only you and Public Enemy Number Thirteen left.'

'And get this, kid,' said Eddie. 'Who —'

'Yes, get this, kid,' said Fred. 'Who do you think —'

'Yes, tilt up your ears for the big smash, kid,' said George. 'Who do you think Public Enemy Number Thir-

teen turns out to be? Just your long-lost father. That's all.
Nothing but that. Maybe that ain't a smacko? There's a
locket you're wearing round your neck – see —'

'And this bozo takes a slant at it while you're asleep –
see —'

'And,' said George, 'it's yessir sure enough the picture of
the dead wife he loved . . .'

At this point I interrupted the story conference.

'Hands up!' I cried, pointing the pistol which George,
the silly juggins, had left lying by his cup. 'Hands up,
you frightful bounders!'

Chapter 25

I DON'T know when I've seen three bearded blokes so thoroughly taken aback. And I wasn't surprised. I don't know much about kidnappers, but I imagine it can't be often that they have their victim turning round on them and putting them on the spot like this. To George, Eddie, and Fred, you could see that this had come as a totally new experience. They scrambled to their feet and stood gaping.

Fred was the first to speak.

'Hey!' he cried. 'Be careful what you're doing with that gat!'

'Didn't your mother teach you it's dangerous to point guns at people?' asked Eddie, a bit severely.

And George wanted to know if this was any way to act. Was that, he demanded, a system?

All this shook me a good deal, of course. I found it hard to meet their reproachful eyes. A minute before, I mean to say, we had been all pals together, and I could not deny that I was bursting with their pancakes. In a way, it was a bit as if the guest of honour at a civic banquet had risen in his place and started throwing plates. One felt the same sense of social strain.

But I crushed down the momentary weakness and was firm again.

'I don't care,' I said. 'You shouldn't have kidnapped me. It's a dashed low trick, kidnapping people. Ask anybody.'

They seemed stunned. George particularly.

'But wasn't you told?' he said.

'Told what?'

'Wised up, George means,' explained Eddie. 'Wised up that this was all sim'ly a publicity stunt.'

'What!'

'One of those press gags,' said George. 'The lady came to us —'

'What lady?'

'We never got her name, but she says: "I'm representing this big star —" see —'

'What big star?'

'We never got her name, either. But it seems where the lady that come to us is the press agent for some big star and she wants us to snatch you – see – and hide you away somewheres – see – and then just as all the mothers in America is running around in circles and saying: "Oh, Hell! Can no one save our darling boy?" this big star's going to come along and rescue you – see – and that'll put her on the front page.'

I smiled a cynical smile. I wasn't going to swallow bilge like that. I may be an ass, but I'm not a silly ass.

'Ha!' I said. 'A likely story!'

'It's true,' insisted Eddie. 'See that's wet, see that's dry . . .'

I smiled again.

'Perfect rot, my dear chap.'

'But —'

'If this was just a press stunt, why didn't you simply ask me in a quiet and civil manner to come along with you, instead of soaking me to the gills in your beastly chloroform?'

George looked at Fred reproachfully.

'There! You see!'

Eddie looked at Fred reproachfully, too.

'You see! There!'

'I knew that chloroform of yours would get us into trouble,' said George.

Fred's beard drooped. You could see he felt his position acutely. He muttered something about technique.

'I don't believe a single dashed word,' I said. 'You talk about this press agent and you don't know her name, and you talk about this star and you don't know her name either. I never heard anything so bally thin in my life.

No,' I said, summing up, 'what the thing boils down to is this – you're simply a lot of low twerps who kidnapped me in order to cash in, and you can jolly well march out of this room into the cellar, if you've got a cellar, after which I shall telephone to the constabulary and lodge a complaint.'

This got in amongst them. It isn't easy to be sure, when fellows are bearded to the eyebrows, but I rather think they blenched.

'No, say, don't do that,' urged George.

'You wouldn't do that,' pleaded Eddie.

'Yes, I would,' I said. 'And I'm dashed well going to.'

'What, after all those pancakes?' said George.

'Pancakes have nothing to do with it,' I snapped testily, for I knew that I was on thin ice there. I could see that, in a sense, I was outraging the sacred laws of hospitality, which, as everyone knows, is a rotten sort of thing to do, and, if persisted in, gets one cut by the County. I changed my mind about telephoning the police. I preserved unimpaired the austerity of my demeanour, but inwardly I decided that after I had shut them up in the cellar I would just go off and call it a day.

Not being able to read my thoughts, however, these blighters continued to be in a twitter.

'Gee!' said Eddie.

'Gosh!' said Fred.

'If he does phone the cops,' said George, 'you know what will happen?'

'Gosh!' said Fred.

'Gee!' said Eddie.

'I'll tell you what'll happen,' said George. 'We'll be left to take the rap. The dame that hired us – see – is going to swear she never did no such thing – see – and then where'll we be? In the cooler, facing a kidnapping charge.'

'Gee!' said Fred.

'Gosh!' said Eddie.

They paused a while in thought.

'Seems to me,' said George, 'one of us had best rush him and get that gun away.'

'That's right,' said Fred. 'You rush him, Eddie.'

'You rush him, George,' said Eddie.

'You rush him, Fred,' said George. 'Or, listen, we'll do it perfectly fair, so's there won't be any complaints. We'll count out. Eeny, meeny, miney, mo, catch a nigger by the toe, tiddly-iddly-umpty-whatever-it-is . . . You're it, Fred.'

'Snap into it, Fred,' said Eddie.

'Yes, no sense in wasting time,' said George. 'Make one of those quick springs of yours.'

'Like a leopard,' said Eddie.

'Yes, say, I know, but listen,' said Fred.

At this tense moment a voice spoke.

'What is all this?'

April June was standing in the doorway.

Chapter 26

IT was a nasty shock. I think if I hadn't been so full of
pancakes, I should have tottered. I decided to take a firm
line from the start.

'Stand back, woman,' I cried. 'I am armed!'

Her agitation seemed to equal mine.

'You little bonehead,' she said feverishly, 'what do you
think you're doing? Haven't you any sense? At any
moment my press agent will be here with the reporters
and camera men, and what sort of a rescue party is it going
to be if they find you carrying on in this way? And haven't
you any sense?' she proceeded, turning to George and
Eddie and Fred with gleaming eyes. 'My press agent tells
me that she explained most carefully exactly what you
were to do, and here you are, simply fooling about. The
reporters aren't supposed to find you romping with the
child. He ought to be tied to a chair and you ought to be
menacing him with threats. The first thing the camera
men will want is a shot of him tied up and you menacing
him with threats and me standing there with the gun?'

'But, lady,' said George. 'Pardon me, lady, are you the
lady the lady said was the lady she was press agent for?
The big star?'

'Of course I am, you poor fish.'

'Pleased to meet you, lady.'

'Never mind about being pleased to meet me —'

'Say, it's April June,' said Eddie.

'That's right,' said Fred.

'Of course I'm April June.'

'Listen, George,' said Eddie. 'What was that story we
were doping out couple days ago – the one you said would
be a natural for Miss June?'

'You remember, George,' said Fred. 'The one about —'

'Why, sure,' said George. 'Listen, lady, if you've a

minute to spare, I'd like to approach you on a little scenario me and the boys have sort of thrown roughly together. It's where this big business man has a beautiful secretary —'

April June stamped what, if I hadn't felt it on my trouser seat, I would have called a dainty foot.

'I don't want to hear any stories. I want to know why you haven't tied him up.'

George waggled his beard apologetically.

'We hadn't the heart, lady.'

'Not,' added Eddie, 'while he was eating pancakes.'

'We was aiming to get around to it later,' said Fred.

'And then,' explained George, 'we got to mulling over a story sequence —'

April stamped again.

'And now you've probably ruined the whole thing. Tie him up, quick. Hurry. Even now it may be too late.'

'But, lady, that Roscoe he's got is loaded.'

'What on earth did you want with a loaded gun?'

'That's Fred,' said Eddie, directing another reproachful glance at him. 'He's so thorough.'

'He likes doing things right,' said George.

'I'm an artist,' said Fred defiantly. 'I saw that gun as loaded. That's how I felt it – felt it *here*,' he said, slapping his chest.

'The fact of the whole matter is,' said George, 'Fred's never been the same man since he was an extra in *Lepers of Broadway*.'

April June turned on me with a look which in its way was almost as bad as a paper-knife.

'Give me that gun!'

I hesitated. I wanted to be very sure of my facts before I did anything drastic.

'Is it true,' I asked, 'what these birds were saying? This is simply a publicity stunt?'

'Of course it is. Haven't you had it explained to you over and over again? Miss Bannister told me she had thoroughly coached you and that you understood.'

'By Jove, yes, of course,' I said. I saw the whole thing now. This was the meaning of all those occasional observations which I had found cryptic. You remember. When Ann had said about my having a busy day to-morrow and all that, and when the kid Cooley had mentioned something about putting me wise.

'All the papers were notified last night that you had been kidnapped. . . .'

Of course, yes. That was why Ann had been so sure that all my crimes in the matter of frogs and statues would be forgotten next day.

'. . . And this morning I am to find you and rescue you. Give me that gun and get yourself tied up, quick. I hear the car.'

And yet, in spite of everything, I still hesitated. It was all very well for her to tell me to get myself tied up, but how was I to be certain that this was not a ruse? I knew what a formidable adversary this woman was, even when one had full possession of one's limbs and was in a position to dodge. To expose myself to her fury in a tied-up condition might quite easily be simply asking for it. I didn't want another of those unilateral infractions of hers.

This tense meditation caused me to relax my vigilance. I lowered the weapon, and the next moment the squad of beavers were on me. I was assisted to a chair, and ropes were coiled around me. Footsteps sounded outside. April secured the gun. The beavers raised their hands and registered alarm.

'Move a step and I shoot, you scoundrels!' cried April. And so saying, she cocked an expectant eye at the door. But it was not a gaggle of reporters and camera men who entered. Simply Ann Bannister by herself.

A bit of an anti-climax, what? I thought so, and I could see that April June thought so, too. I mean to say, rather like somebody in a comic opera saying 'Hurrah, girls, here comes the royal bodyguard!' and one drummer-boy entering left.

April stood there with her eyes swivelling round in their sockets.

'Where are the reporters?' she cried.

'I haven't brought them,' said Ann shortly.

'And the camera men?'

'I haven't brought them.'

'Not brought them?' I don't say April was foaming at the mouth, but it was a near thing. 'What do you mean, you haven't brought them? Great heavens!' she cried, registering about six mixed emotions. 'Don't I get *any* co-operation?'

The beavers looked at one another.

'No reporters, lady?' said George, pursing his lips.

'No camera men, lady?' said Fred and Eddie, raising their eyebrows.

'No,' said Ann. 'Not one. And if you will give me a moment to explain, I will tell you why not. It's no use going on with this thing. It's cold.'

'Cold?'

'Cold,' said Ann. 'There's not a cent's worth of publicity in rescuing Joey Cooley now. The poor kid's name is mud and his screen career finished.'

'What!'

'Yes. You have a Sunday paper there. Haven't you seen? On the front page?'

'We've only read the movie section and the funnies,' said George.

'Oh? Well, take a look at it now. You are an old chump, Joseph,' said Ann, eyeing me commiseratingly. 'Why on earth did you want to go and be funny with a female interviewer? I told you your sense of comedy would get you in trouble some day. You didn't expect her to know you were kidding, did you? And do you think the fans will believe you said it just for a laugh? I'm afraid you'll never be able to live this down. There is a photograph on the front page of the *Los Angeles Chronicle*,' she said, turning to April, 'showing Joey Cooley smoking a cigarette with a highball in his hand. In the accompanying letter-

218

press he states that he is twenty-seven years old and prefers a pipe.'

April snatched up the paper and began to read. George looked at Eddie. Eddie looked at Fred.

'Seems to me, boys,' said George, 'the deal's off.'

'Ah,' said Fred.

Eddie nodded briefly.

'No sale,' he said.

'Nothing to keep us here now,' said George. 'If we hurry, we'll just be in time for church.'

'Ah,' said Fred.

'Ah,' said Eddie.

They shook their heads at me reproachfully, removed their beards, put them away in a cupboard, and taking prayer-books from this cupboard, withdrew in what I thought rather a marked manner.

Ann turned to me, angelically sympathetic.

'Poor old Joseph!' she said. 'It's your old weakness – anything for a laugh. And it must have been funny, too. But I'm afraid you've done for yourself. American Motherhood will never forgive this. As a matter of fact, when I left, there were six hundred Michigan Mothers gathered outside Mr Brinkmeyer's house, calling on him to bring you out so they could tar and feather you, and demanding that he pay their expenses to and from Detroit. So I'm afraid —'

There was a sort of low, whistling sound, like an east wind blowing through the crannies of a haunted house. It was April June drawing in her breath.

'Not a word about me in the whole interview from beginning to end,' she said, in a strange, hard, quiet voice that suggested the first whisper of a tornado or cyclone. 'Not – one – word! Not so much as a single, solitary, blanked, by-golly syllable. *My* interview!' she proceeded, her voice gathering volume. '*My* private and personal interview. *My* individual and exclusive interview, and this little bohunkus wriggles in and hogs the whole shooting-match! Let me get at him!'

A sort of shiver passed through her frame and she began to slide across the room, clenching and unclenching her hands. Her teeth were set, her eyes large and luminous, and it seemed to me that Reginald was for it.

And then with a quick movement Ann stepped between us.

'What are you going to do?'

'Plenty.'

'You won't touch this child,' said Ann.

I couldn't see April now, for Ann was in the way, but I heard her do that drawing-in-breath business again, and most disagreeable it sounded. I thought she was going to say 'Huh?' but she didn't. She said 'No?'

'No?' she said.

'No,' said Ann.

There was a silence. I remember once, years ago in the old silent days, seeing a picture where the heroine, captured by savages, lay bound on an altar, and all that stood between her and the high priest's knife was the hero, who was telling the high priest to unhand her. I knew now how that heroine must have felt.

'Get out of my way,' said April.

'I won't,' said Ann.

April whistled a bar or two.

'You're fired,' she said.

'Very well,' said Ann.

'And I'll see that nobody else engages you as a press agent.'

'Very well,' said Ann.

April June stalked to the door. She paused for an instant on the threshold, glared at Ann, glared at me, and stalked out.

An unpleasant girl. I can't think why I ever liked her.

Ann cut my bonds, and I left my seat. I turned to her and opened my mouth, then shut it again. It had been my intention to thank her with all the eloquence I could scoop up for her splendid conduct in thus for a second time saving me from the powers of darkness, but the sight of her face stopped me.

She was not bathed in tears, for she was not the sort of girl who weeps to any great extent, but she looked licked to a splinter, and I realized what it must be meaning to her, losing like this the job for which she had worked so hard and on which she had been counting so much. Whole thing unquestionably a pretty nasty jar.

And she had dished her aims and dreams purely in order to save me from the fury of A. June. My admiration for her courage and unselfishness, seething on top of all the pancakes I had eaten, threatened to choke me.

'I say,' I said, foozling the words a bit, 'I'm frightfully sorry.'

'It doesn't matter.'

'But I am.'

'That's all right, Joseph.'

'I – I don't know what to say.'

'It's quite all right, Joey dear. You don't suppose I was going to stand by and let her —'

'But you've lost your job.'

'I'll get another.'

'But she said —'

'Perhaps not as a press agent – I suppose she has enough influence to queer me in that way – and, anyhow, press agent's jobs don't come along all the time – but something.'

An idea struck me, enabling me to look on the bright side. If you could call it the bright side.

'But, of course, you don't really need a job. You're going to get married,' I said, wincing a bit as I spoke the words, for the idea of her getting married was dashed unpleasant – in fact more or less like a spear-thrust through the vitals.

She looked at me in surprise.

'How do you know that?'

I had to think quick.

'Oh – er – Eggy told me.'

'Oh, yes. He came to give you an elocution lesson yester-day, didn't he? How did you get on?'

'Oh, fine.'

'You must have done, if you call him "Eggy" already.'

'He's got quite a bit of money.'

'So I believe. But it won't be any use to me, because the engagement is off.'

'What!'

'Broken. Last night. So I shall have to be looking out for a job, you see. I have an idea that I shall end up as a dentist's assistant. The girl who helps Mr Burwash told me she was leaving. I might get her place.'

I was unable to speak. The thought of Eggy's foul treachery in tying a can to this noble girl, and the thought of Ann – my wonderful Ann – wasting her splendid gifts abetting B. K. Burwash in his molar-jerking, combined to tangle up the vocal cords.

'But we won't waste valuable time talking about that now,' said Ann. 'What we've got to think of is what is to become of you.'

'Me?'

'Why, yes, my poor lamb. We shall have to dispose of you somehow. You can't go back to Mr Brinkmeyer.'

I saw that she was right. Contemplating her swivet, had rather given a miss to the fact that I was in no slight swivet myself. And the mental anguish of sitting tied up in a chair with April June bearing down on me had helped to take my mind off it. When an angry woman is spitting on her hands and poising herself to give you one on the submaxillary, you find yourself concentrating on the immediate rather than the more distant future. Into this was now at liberty to peep.

'Gosh!' I said.

'It's a problem, isn't it? Have you any views?'

'I had thought of going to England.'

'England?'

'If, of course, I could collect the necessary cash.'

'But why England?'

222

Not, in the circs, easy to answer that.

'Oh, I just thought of it.'

'Well, think of something else, my poor child. You certainly get the craziest ideas, Joseph. Apart from the fact that you would have nowhere to go when you got there, you couldn't so much as begin to get there. Where's your passport? Do you think a shipping office would sell transportation to anyone of your age? You would be detained for enquiries and then mailed back to Miss Brinkmeyer.'

I hadn't thought of that. In conceiving the plan of going to England and settling down at Biddleford, I had, I am free to admit, merely sketched out the broad, general outlines of the thing, leaving the details to be filled in later.

'There's only one thing. You must go home to your mother at Chillicothe, Ohio. So listen. I can't drive you there myself, because my car's only borrowed, but I'll go to the nearest garage and hire something to take you home. Your mother can pay when you arrive. I will explain to them. All right, then, I'll be going. Good-bye.'

'Good-bye.'

'I'll be back to see you off. Cheer up, Joseph. Things will dry straight one of these days.'

She pushed off. There was a pancake left on the dish. I ate it moodily. Then, feeling stifled indoors, I wandered out of the house and started to walk up the lane, kicking stones.

She had told me to cheer up, but I was dashed if I could do it. She had said that things would dry straight one of these days, but I was blowed if I could see when. The more I contemplated the general outlook, the ballier it seemed.

I mean to say, leaving Ann's swivet out of it and concentrating on my own, what was the position of affairs? Hopeless love gnawed at my heart, and would doubtless continue so to gnaw. But, even apart from that, how about it?

The future seemed to me to look about as black as it could stick. I hadn't been any too keen on being a child star, when all my tastes and habits lay in the direction of being a third earl, but it would have been a dashed sight better than being an ex-child star, as I was now.

There might have been some faint satisfaction to be gained from feeling that one was the Idol of American Motherhood. Of this I was now deprived. Taking a line through the attitude of those Michigan specimens, it was only too plain that the sole emotion American Motherhood would feel towards me from now on would be a strong desire to bounce a brick off my head.

Presumably I would have to settle down to a life of retired obscurity with Joey Cooley's parent in Chillicothe, Ohio. And while he had told me that this parent cooked an excellent fried chicken, Southern style, I can't say I found myself relishing the prospect much. You know how it is, getting to know a strange woman. It takes you a long time to feel at your ease. Difficult at the outset to discover mutual tastes and congenial subjects of conversation.

With all this on my mind it is not surprising that as I turned into the main road I was in a pretty profound reverie. What jerked me out of it was the sound of a motor bicycle coming along at the dickens of a speed. And, looking round, I found the bally thing right on top of me.

I had just time to note that the occupant of the saddle was clad in a quiet grey suit and that his socks, which were of powder blue, melted into tasteful suède shoes, when there was a yell and a toot, one of the handlebars biffed me on the head, and I turned three somersaults and knew no more.

Chapter 27

WHEN I came to, I was lying by the side of the road with my eyes shut and a nasty lumpy feeling in the skull. A voice was speaking.

'Hey!' it said.

My first idea was that I was in Heaven and that this was an angel trying to get acquainted, but I was too occupied with skull to take a look and ascertain. I just lay there.

'Hey,' said the voice again. 'Are you dead?'

A moment before, I should have replied 'Yes' without hesitation, but now doubts were beginning to creep in. The bean was clearing. I thought it over a bit longer and was convinced.

'No,' I said.

And by way of producing evidence to back up the statement, I opened my eyes. They fell upon something which brought me up with a round turn.

For an instant, I thought that I was having those things chaps have that begin with 'h'. Then the bean cleared still further and I saw that this was not so.

Standing before me was little Joey Cooley in person. There was no possibility of error. There were the knicker-bockers, there were the golden curls. And at the same moment I caught sight of my legs, stretching out towards the horizon. They were long and beefy and clad in quiet grey trousers, terminating at the ankles in powder-blue socks that melted, as it were, into tasteful suède shoes.

I suppose some fellows would have been non-plussed. Possibly a day or so earlier I might have been non-plussed myself. But the vivid life which I had been living of late had sharpened my faculties, and I was on to what had happened in a flash.

We were back again as before.

I could see quite easily how the thing had been worked. It was that smash that had done the trick. At the precise moment when it had laid me out cold, it must have laid the kid Cooley out cold, and while we were both laid out cold we had done another of our switches. I had no recollection of the incident, but no doubt we had got together in the fourth dimension, talked the things over briefly, and decided that now was an admirable opportunity of getting back to what I believe, though I wouldn't swear to it, is called the *status quo*.

'What ho!' I exclaimed.

After what had passed between this young shrimp and myself at our last meeting, I would have been well within my rights, no doubt, in being a bit stand-offish. We had parted, I mean to say, if you remember, on distant terms, he having shrugged my shoulders and sneered at me and gone off and left me alone with the ravening Murphy. But I was feeling much too bucked to be sniffy. I fairly beamed at the little Gawd-help-us.

'What ho, what ho!' I said. 'I say, do you notice anything?'

'Notice what?'

'Why, the old *status quo*, if that's the expression I want. Have you observed that we're back again?'

'Oh, yes. I got that. How do you suppose it happened?'

I hadn't had time to think it all out, of course, but I gave my view for what it was worth. He nodded understandingly.

'I see. Same old routine. It wasn't my fault,' he went on, with a touch of sullen defensiveness in his voice. 'I blew my horn.'

'Oh, quite.'

'What were you doing, wandering around on the road that way?'

'Just musing.'

'And how do you come to be here at all?'

'This is where George and Eddie and Fred brought me.'

'Who are George and Eddie and Fred?'

'Rather decent coves. Kidnappers.'

His face cleared.

'Oh, that kidnapping stunt came off, all right, did it?'

'Not a hitch.'

'And this is their hide-out? That house down the lane there?'

'That's right.'

'What happened?'

'Well, it's a long story. We started off with some break-fast —'

He uttered an exclamation.

'Breakfast! So that was it? The moment I got back into this body of mine, I thought you must have been doing something to it since I had it last. It seemed fuller. It had kind of lost that hollow feeling. Breakfast, eh? What did you have?'

'Sausages, followed by pancakes.'

His eye lit up.

'Any left?'

'You can't want any more already.'

'I do too.'

'There may be some in the kitchen. Can you cook sausages?'

'I'm not sure. But I can try. And maybe there'd be some bacon, as well. And eggs. And bread. If I've got to go back to Ma Brinkmeyer, with Clause B of my contract operating, I'll need to stoke up.'

The time had come, I saw, to break the news to him.

'I wouldn't go back to the Brinkmeyers, if I were you.'

'Talk sense. My contract's got three years to run.'

'Not now.'

'Eh?'

'Haven't you seen the Sunday paper?'

'No. Why?'

'Well, I'm sorry to say,' I said, 'that inadvertently, if you know what the word means, I've rather let you in a bit.'

And in a few simple words I informed him of the state of affairs.

I needn't have worried. I've never seen a child so profoundly braced. In supposing that he would be all broken up at the news that his professional career had been ruined, I had been right off the mark. Nowhere near it.

'Well, sir,' he said, regarding me affectionately, 'I'll say you've done me a good turn all right. You couldn't have done me a better turn if you'd sat up nights studying how to. No, sir!'

I was astounded.

'You're pleased and gratified?' I said, quite unable to grasp.

'You bet I'm pleased and gratified. This lets me out nicely. Now I can go straight back to Chillicothe.' He broke off, his exuberance waning a bit. 'Or can I?'

'Why not?'

'How am I to get there?'

I waved a hand lightly. And the relief of being able to wave my own hand was simply terrific.

'Oh, that's all arranged.'

'It is?'

'Oh, rather. There will be a car here shortly to take you.'

'Well, that's swell. Whose idea was that?'

'Ann Bannister's.'

'It would be. What a girl!'

'Ah!'

'There's a girl that's got a head on her shoulders.'

'And what a head!'

'I love Ann.'

'Me, too.'

He seemed surprised.

'You?'

'Certainly.'

'Do you love two of them, then?'

'I beg your pardon?'

'You told me you were that way about April June.'

228

I shuddered.

'Do me a favour,' I said. 'Don't mention that name to me. How right you were, young Cooley! How unerring was your judgement of character. When you called her a pill.'

'She's a pill, all right.'

'Definitely a pill.'

'A whale of a pill.'

'A frightful pill.'

'Yessir!'

'Yessir!'

We seemed to be pretty straight on that point. I turned to another.

'Rummy,' I said, 'that you hadn't seen the Sunday paper. Don't you read it as a rule?'

It seemed to me that a slight shadow passed over his brow again. He appeared a trifle embarrassed, I thought.

'Why, yes,' he said, 'I do. Only to-day I was stopped – sort of.'

'Stopped – sort of?'

'Yes, interrupted – kind of – before I could get down to it.'

'Who interrupted you?'

'This cop.'

'Which cop?'

His embarrassment increased.

'Say, listen,' he said, 'there's something I ought to tell you. I was meaning to let you have it before this, but we got to talking of other things. It was this way. I'd just bought the paper this morning, and I was starting to read it on the street outside the Garden of the Hesperides, when up comes a cop on a motor-bicycle and asks me am I Lord Havershot.'

'To which you replied —?'

'Yessir. He then ups and pinches me for assaulting Ma Brinkmeyer. It's an open-and-shut case, he says, because it seems where when I was chasing her around that pool I dropped your card-case.'

'Great Scott!'

'Sure. But wait. You ain't heard nothin' yet. You know that lovely wallop of yours, the one that travels about eight inches, with a sort of corkscrew twist on it?'

I tottered.

'You didn't —'

'Yessir. Plumb on the snoot. Down he went, and I swiped his motor-bike and lit out. I was heading for Mexico. And let me tell you sump'n. If I was you, if that motor-bike is still working, why, I'd keep right on heading for Mexico. If I was you. Yessir. And now I think I'll be going along and snaring myself a sausage. These pancakes of yours seem to be kind of wearing off a little.'

He disappeared down the lane, and I made a beeline for the motor-bike to look it over. If this body of mine, for whose rash acts I must now once more take the responsibility, had been going about hitting policemen, I could see that his advice about getting over the border into Mexico was sound.

It was a dashed sight more than the bike was. The thing was a mere *macédoine*. I concluded my post-mortem and turned away. Not by means of this majestic ruin could I win to safety.

It seemed to me that the best thing I could do would be to wait till the hired car came to fetch the kid and get him to give me a lift to this Chillicothe place of his, which would at least take me into another State, and I went to the house to ask him if this would be all right. I found him in the kitchen, preparing to get busy with a large frying-pan, and he said it would be quite all right. Glad of my company, he was decent enough to say.

'And you'll be sitting pretty, once you're over the State line,' he said. 'They can't get at you there.'

'You're sure of that?'

'Sure I'm sure. They'd have to extradite you, or whatever it's called.'

A horn tooted without.

'Hello,' he said. 'Somebody at the door. If it's for me, tell 'em I'm not ready yet.'

I was struck by a disquieting thought.

'Suppose it's somebody for me?'

'The cops, you mean? Couldn't be.'

'It might.'

'Well, if it is, poke 'em in the snoot.'

It was with a good deal of uneasiness that I made my way to the front door and opened it. I had not this child's simple faith in snoot-poking as a panacea for all ills. Outside, a car was standing, and my relief was substantial on perceiving that it was not a police car, but just one of those diseased old two-seaters which are so common in Hollywood.

Somebody was getting out of it. Somebody who seemed strangely familiar.

'Golly!' I exclaimed.

I had recognized our caller. It was my cousin Eggy.

Chapter 28

THIS human suction-pump being absolutely the last chap I was expecting to see, I just stood there and gaped at him as he wriggled out. It took him a moment or two to get clear, for this was a pint-size two-seater and he is one of those long, thin, straggly fellows, built rather on the lines of a caterpillar or a hose-pipe. However, he managed it at last and came forward with a cheery 'What ho!' Or, rather, with a cheery 'What' and a sort of gargling gurgle. For before he could add the 'ho!' he saw me standing in the doorway and the spectacle seemed to wipe speech from his lips. He shot back as if he had collided with something red-hot, and for perhaps a quarter of a minute stood blinking and making a low rattling noise in the recesses of his throat.

Then he smiled a sickly smile.

'Hullo,' he said.

'Hullo.'

'Good morning, George.'

'George?'

'I mean, Good morning, Eddie.'

'Eddie?'

'That is to say, Good morning, Fred.'

I snatched at what appeared to me the only possible explanation, though even at his best I had never seen the old boy quite like this.

'You're blotto,' I said.

'Nothing of the kind.'

'You must be. If you can't see that I'm Reggie. What's all this rot about George and Eddie and Fred?'

He blinked again.

'You mean you really *are* Reggie?'

'Of course.'

He stood for a moment mopping his forehead, then spoke in an injured voice.

'I wish you wouldn't do this sort of thing, Reggie. I've had to speak to you about it before.'

'What sort of thing?'

'Why, suddenly popping up in places where no one would ever dream you could possibly be and confronting a chap who's expecting to see somebody totally different. A most unpleasant shock it gave me, seeing you standing there, when I had expected to see George, or Fred or Eddie. Naturally I thought that you must be George or Fred or Eddie and that my eyes had gone back on me again. You ought to have more consideration. Put yourself in the other fellow's place. Think how you would feel in his position.'

I was astonished.

'Do you know George and Fred and Eddie?'

'Of course I do. Splendid chaps.'

'Are you aware that they are kidnappers?'

'They may be kidnappers in their spare time. I met them at the Temple of the New Dawn. They're church-wardens there, and pretty highly thought of by the flock. Eddie lent me his hymn-book at evensong yesterday, and we had a lemonade after the service, and they asked me to look in this morning for lunch and a round of golf. Nice fellows. No side about them. Do you know the Temple of the New Dawn, Reggie?'

'I've heard of it.'

'You ought to join us. Wonderful place. A girl called Mabel Prescott put me on to it. It's a sort of combination of a revival meeting and a Keeley Cure Institute. I signed on yesterday.'

'About time, I should think.'

'The nick of time. I was pretty far gone.'

'You've been pretty far gone for years.'

'Yes, but in these last two days things have come to a head, if you know what I mean. It's really been most extraordinary. I was going along just the same as usual, without a care in the world, mopping it up here, sopping it up there, when all of a sudden I had a sort of collapse. I went right to pieces.'

'Yes?'

'I assure you. It was like Mabel was saying. I didn't stop at way-stations: I went right on and hit the terminus. The first thing I knew, my eyesight had gone phut. The symptoms were rather odd. I started seeing astral bodies. Have you ever been annoyed by astral bodies, Reggie? Most unpleasant. They poke their heads up from behind chairs.'

'What do they do that for?'

'I can't imagine. A whim, no doubt.'

'May be just a hobby?'

'Call it a hobby if you like. Anyway, they do. Mine did. It was the astral body of a child star named Joey Cooley. I happened to be out at your bungalow at the Garden of the Hesperides, and there he was, right behind the chair. When I say "he", I mean, of course, his wraith or phantasm.'

'I see.'

'So did I, and it gave me a hell of a jolt. But I think I should have carried on, considering it a mere passing weakness, had it not been for what occurred the very next day. I'm going to tell you something now that you will find it very hard to believe, Reggie, old man. Yesterday morning I had to go and give an elocution lesson to this same Joey Cooley, and after the natural embarrassment of seeing in the flesh one whom I had met only the day before as a phantasm or wraith, we got down to it. I said to him: "What you want to do, laddie, is to watch your '*ow's*'. They're rotten. Say: 'How now, brown cow, why do you frown beneath the bough?' " and do you know what I could have sworn I heard him reply?'

'What?'

'That he was you! Just imagine! "It may interest you to know," he said, "that I am your cousin Reggie Havershot." '

'He did?'

'Positively. "I might mention in passing," he said, "that I am your cousin Reggie Havershot." '

'Well, well.'

'Exactly. I saw at once what it meant. In addition to my eyes handing in their portfolio, my ears had gone west also. Well, I know when I'm licked. I tooled straight round to the Temple of the New Dawn and asked for an entrance form. And as I say, that's how I came to know George and Fred and Eddie. Where are they, by the way?'

'They said something about going to church.'

'Ah? They meant the Temple. Matins start at eleven. I'd better go and join them there. And now tell me, Reggie, how on earth do you come to be —' He broke off, and started to sniff. 'I say, do you smell something burning?'

I sniffed, too.

'Yes, I do seem to — What's the matter?' I asked, for he had given a sudden jump and was now stepping slowly back, his eyes a bit enlarged and his tongue moving over his lips.

He seemed to brace himself.

'It's nothing,' he said, 'nothing. Just a trifling relapse. A slight return of the old trouble. I suppose I must expect this sort of thing for a little while. You remember we were speaking of Joey Cooley's astral body? Well, it's in again. Just behind you. Don't encourage it. Pretend not to notice it.'

I turned. The Cooley kid was standing in the doorway, holding a smoking frying-pan from which proceeded a hideous niff of burned sausages.

'Say,' he said.

'Voices,' said Eggy, wincing. 'It spoke.'

'Say, I don't seem to be fixing these sausages just right,' said the kid. 'They sort of curl up and turn black on me. Hello, who's this?'

I gave him a warning glance.

'You haven't forgotten your elocution teacher?' I said meaningly.

'Eh?'

'Yesterday morning. Your elocution teacher. Chap who came to teach you elocution.'

'Oh, sure. Sure. Yes, my elocution teacher. I remember. How are you, elocution teacher? How's tricks?'

Eggy came forward cautiously.

'Are you real?' he asked.

'I guess so.'

'Do you mind if I prod you?'

'Go ahead.'

Eggy did so, and heaved a relieved sigh.

'Ah! It wasn't that I doubted your word. It was only — It's all most confusing,' he said, a little petulantly. 'I mean, sometimes you're real and sometimes you're not. There seems to be no fixed rule. Well, I still don't see what you're doing here.'

'I'm trying to cook me some sausages, but I don't seem to do it so good. Can you cook sausages?'

'Oh, rather. At school, I was an adept. I could fry a sausage on the end of a pen. Would you like me to come and help you?'

'Will you?'

'Certainly.'

He started off, and I leaped forward and detained him by grabbing at his coat. Until this moment, what with talking of other things, I had forgotten that this was the man who had let Ann down with a thud by callously breaking off their engagement.

'Wait!' I said. 'Before you go, Egremont Mannering, I want a full explanation.'

'What of?'

'Your scurvy behaviour.'

He seemed surprised.

'What do you mean? I haven't been scurvy.'

'Ha!' I said, laughing a hard laugh. 'Your engagement is broken, isn't it? You've oiled out of marrying Ann, haven't you? If you don't call it scurvy, winning a girl's love and then saying: "April fool, it's all off!" there are some who do. I appeal to you, young Cooley.'

'Sounds pretty scurvy to me.'

'As it would to any fine-minded child,' I said.

Eggy seemed all taken aback.

'But, dash it, all that has nothing to do with me.'

'Ha! You hear that, Cooley?'

'I mean, it wasn't I who broke off the engagement. It was Ann.'

I was stunned.

'What!'

'Certainly.'

'She broke off the engagement?'

'Exactly. Last night. I looked in to tell her about my joining the Temple, and she gave me the push. Very sweetly and in the kindliest spirit, but she gave me the push. And if you want to know what I think was the reason, throw your mind back to what I was telling you a couple of nights ago at that party. You were urging me to swear off, and I said that if I did Ann would chuck me, because it was only to reform me that she had taken me on at all. You follow the psychology, Cooley?'

'Sure.'

'If a girl gets engaged to a chap to reform him and he goes and reforms on his own, it makes her feel silly.'

'Sure. It's what happened in *Pickled Lovers*.'

'That's what it must have been, you see. Come on, young Cooley. Sausages ho!'

I grabbed his coat again.

'No, wait!' I said. 'Wait! Don't go yet, Eggy. You don't appreciate the nub.'

'How do you mean, the nub?'

'I mean the poignancy of the situation. When Ann gave you the push last night, she was self-supporting. She had a good job in prospect. To-day, she is on the rocks. The job has fallen through. I happen to know that she is more or less broke. So somebody's got to look after her. Otherwise, all that stands between her and the bread-line is the chance of really getting taken on as a dentist's assistant.'

'Not really?'

'Absolutely. She would have to wear a white dress and say: "Mr Burwash will see you now".'

'She wouldn't like that.'

'She would hate it.'

'It would make her feel like a bird in a gilded cage.'

'Exactly like a bird in a gilded cage. So there's only one thing to be done. You must go to her and ask her to take you on again.'

'Oh, but I can't do that.'

'Of course you can.'

'I can't. There are technical difficulties in the way. The fact is, old man, immediately after Ann had given me the air last night, I toddled round to Mabel Prescott and I'm now engaged to her.'

'What!'

'Yes. And she isn't the sort of girl you can go to the day after you've become betrothed to her and tell her you've changed your mind. She's – well, I would call her rather a touchy girl. A queen of her sex, mind you, and I love her madly, but touchy.'

'Oh, dash it!'

'The best I could expect if I went and told her there was a change in the programme would be to have my neck wrung and my remains trampled on. But listen,' said Eggy. 'Ann's all right. Why can't she just go on being nursemaid to this young sausage merchant here?'

'She was fired yesterday.'

'By Jove, she does keep getting fired, doesn't she? It's what I always say. What's the use of getting jobs? You only lose them.'

The Cooley child, who had been standing frowning thoughtfully and scratching his chin with the handle of the frying-pan, now spoke.

'Here's a suggestion, boys. May be nothing in it, but

we're all working for the good of the show. Why don't *you* marry Ann?'

I quivered.

'Who, me?'

'Yay. You told me you loved her.'

'Does he? Well, that's fine,' said Eggy.

'Swell,' said the child. 'Couldn't be better.'

At this point, they appeared to notice that I was ha-ha-ing hollowly.

'What's the matter?' asked Eggy.

'Ann wouldn't look at me.'

'Of course she would.'

'Sure she would,' said the child. 'He's an Oil,' he added to Eggy.

'I know he's an Oil. And the type of Oil of which England is justly proud.'

'Any dame would like to marry an Oil.'

'I cannot conceive anything more calculated to buck the average dame up like a week at Skegness,' assented Eggy heartily.

They seemed to have got it all reasoned out between them, but I still shook my head.

'She wouldn't look at me,' I repeated. 'I'm the very last chap in the world she would dream of marrying.'

The Cooley half-portion addressed Eggy in what I imagine he intended to be a confidential whisper. It sounded like somebody calling coals.

'He's thinking of his face.'

'Oh?' said Eggy. 'Oh, ah, yes, of course. Yes, to be sure.' He coughed. 'I wouldn't worry about your face, Reggie,' he said. 'I can assure you that from certain angles – in certain lights – what I mean is, there's a sort of rugged honesty . . .'

'What does a fellow's face matter, anyway?' said Joey Cooley.

'Exactly.'

'Looks don't mean a thing. Didn't Frankenstein get married?'

'Did he?' said Eggy. 'I don't know. I never met him. Harrow man, I expect.'

'It's the strong, passionate stuff that counts,' said the Cooley child. 'All you got to do is get tough. Walk straight up to her and grab her by the wrist and glare into her eyes and make your chest heave.'

'Exactly.'

'And snarl.'

'And, of course, snarl,' said Eggy. 'Though when you say "snarl" you mean, I take it, not just make a noise like a Pekingese surprised while eating cake, but add some appropriate remark?'

'Sure. Like "Sa-a-ay, listen, baby!" If he does that, she'll fall.'

'Then we'll leave you to it, Reggie. The only thing that remains is to find her. Does anybody know where she would be at this hour?'

'She'll be right back any moment now.'

'Then all is well,' said Eggy. 'You just potter about and brush up your snarling, old man, while I repair to the kitchen with young Goldilocks here and show him how to cook a sausage which his astral body will appreciate. Are you with me, kid?'

'I'm in front of you, buddy. Let's go.'

They moved off in the direction of the kitchen, and I wandered up the lane again and stood staring dumbly down the road. And presently I saw a car coming along, with Ann at the wheel.

I stepped out into the road, and she shoved the brakes on with a startled yip.

Chapter 29

'REGGIE!' she cried.

Surprised to see me, of course. I don't blame her. Probably the last fellow she had anticipated barging into.

'*Reggie!*'

'Hullo, Ann,' I said.

She got slowly down and gave me the astonished eye. Her face had gone a bit pink, and then it had gone a bit pale, and now it had started going pink again. What mine was doing over this period, I can't say. No doubt looking perfectly foul.

There was a long silence. Then she said:

'You've shaved your moustache.'

'Yes.'

There was another long silence. I gazed at her in the sort of agonized, hopeless way young Joey Cooley would have gazed at a sausage if there had been an insurmountable barrier between him and it. Because I knew I hadn't a chance. All those things she had said to me at Cannes two years ago, when severing our relations, came back to me. No girl was going to take on a chap who answered to the description she had given of me in those few tense moments immediately following the impact of my lighted cigar on the back of her neck.

She started speaking again.

'Whatever —' she began, and I think she was going to add 'are you doing here?' but she stopped. A chilliness came into her manner. 'If you have come bleating after April June, she left long ago. You will probably find her at her home.'

I was definitely incensed.

'I did not come bleating after April June.'

'Really?'

'It is not my practice to bleat after the lady you mention.'

'Oh, but surely? The story going the round of the clubs —'

'Curse the clubs and blast the story that's going round them.' I laughed another of my hard ones. 'April June!' I said.

'Why do you say "April June" like that?'

'Because it's the only way to say it. April June is a pill.'

'What!'

'Slice her where you like, she's still boloney.'

She raised a couple of eyebrows.

'Reggie! The woman you love?'

'I don't love her.'

'But I thought —'

'I dare say you did. But I don't. Whole story much exaggerated.'

I was pretty shirty. Enough to make a chap fly off the handle a bit, all this rot about my loving April June. There was only one girl I loved – or, as I could see now, ever had loved. The above Ann, to wit.

For the first time since this spot of conversation had started, she smiled.

'Well, your words are music to my ears, Reggie, but you can't blame me for being a little surprised. After the way you were raving about her two days ago —'

'Much can happen in two days.'

'Don't I know it! What did happen?'

'Never mind.'

'I merely asked. Well, thank goodness you've seen through her. That's off my mind.'

I shook a trifle, and my voice became a bit throaty.

'Were you worried about me, Ann?'

'Of course I was worried about you.'

'Ann!'

'I would have been worried about anybody who was thinking of getting married to April June.'

'Oh?' I said, a bit damped, and silence fell again.

She looked down the road.

'I'm expecting a car,' she said.

I nodded.

'I know.'

'Clairvoyant?'

'No. I've been talking to the Cooley kid.'

'What! But you don't know Joey Cooley?'

I nearly laughed when she said that.

'Yes, I've met him.'

'When? Where?'

'We were having mutual teeth out that day, and we fraternized in the Zizzbaum-Burwash waiting-room.'

'Oh, I see. And you've been talking to him now? Reggie, you haven't explained yet. How on earth do you happen to be here like this? I took it for granted that you had come after April June, but you say —'

I had to do a bit of quick thinking.

'I just chanced to be out for a ride on my motor bicycle and saw him and stopped to pass the time of day.'

'You mean he was out here in the road?'

'Yes.'

She looked anxious.

'I hope he's not roaming about all over the countryside. He ought to have stayed in the house till I got back.'

'He is in the house now. He's in the kitchen with Eggy.'

'Eggy! Eggy's not here?'

'Yes. He came to spend the day with some pals of his who own the house.'

'I see. It sounded like a miracle at first. Have you been talking to him?'

'Yes.'

She looked down and slid her foot about on the concrete road. Her air was that of one who would have kicked a stone, if there had been a stone to kick.

'Did he tell you —?'

'Yes.'

'Oh, so you know about that, too?' She laughed, though not too bobbishly. 'Well, you were right just now when you said that much can happen in two days, Reggie. Since I saw you at that party, I've broken my engagement and lost a couple of jobs.'

'So I hear.' I hesitated. 'You're a bit up against it, Ann, aren't you?'

'Yes, a little.'

'Any money?'

'Not much.'

'And no job in prospect?'

'Not a very dazzling one, anyway.'

'What are you going to do?'

'Oh, I'll be all right.'

I passed a finger round the inside of my collar. Something told me it was no good, but I had a pop at it.

'You wouldn't consider marrying me, would you?'

'No.'

'I thought not.'

'Why?'

'Oh, I just thought you wouldn't.'

'Well, you were right. I don't like charity.'

'What do you mean, charity?'

'I mean what you are offering me. "Cophetua swore a royal oath – 'This beggar maid shall be my queen.'" If I'd been here I'd have said: "Oh, yeah?" '

'I don't know what you're talking about.'

'Oh, yes, you do, Reggie. You haven't changed. I told you you had a heart of gold, and you're just the same sweet old thing you always were. You're sorry for me.'

'Nothing of the kind.'

'Oh, yes. And don't think I don't appreciate it. It's dear of you, and just like you. But the pride of the Bannisters is something frightful. No, I won't marry you, Reggie – bless you all the same and thanks for asking me.'

She gave herself a little shake, like a dog coming out of a pond. It was as if she were chucking off her all this rot of marrying me. 'Well, that's that!' the shake seemed to say.

She turned to other topics.

'Did you say Joey was in the kitchen?'

'He was heading that way when I saw him last.'

'I'd better go and tell him there will be some delay before his car arrives, or he may be worrying. Not that I can imagine anything capable of worrying young Joseph. I wouldn't call him a neurotic child. I'm hiring a car to take him back to his Ohio home, you see, because he has got to get out of these parts quick. Did you read the paper this morning? That interview?'

'Oh, yes.'

'It will finish him on the screen, poor mite.'

'He doesn't seem to mind that much.'

'I'm glad.'

'In fact, he's thoroughly bucked. He wants to get back to his mother. She cooks fried chicken, southern style.'

'I know. He's often told me about it. Well, he can start as soon as the car comes. The garage people are tuning it up.' She gave a little sigh. 'I shall miss old Joseph. It's a nuisance when people go out of your life, isn't it?'

'And when they come back, what?'

She gave me a queer look.

'Well, it's ... upsetting sometimes. Funny our meeting again like this, Reggie.'

'Dashed droll.'

'I didn't mean quite that — Well, good-bye.'

She broke off rather abruptly and shoved her hand out. And here, of course, if I had wanted to, was an admirable opportunity of grabbing her wrist and glaring into her eyes and making my chest heave, as the Cooley kid had advised. But I let it go. Quite possibly he was right in claiming that this procedure would bring home the bacon – nobody could say he was not an intelligent child – but I gave it a miss. A ghastly, dull, grey, hopeless sort of feeling had come over me.

'Good-bye,' I said.

She uttered a little choking cry.

'Reggie!'

She was staring at me, her breath coming jerkily. I

couldn't imagine why. I squinted down at my waistcoat. It seemed all right. I took a look at my legs. The trousers seemed all right. So did the socks. And the shoes.

'Reggie! What is that on your head?'

Well, it wasn't my hat, because I hadn't got one on. I put up my hand and felt.

'Why, hullo!' I said. 'Blood, by Jove!'

She was pointing at the ditch. A bit on the distraught side it seemed to me.

'What is that?'

I took a dekko.

'Oh, that? That's what's left of a motor-bicycle.'

'Yours?'

'Well, I was riding on it.'

'You – you had an accident?'

'A bit of a spill, yes.'

A sort of greenish pallor had spread over her map. Her eyes were goggling, and she was having trouble with the vocal cords. She clucked like a hen and came groping at me with her hands out in a blind sort of way.

'Oh, Reggie, darling! You might have been killed, Reggie darling! You might have been killed! You might have been killed!'

And here she buried her face in her hands and broke into what I believe are called uncontrollable sobs.

I was stunned – (a) by her words, (b) by her behaviour. Neither seemed, as it were, to check up with her recent attitude.

'Did you say "Darling"?' I said, groping.

She raised her face. It was still greenish, but her eyes were shining like . . . well, more like twin stars than anything I can think of.

'Of course I said "darling".'

I continued to grope.

'But you don't love me, do you, by any chance?'

'Of course I love you, you silly ass.'

'But at Cannes you said —'

'Never mind about Cannes.'

'And just now —'

'And never mind about just now.'

I got right down to it.

'But do you mean – I just want to check up my facts – do you mean you *will* marry me, after all?'

'Of course I'll marry you.'

'Good egg!'

'Do you think I'm going to let you run around loose after this? I don't care if you are just marrying me out of pity and – and charity.'

I said something about pity and charity so crisp and incisive and so wholly unfitted for the delicate ears of woman that even in the midst of her emotion she gave a little startled jump. Then I began to speak.

You've probably had the experience of taking the cork out of a bottle of champagne and seeing the liquid come frothing out. Well, at this juncture it was as if I had been the said bot. and someone had uncorked me. I opened my mouth, and out it all came. I'm not much of a flier at molten eloquence, as a rule, but I managed it now. I cut loose with everything I had. I never paused for a word. I said this and that and so on and so forth, at the same time kissing her a good deal.

And then, right plumb spang in the midst of my ecstasy, if that's the word – at the very moment, in fact, when I was kissing her for the forty-fifth time – a chilling thought intruded – viz., that, now that we had got everything fixed up on this solid basis, she would, of course, expect me to return to Hollywood with her, there to put in train the preparations for the forthcoming nuptials.

Hollywood, mind you, where the police, I presumed, were even now spreading a drag-net and combing the city for me.

How the dickens was I to explain that I must now leave her and push on to Chillicothe, Ohio?

I mean to say, what reason could I give? How could I make plausible this sudden passionate desire to go to Chillicothe, Ohio? It would mean issuing a statement, after all. In which event, she would most certainly think I was looney and break off the match in case it was catching.

And then I saw the way. I must say that I didn't like the idea of a kid of Joey Cooley's tender years going all that way alone. It would sound thin, of course, but ...

I became aware that she was speaking.

'Eh?' I said.

A slight whiffle of impatience escaped her. The old Ann.

'Haven't you been listening?'

'Awfully sorry. My attention wandered a bit.'

'Well, do listen, my precious imbecile fathead, because it's important. It's about young Joseph.'

'Oh, yes?'

'Something has just occurred to me. He's such a child. I don't really think he ought to make that long journey all alone. So —'

My heart gave a leap like a salmon in spawning time.

'You want me to go with him?'

'Would you?'

'Rather!'

The air seemed full of pealing bells. I was saved. No tedious explanations. ... No issuing of statements ... no breaking off of the match on account of lunacy of one of the contracting parties ...

I kissed her a good deal more.

'You're an angel, Reggie,' she said. 'I don't know how many men who would be so unselfish and put themselves out like this.'

'Not at all,' I said. 'Not at all.'

'I think you ought to get away as soon as possible.'

So did I. I kissed her again.

'And then you could come back to Hollywood —'

'No,' I said. 'I'll meet you in New York.'

'Why?'

'I'd rather.'

'Perhaps it would be better.'

'Much better.'

I kissed her again, bringing the total, I should say, about up to the level hundred. Then, hand in hand, we walked down the lane, guided by the scent of frying sausages which told me that Eggy had not overestimated his culinary skill and that little Joey Cooley was busy victualling up against the new day.

THE WORLD OF
P. G. WODEHOUSE

For most of the 20th century, readers in their millions have been losing themselves in the sunlit world of enchantment and entertainment Wodehouse has created—a world of elegant living, gaily complicated romance, intricate intrigues and crimes. P. G. Wodehouse has been hailed by critics as the most masterful writer of English prose today—and, more to the point, close to 30 million copies of his books have found their way to a delighted public. Here are three Wodehouse classics in new paperback editions—fresh as ever for today's reader.

BRINKLEY MANOR. A Jeeves Novel. The immortal Jeeves sorts out the tangled love affair of a man who knew more about newts than about girls.

LEAVE IT TO PSMITH. A Blandings Castle Novel. Psmith offered his services for any assignment—crime not objected to. And Freddie Threepwood was dumb enough to take him up on it in his pursuit of Eve—the result, a mad mix of pearls, pigs, and pandemonium.

THE SMALL BACHELOR. George Finch came to Greenwich Village to live the free life of an artist. He was no good at it—but that didn't matter when Molly came into his life like lightning. And so did a fortunehunting fortuneteller, a thieving valet, a Western-movie fan, and the New York Police Department.

FICTION

for all seasons... for people of all ages.

STEP THIS WAY TO THE LAND OF ENCHANTMENT... J.R.R. TOLKIEN'S MIDDLE EARTH!

Available at your bookstore or use this coupon.

Lighten up...
try some funny fiction!

___ **THE PRINCESS BRIDE**, William Goldman   25483   1.95
The author of *The Marathon Man* here creates a tangle
of unbelievable feats and narrow escapes in this charm-
ing spoof on the historical romance.

___ **HAPPINESS IS TOO MUCH TROUBLE,**
Sandra Hochman   25509   1.75
The outrageously liberated life and loves of the first
woman to head the world's largest film studio. "Funny
...powerful...a tour de force!"—*L.A. Times*

___ **ANOTHER ROADSIDE ATTRACTION,**
Tom Robbins   24935   1.95
From the author of *Even Cowgirls Get the Blues.* The
hilarious account of the second coming as witnessed by
a band of spaced-out, but sincere hippies. Full of "humor
and lust."—*Playboy*

___ **THE MILAGRO BEANFIELD WAR,**
John Nichols   24758   1.95
An insanely comic battle waged between the poor of
Milagro and the wealthy Anglos over lost lands, water
and human dignity. By the author of *The Sterile Cuckoo.*

___ **MONEY IS LOVE**, Richard Condon   24971   1.95
A hilarious satire on America's =1 obsession (next to
which sex is a mere hobby)—money! "Wonderful...a
funhouse mirror."—*Newsweek*

___ **HOLLYWOOD AND LE VINE,**
Andrew Bergman   25006   1.75
Set in Hollywood at the time of the Red scare, this spoof
of the hardboiled-detective novels features such charac-
ters as Humphrey Bogart, Lauren Bacall and Richard
Nixon! "Entertaining...fast-paced, original, and tense!"
                                        —*Chicago Sun-Times*

 **Ballantine Mail Sales
Dept. LE, 201 E. 50th Street
New York, New York 10022**

Please send me the books I have checked above. I am enclosing
$..........................(please add 50¢ to cover postage and handling).
Send check or money order—no cash or C.O.D.'s please.

Name_____

Address _____

City_____State_____Zip_____

Please allow 4 weeks for delivery.   L-57

Available at your bookstore or use this coupon.